Hot Fudge
Murder

Books by Cynthia Baxter

MURDER WITH A CHERRY ON TOP

HOT FUDGE MURDER

Published by Kensington Publishing Corporation

Hot Fudge Murder

Cynthia Baxter

KENSINGTON BOOKS
www.kensingtonbooks.com

KENSINGTON BOOKS are published by

Kensington Publishing Corp.
119 West 40th Street
New York, NY 10018

Copyright © 2019 by Cynthia Baxter

All Kensington titles, imprints and distributed lines are available at special quantity discounts for bulk purchases for sales promotion, premiums, fund-raising, educational or institutional use.

Special book excerpts or customized printings can also be created to fit specific needs. For details, write or phone the office of the Kensington Special Sales Manager: Kensington Publishing Corp., 119 West 40th Street, New York, NY, 10018. Attn. Special Sales Department. Phone: 1-800-221-2647.

Library of Congress Catalogue Number: 2018952807

Kensington and the K logo Reg. U.S. Pat. & TM Off.

ISBN-13: 978-1-4967-1415-2
ISBN-10: 1-4967-1415-6
First Kensington Hardcover Edition: February 2019

ISBN-13: 978-1-4967-1417-6 (e-book)
ISBN-10: 1-4967-1417-2 (e-book)

10 9 8 7 6 5 4 3 2 1

Printed in the United States of America

To Nancy Mendell,
a friend extraordinaire

Chapter 1

There are multiple stories about the invention of
the ice cream sundae. One is that it originated in
Ithaca, New York, in 1892 when Chester Platt,
who ran a drugstore with a soda fountain called
Platt & Colt's, created a cherry sundae. It
consisted of vanilla ice cream, cherry syrup, and a
candied cherry and sold for ten cents.

—*https://whatscookingamerica.net/History/
IceCream/Sundae.htm*

"Six dozen mini ice cream sandwiches, three dozen
made with Classic Tahitian Vanilla and three dozen
made with Dark Chocolate . . ."

"Check."

"Six dozen ice cream cupcakes in assorted flavors . . ."

"Check."

"Four three-gallon tubs of ice cream. That's one Classic
Tahitian Vanilla, one Chocolate Almond Fudge, one Peanut
Butter on the Playground, and one Cappuccino Crunch."

"Check."

"And hot fudge," I added, lowering my clipboard. "An entire gallon of the best chocolate fudge sauce imaginable,
whipped up in my very own kitchen. We can *not* forget that!"

As I fought off the butterflies that had been break-dancing

in my stomach since early that morning, I surveyed my staff. Just looking at them had a calming effect, reminding me that I wasn't alone in undertaking this terrifying, first-time venture.

I was still having trouble comprehending the fact that I was about to serve up a selection of my handmade ice cream treats at what could well turn out to be the Hudson Valley's most glamorous event of the summer.

I was glad I wasn't alone in taking on this daunting challenge.

My personal team of Three Musketeers included my best friend since elementary school, Willow; my eighteen-year-old niece, Emma; and Emma's boyfriend for the past few weeks, Ethan.

Today I felt a surge of real pride over how professional they looked. For tonight's event, they had donned the spanking-new, bubble-gum-pink polo shirts I'd recently ordered for all four of us. The breast pockets were emblazoned in white with the name of my similarly spanking-new ice cream emporium, the Lickety Splits Ice Cream Shoppe. They were also wearing white pants—although Emma had opted for white jeans.

As the three of them looked at me expectantly, I found myself thinking about George Washington in 1776. I imagined him addressing his troops right before they climbed into a rickety boat to spend Christmas sneaking up on the British instead of chugging eggnog and merrily tossing tinsel onto an evergreen tree.

But I didn't *feel* like George Washington. In fact, I desperately hoped that my Ice Cream Team's bright, eager-to-please expressions would buoy up my confidence enough to get me through the night ahead.

Instead I could feel whatever small amount of it that I'd possessed when I'd walked into my shop that morning melting away like a chocolate ice cream cone that had been dropped on the sidewalk on a hot summer day.

"Do you think this will be enough for seventy-five guests?" I asked in a wavering, not-at-all-George-Washington-like voice.

"We definitely have enough," Willow assured me. "We've gone over this a hundred times, Kate. We'll be fine."

"I'm even expecting leftovers," Emma said.

"Are you kidding?" Ethan chimed in. "I'm counting on them! Leftover ice cream sounds dope!" He pushed aside the curtain of dead-straight black hair that permanently hung over his face long enough for me to make sure that he actually possessed eyes.

"And do you think I made good choices?" I asked, nervously smoothing back my shoulder-length brown hair, today worn in a neat ponytail. "I mean, not everyone likes peanut butter. Or at least not peanut butter as an ice cream flavor. And just because we all think the ice cream cupcakes are the cutest thing since puppies, with their different-colored sprinkles and their pastel-colored papers . . ."

"People go crazy for the mini cupcakes!" Emma insisted. "Everybody from the Chamber of Commerce loved them. And that day at the shop when you handed them out as freebies so people could try some of the more exotic flavors, everyone was over the moon about them. The entire concept is pure genius!"

"Emma's right," Willow seconded. "It's impossible not to like the ice cream cupcakes."

"I'm *definitely* hoping for leftovers on those!" Ethan exclaimed. "Those dudes are totally chill!"

"And the hot fudge?" I couldn't resist adding, even though I knew I was bordering on being truly annoying. "Do you think they'll like it? This is a pretty sophisticated crowd, after all. They're used to the very best . . ."

"Kate," Emma replied with remarkable patience, "your homemade Heavenly Hot Fudge Sauce is the best in the entire universe. It's what put your Hudson's Hottest Hot Fudge Sundae on the map!"

I let out a long, appreciative sigh. My crew. Perhaps not the most professional, at least in terms of training or even appearance. Willow Baines, for example, was about as far away from an ice cream entrepreneur as you can get. She was a yoga instructor, the owner of the Heart, Mind & Soul yoga studio a few blocks away from Lickety Splits. She also held classes in meditation and relaxation.

She even looked the part. Willow had pale blond hair she wore in a cute pixie cut, the perfect complement to her tall, slender frame. And the tailored outfit she was wearing today was completely out of character for her, since she usually wore loose, comfortable clothes. The woman owned an entire wardrobe of yoga pants.

Willow didn't just teach others how to be calm and centered; she was those things herself. I found that pretty impressive, given her rocky childhood. She had grown up with a drug-addicted mother and two brothers who took off as soon as they could. The instability of her early years had instilled in her a strong need to create order in her life, something I'd picked up on when I first met her back in middle school.

Her personal struggle to find balance had made her one of the kindest, most generous people I'd ever met. For example, she was big-hearted enough to spend her Saturday night helping out her BFF as a favor. And while she was committed to maintaining a healthy lifestyle, there were two exceptions: coffee and—fortunately—ice cream.

My niece, Emma, a computer whiz and a talented artist, was one of the most creative people I'd ever met, a personality trait that was reflected in the blue streaks she'd incorporated into her wild, curly black hair. At the beginning of the summer, she'd run away from her home in the Washington, D.C., area and appeared on my doorstep—literally. She announced that she didn't want to rush off to college in the fall, as expected by her parents, my oldest sister, Julie, and her husband, Ron. Instead, she wanted to take some time off to decide exactly what direction she wanted her life to go in. She felt that living with Grams and me would provide her with the perfect way to do that. She had instantly turned into my right-hand person, helping me run Lickety Splits and doing a first-rate job thanks to her quickness to learn, her organizational skills, and her strong sense of responsibility.

As for Ethan, I knew nothing about him except that he worked at a local organic dairy that was one of my suppliers and that he generally dressed completely in black no matter how hot the summer day was. His latest thing was carrying around a tattered paperback, usually one of the classic novels devoured by young men who are on a quest to find themselves. Last week, it had been Jack Kerouac's *On the Road*. This week, it was Dostoevsky's *The Brothers Karamazov*. Frankly, I had yet to figure out why he'd become an object of affection for my otherwise-reasonable niece, since his level of conversation was generally as far away from Kerouac and Dostoevsky as you can get. In fact, I didn't think it was even possible to translate the primary words that constituted his vocabulary—"awesome," "dope," "chill," and "dude"— into Russian.

But what my crew lacked in professional deportment and experience in the world of ice cream, they more than made up for in enthusiasm, energy, creativity, and general cheerleading abilities when it came to spurring me on. They also looked pretty cool in those pink Lickety Splits shirts. I had no doubt that they would help me carry the day.

"Then I guess we're all set." I took a deep breath. "Okay, gang. Let's get this party started!"

I must admit that a tidal wave of pride washed over me as I surveyed the spread of goodies laid out before me on the counter of my shop. And not only pride: surprise, too, bordering on shock. After all, it was still hard for me to believe that I'd really opened an ice cream shop just a few weeks earlier.

Six weeks earlier, to be exact.

During that time, I'd lived out every ice cream fantasy I could think of, creating fun, exotic, and not-always-successful flavors like Peanut Butter on the Playground, which is peanut butter ice cream made with freshly ground peanuts and dotted with plump globs of grape jelly; lusciously smooth and surprising Honey Lavender; and chunky Prune 'n' Raisin. (That last one turned out to be one of the not-so-successful ones.)

I'd forced myself to master the tedious, day-to-day aspects of running a small business, wrapping my head around tasks like routinely entering every single expense on an Excel spreadsheet and keeping all my receipts carefully sorted for when tax time came around.

I'd even gotten used to the demanding schedule that running an ice cream shop requires, pulling myself out of bed before sunrise practically every day of the week in order to have enough time to make fresh new batches of ice cream before opening at eleven, then staying at the shop as late as necessary to clean up.

But I'd never catered an event of this size before.

True, since opening Lickety Splits, I'd put on two children's parties, complete with ice cream clowns made with scoops of vanilla, chocolate, and strawberry topped with ice cream cone hats, gumdrop faces, and hair made from colored sprinkles.

I'd catered a fortieth birthday party at the home of a local art gallery owner, putting together an ice cream social for fifteen women. As soon as they surveyed the buffet-style spread

I'd set up on the hostess's dining room table, they all solemnly agreed to abandon their diets for the evening. Then they set about making the most outrageous ice cream concoctions imaginable from three flavors of ice cream, three kinds of syrup, a mound of whipped cream the size of a sand dune, and an array of mix-ins that included mini M&Ms, nuts, chocolate sprinkles, strawberries, blueberries, bananas, bacon, marshmallows, pretzels, popcorn, peanut butter chips, and, of course, classic maraschino cherries.

I'd also hosted the monthly meeting of the local Chamber of Commerce. That was when I'd invented Ice Cream Incidentals, my hors d'oeuvre-style ice cream mini treats that included the tiny ice cream cupcakes and bite-sized ice cream sandwiches I'd prepared for today. They were perfect for passing around at a gathering since people could pop them into their mouths without needing a spoon—or, in most cases, even a napkin.

But all of those events had been kid stuff compared to the gala event I was catering tonight.

And it wasn't even the fact that there would be upward of seventy-five guests at this Saturday night gala that was giving me pause. Even more nerve-wracking was the aforementioned glam factor.

The party I was catering was being held at the weekend retreat of a famous fashion designer.

I'm talking about someone so well-known that his line of expensive purses and wallets is one of the first things you see when you walk into any Macy's or Nordstrom in the country. Someone whose name is regularly mentioned at the Academy Awards when one of the interviewers asks one of the spectacularly dressed nominees, "Who are you wearing tonight?" Someone who regularly appears on TV as a judge on a weekly fashion design competition, making or breaking the careers of some monstrously talented hopefuls.

Omar DeVane was as much a household word as Mr. Clean.

And it wasn't just Omar whom I found intimidating. It was the guest list. When his assistant, Federico, had called to engage my services, he'd casually dropped a couple of names that I immediately recognized. One was Gretchen Gruen, a gorgeous blond, blue-eyed supermodel who has been featured in ads for everything from makeup to luxury cars to Greek yogurt. The other was Pippa Somers, the editor of *Flair*, a fashion magazine that's right up there with *Vogue*, *Elle*, and *W*.

And Omar DeVane wasn't even throwing this extravagant event for any particular reason, as far I could tell. It wasn't as if he was splurging because of a birthday or an anniversary or even the release of a new line of pocketbooks or evening gowns or any of the other items he was famous for putting his easily recognizable ODV logo on.

"Is tonight some sort of celebration?" I'd asked his assistant as I'd jotted down notes during our phone call.

Federico was silent for a few seconds. "I suppose we're celebrating Omar's life," he'd finally replied. "And Omar's estate, Greenaway, is the perfect venue."

Omar's house even had a name.

Yet despite the glamour factor, one simple fact had kept me grounded through the process of planning this glitzy event. And that was that Omar DeVane's favorite food was ice cream.

Hot fudge sundaes, to be specific.

So despite his fame, despite his fortune, despite his star-studded guest list, when you came right down to it, this Omar guy was pretty much the same as you and me. Maybe he was an internationally known fashion mogul, but deep down he was still a little kid who got excited by a dish of ice cream.

In an attempt at reining in those frisky butterflies, I reminded myself of this reality for the hundredth time. Or perhaps the thousandth.

At the same time, I tried *not* to think about the fact that six weeks isn't a very long time to be in business. Especially a brand-new business, one I'd actually known little about when I decided to jump in and give it a try.

Before running my ice cream empire—or at least a nine-hundred-square-foot ice cream parlor in a charming small town in the Hudson Valley, just north of New York City, called Wolfert's Roost—I'd been living in Manhattan, working in public relations. And I loved it, for the most part. The challenges of the job, renting a shoebox-sized but fabulously located apartment in the Big Apple, knowing that a seemingly unlimited array of opportunities lay right outside my door, everything from Broadway plays to ballet to some of the world's best restaurants, museums, shops . . .

Then Grams fell.

The arthritis in her knees had been getting worse over the years. And then, while she was completely alone in the house except for her dog, Digger, and her cat, Chloe—neither of whom possess any caretaking abilities aside from all the emotional support and comic relief they both provide—she slid down three steps at the bottom of the big wooden staircase in the front hall.

Fortunately, she was able to get to a phone to dial 911. But even though Grams thankfully didn't break any bones, she was still faced with the harsh reality that taking care of herself and running her household was becoming increasingly difficult. In some ways, impossible. The woman who'd raised my two older sisters and me ever since our mother died the summer I was ten years old was clearly in need of live-in help.

That was where I came in.

I immediately decided that I would come back to the Hudson Valley. Once again, I took up residence in the riverside town I'd left fifteen years earlier, right after high school graduation. I'd moved back to the very same house, in fact, the dilapidated yet utterly charming Victorian at 59 Sugar Maple Way.

Of course, that also meant leaving behind my job in public relations. But when it came time to start thinking about what to do next job-wise, I found that the idea of going back to a schedule of working in an office from nine to five—actually, more like five AM to nine PM—held little appeal. Instead, I decided to live out a lifelong fantasy.

In June, the Lickety Splits Ice Cream Shoppe opened its doors on Hudson Street, Wolfert's Roost's main thoroughfare, less than a hundred feet from the town's busiest intersection.

And what a shop it was! Even now, every time I walked inside, I had to practically pinch myself to make myself believe this wasn't just a dream.

It was particularly thrilling that the store I'd created looked exactly the way I thought an ice cream emporium should look. I'd made sure of that. It helped that the space I was able to rent wasn't only in a great location. It also reeked of the turn-of-the-century charm that the downtown area itself possessed, with its quaint red-brick buildings, old-fashioned streetlights, and line of lush green trees.

Besides being just the right size, the storefront had a black-and-white tile floor that I'd had refinished, a tin ceiling that reflected the light, and—my favorite part—an exposed brick wall that added warmth along with a delightful old-fashioned feeling.

As soon as I signed the lease, I got busy turning the space into the perfect ice creamery. I'd had the walls painted pink and hung huge paintings of colorful, almost cartoonish ice cream concoctions—a three-foot ice cream cone, a gigantic banana split, and an ice cream sandwich the size of a crib mattress—that Willow had created. I'd outfitted the front with a long glass display case and brought in six small, marble-topped tables, three lining each wall. Each one was accompanied by two black wrought-iron chairs with pink vinyl seats.

Even the shop's exterior was cute. The building itself dated back to the Victorian era, so the shop had some delightful features, like two hand-carved wooden columns on either side of the front door and window boxes below the display window that dominated the front.

But I took its feeling of Disneyland's Main Street a few steps further by painting the façade a soft shade of pink, then making the wooden columns and the window box lime green. I'd also put a pink-and-green wooden bench in front of the display window. All summer, I'd kept the window box filled with pink-and-white petunias. The pastel-colored blossoms spilled over the front and sides so that the pink of the petals and the green of the leaves echoed the building's colors.

I'd planned on running the shop by myself, with occasional help from Willow. Then Emma showed up and turned out to be the perfect employee. She never missed a day or even showed up late. She was full of great ideas, dreaming up new flavors of ice cream that even I had never thought of. And her mastery of both computers and images had already proved invaluable. She'd designed fliers and created other graphics for the store. In addition, she was a master at surfing the Internet, which turned out to be particularly handy not only for my business but also when I'd investigated a murder a few weeks earlier.

At the moment, however, what I needed from my niece was for her to start packing up all the Ice Cream Incidentals.

"Emma, could you please—Emma?"

I glanced up to find that my niece had drifted over to the front of the shop, where she was staring out the huge win-

dow. Ethan was standing right next to her. True, it wasn't unusual for him to glom onto her. They had been inseparable
practically since that balmy evening in early July when he'd
dropped over at the house soon after they'd met at the dairy.
He claimed he'd stopped by to show her some sketches of
Japanese animation-style cartoons he'd been working on. But
the two of them ended up sitting on the front porch, talking,
until three AM. From that day on, they were what in the old
days was called an item.

At the moment, Ethan was also transfixed by whatever
was on the other side of this window.

"Hey, Kate? Check this out," Emma called.

Even though we were on a tight schedule, I strode over to
where the two gawkers were standing. Willow drifted over,
too, unable to resist the temptation of finding out what
Emma and Ethan were finding so fascinating.

I immediately saw what had grabbed their attention. From
the looks of things, the construction crew that had been
working on the store directly across the street from Lickety
Splits for weeks was finally wrapping things up. The four of
us watched as three burly guys struggled to affix a green canvas awning to the front, a sure sign that their renovations
were about to come to an end.

For five years, that shop had been the home of the Sweet
Things Pastry Palace. Soon after I'd opened Lickety Splits,
however, the bakery's owner had met with an unfortunate
fate. The owner, Ashley Winthrop, had been a longtime acquaintance, someone I'd known ever since kindergarten.

Notice I said "acquaintance," not "friend." There's a story
there. However, it's much too long to go into here. In fact,
telling that tale would require writing an entire book.

But for the past few weeks, the storefront had been empty.
That is, until early July, when construction crews began
showing up first thing every morning.

Since my shop was directly across the street, how could I not keep careful track of what was going on right before my eyes?

So along with Emma and Ethan and Willow, every day I had watched the muscle-bound workmen in jeans and tight T-shirts who showed up at seven. First they hauled out the glass display cases and kitchen equipment that had been part of the store's former incarnation. Then came demolition and construction. Old walls went out, new walls went in . . . you get the picture.

On one especially steamy afternoon, in an act of what I thought was pure inspiration, I'd sashayed over with an armful of ice cream cones. I was so desperate for some information about who my new neighbor would be that I was attempting to bribe the workers. They just shrugged, insisting that they were only following the plans the contractor had given them. Then they proceeded to devour more ice cream than you'd think was humanly possible.

The arrival of the painters a few days later piqued my curiosity even further.

Whoever was moving in was clearly a big fan of earth tones, since he or she had chosen dark green for the walls. The construction guys also put up lots of natural wood accents, which lent a fresh, outdoorsy touch.

But I still didn't have a clue as to what kind of establishment the new shop was going to be. And the addition of an awning that simply replicated the forest green of the walls didn't help.

"I can't wait to find out what kind of shop that's going to be," Emma said, as if she'd been reading my mind.

"As long as it doesn't sell ice cream," Willow commented. She cast me a meaningful look, a reminder that Lickety Splits had had to deal with some head-to-head competition once before. And it hadn't exactly gone well.

Emma leaned forward so she could see better. "I don't think it's going to sell food," she said. "Not with those dark colors. That place looks more like the Amazon rain forest than a café."

"It could be a restaurant that specializes in healthy food," Ethan said. Brightening, he added, "It would be totally sick if it was one of those places that makes those awesome smoothies. I'm really into kale."

I immediately started fantasizing about kale ice cream, wondering if that would turn out to be another Prune 'n' Raisin fiasco. Which reminded me that I was in the ice cream business—and that I had better get busy with that business.

"Okay, 'Cream Team," I said, clapping my hands. "Let's get back to work. We've got a party to put on!"

My crew immediately turned their attention back to me. At that moment, I felt as if George Washington would have been proud.

Standing up a little straighter, I said, "Willow, take the keys and pull the truck up in front of the shop. Emma, start packing up all this ice cream in dry ice. Ethan, get ready to start loading the heavy stuff."

My heart was pounding with a combination of excitement and terror as my three assistants scurried around, helping me realize an entirely new chapter in what had once upon a time been a mere fantasy.

I still couldn't quite believe all this was really happening.

"Let's load up the truck," I said. "It's show time!"

We drove to Greenaway in two vehicles. Willow sat beside me in my ice-cream–laden pickup truck, while Emma and Ethan followed in Ethan's dilapidated Saab. And as we wove our way through the hills above Wolfert's Roost, I actually found myself looking forward to the evening ahead.

This is going to be an adventure, I told myself, only half-listening to Willow as she chattered away about a yoga conference she'd just attended.

In fact, I was starting to feel pretty excited about the evening ahead when Willow announced, "Here it is! Twenty-two-fourteen Riverview Drive. And there's a sign that says Greenaway, so we're definitely in the right place. That must be the driveway. Turn right."

I did—and all my anxieties came back in a sudden swoosh. Whatever I'd been picturing in my mind had been nothing compared to what was in front of me.

What was looming ahead of me wasn't a house. It wasn't even a mansion.

This was an estate—one that made Downton Abbey look like a rustic cabin in the woods.

Chapter 2

Another story about the invention of the ice
cream sundae is that in 1881, Edward Berners,
who owned Ed Berners's Ice Cream Parlor in Two
Rivers, Wisconsin, tried serving ice cream with
chocolate syrup poured over it, even though
chocolate syrup was traditionally used for making
flavored ice cream sodas. Berners liked it enough
to begin selling "ice cream with syrup" for a
nickel, the same price as a plain dish of ice cream.

—*whatscookingamerica.net/History/*
IceCream/Sundae.htm

My throat thickened, and my mouth became uncomfortably dry.

It wasn't as if I'd never seen a residence on this scale before. The entire Hudson Valley was positively littered with them.

Thanks to its proximity to New York City, as well as its spectacular beauty, over the past couple of hundred years a lot of big-time movers and shakers had built humongous estates here. Kykuit—pronounced KYE-cutt—was home to four generations of Rockefellers. It has a jaw-dropping art museum with enough Picassos, Calders, Nevelsons, and other important artists to compete with some of New York City's finest museums. Then there's the Vanderbilt estate in Hyde Park, fronted by tall columns of the sort that are generally described as "stately." And speaking of big names, the Roosevelts, as in Franklin and Eleanor, had houses here. Like the other mansions, they're a major draw for tourists.

Some of the Hudson Valley mansions were constructed by lesser-known but nevertheless remarkable individuals. Olana, for example, my personal favorite. Built by Hudson River School painter Frederick Church, it's a fantastical mixture of Moorish, Persian, and Victorian architecture and furnishings that looks like something out of one of Disney's animated films. It's all you can do to keep from muttering, "Come with me to the Casbah!"

Even beyond the big-name historic sites that the busloads of tourists come to see, there are plenty of other noteworthy residences. On occasion, I've been known to Google "Hudson Valley Real Estate," just for fun. I can dream, can't I? And the listings give a simple gal like me plenty to fantasize about. What pops up are dozens of beautiful homes, ranging from grand Revolutionary War–era houses to Victorian extravaganzas to modern-day architectural wonders. Needless to say, they all have price tags with many, many zeroes.

Greenaway was definitely of that caliber.

The estate sprawled across at least one hundred acres. The three-story stone mansion that was its centerpiece, most likely built in the late 1800s, was perched upon a grassy hill so that it overlooked the Hudson River like a sentry. The house was so big that I couldn't imagine how many bedrooms it had. Or bathrooms.

The façade was rough-hewn gray stone, and a white porch ran along the front. I also spotted a tennis court, a barn, and at least five outbuildings. I noted not one but two swimming pools, the larger one encircled with rustic pieces of stone that matched those on the house. The patio next to it featured half a dozen Adirondack chairs, the biggest grill I'd ever seen, and a circular fire pit.

"Gee," Emma said quietly, "this isn't exactly what I was expecting." Her tone was pinched, reflecting the same level of anxiety I was feeling.

I was in the big league now. Like it or not.

I tried not to think about that as I grabbed one of the gigantic tubs of ice cream out of the back of my truck. It was the Classic Tahitian Vanilla, which may sound like a less than exciting flavor but which I felt strongly had to have a presence at pretty much any event that revolved around ice cream. After all, despite the tidal wave of new flavors that now swamped the shelves of grocery stores and filled the cones of inventive ice cream shops all over the world, vanilla remained the number-one seller.

"Wait here," I told my crew. "I'll make sure we've parked in the right place."

Still lugging the three-gallon tub of ice cream, I walked up an endlessly long red-brick path to the front door, two panels that were probably ten feet high and painted bright yellow. I felt like Dorothy edging toward the Great Oz's castle in the Emerald City.

When I rang the doorbell, I heard what sounded like a harpsichord echo through the house. Mozart, I guessed. A doorbell that played Mozart. On a harpsichord. And here I'd thought it wasn't possible for me to be any more blown away than I already was.

Within a few seconds, the door opened. Standing in front of me was a very tall, very thin man whose reedy appearance made me think of a male runway model.

His hair was blond, but the evenness and brightness of the color made it clear that it hadn't started out that way. The same went for his eyes, which were such a startling shade of green that he had to be wearing tinted contact lenses. And while I couldn't be completely sure, he looked like he was wearing a thin line of eyeliner. And mascara. Definitely mascara.

He was dressed in a pair of gray slacks with a meticulously tailored pale pink jacket. The tiny stitches running along the edge of the collar told me it was hand-sewn. His shoes— suede loafers—were the exact same shade of pink.

"May I help you?" he asked, looking as if he was about to dial 911.

"I'm Kate McKay from Lickety Splits." I shifted the heavy tub from one hip to the other. Not only was it starting to feel heavier; it was also starting to feel colder.

"I'm sorry?" he replied, clearly puzzled.

"The ice cream shop that's catering the party tonight . . . ?"

"Of course," he said. He sighed, giving the impression that he was relieved that he didn't have to deal with anything more challenging than the arrival of one of the caterers. "And I am Federico, Omar's assistant. We spoke on the phone."

Studying me as if I were something he still hadn't quite managed to identify, he continued, "Ms. McKay, before you and your staff even set foot in this house, I want to make it perfectly clear that everything that goes on here tonight—and I mean *everything*—must go through me. If there's one thing we don't want tonight it's any surprises."

Even speaking to him in person, I couldn't place his accent. Definitely European . . . but which corner of that continent it had emanated from wasn't exactly clear.

"Of course," I replied. "By the way," I couldn't help adding, "where are you from?" Not wanting to seem nosy, I quickly said, "I mean your accent sounds so . . . exotic."

A warm smile slowly spread across his face, making me feel as if I'd chosen the right adjective. "I am from the north of Italy," he said. "Right outside of Milano." With a sneer, he said, "You know, what you Americans call Mill-*ann*."

I nodded. Believe it or not, I was tempted to say, some Americans actually know that the Italian name of that small but sophisticated city, a major center of the fashion industry, is Milano. Even if we haven't traveled much, we're big fans of the Milano cookie.

That thought took me in a different direction. I found myself wondering if there was a way to incorporate Milanos and other popular Pepperidge Farm cookies into ice cream. Rich Chessmen broken up and mixed in with cheesecake ice cream, the buttery cookies crushed to play the role of a crust? Or those decadent Geneva cookies, mixed into a smooth, rich chocolate ice cream along with additional chunks of chocolate and big crunchy pecans? As for the classic Gingerman cookies, I realized that one of those crisp little guys would look perfect standing in the middle of a big scoop of ginger ice cream. Perhaps this creation called for some raisins and even a touch of pumpkin pie spice . . .

I had to force myself to focus on the matter at hand.

"Since you're the man in charge," I said brightly, "maybe you can point me in the direction of the kitchen. I've got to unload the ice cream from my truck, and this obviously isn't the best place to do it."

For the first time in my life, I truly understood the expression about "looking down your nose" at someone. Federico literally cocked his head back so that in order to maintain eye contact with me, he had to do exactly that.

"It's that way," he said, dramatically lifting his arm and pointing toward a doorway. "You'll be using the servants' entrance, of course."

I had to resist the urge to allow my eyebrows to jump upward, as they were inclined to do.

It makes sense, I told myself, taking a few deep breaths to calm the fury rising deep inside me. I'm not exactly a guest at this event. I'm here to work, not to sip champagne and make small talk. Besides, the entrance he wants me to use is un-doubtedly closer to the kitchen.

So I just smiled politely and agreed. Then I went back to the truck and climbed in.

"That way," I instructed Willow, pointing toward what I now knew was called "the servants' entrance" rather than simply "the back door." I gestured at Emma and Ethan, telling them to follow.

When I pulled up to the correct spot, I saw that someone was already waiting, holding the door open for me. I was touched by this display of politeness. I'd already told myself that that was something I shouldn't expect tonight.

The tiny woman in the doorway was the exact opposite of Federico, even though they were both probably about my age. Not only because she was female and small, either. She was wearing a uniform that spoke of formality and tradition: an old-fashioned maid's uniform consisting of a plain black dress, a starched white apron, and low-heeled black shoes. Her hair, also black, was pulled back in a neat bun. All that was missing were a few ruffles on the apron and a tendency to mutter, "Yes, mum!" every few seconds.

"Thanks," I said breathlessly as I breezed past her, once again hauling my tub of vanilla ice cream.

"Let me know if there's anything I can do to help," she said. "But it looks like you've got everything under control."

"Thank you," I said. "I'm Kate McKay."

"My name is Marissa," she replied. "I'm the housekeeper. Let me show you around."

"Great," I said, adding, "I really appreciate how helpful you're being."

She seemed to pick up on my meaning. Smiling sympathet-ically, she said, "Federico can be a little hard to deal with, can't he?"

The kitchen was the size of a high school gym. Well, not

quite, but you could certainly have managed a pickup game of basketball in there. The décor was an interesting mixture of old-fashioned and modern. The cavernous room had rough-hewn exposed wooden beams running across the white ceiling, and the floor was made from wide planks of wood that could have used a sanding. Running through the middle was a long, rustic wooden table that looked as if it had spent its early years in the south of France.

Yet in one corner stood two huge state-of-the-art Sub-Zero refrigerators. And the walls on both sides of the cavernous space were lined with sleek black-granite counters. They were dotted with a restaurant-size espresso and cappuccino maker, a juicer, and a giant KitchenAid mixer.

Working in here was going to be a dream.

Once Marissa had given me a quick tour, she said, "I'm going to leave you to it. I've got a million things to do before the guests arrive."

"Of course," I told her. "And thanks again."

With my three crew members still outside unloading the truck, I'd just assumed I would be alone. And I looked forward to scoping out the space where I'd be working, opening cabinets and learning more about the layout.

But a rustling sound made my ears prick up like Digger's whenever there's a squirrel anywhere within a two-mile radius of the house.

I was about to call out a cautious, "Hello?" when I heard a female voice mutter, "*Verdammt!*" Then, with a trace of a German accent: "Where do they keep the ice around here?"

I whirled around. In the back corner of the kitchen, moving around in the shadows, I spotted an extremely thin young woman dressed entirely in black. Black jeans, black T-shirt, black flats. She was randomly opening drawers and cabinets.

"You might check the freezer," I suggested, trying my best not to sound sarcastic. Or even surprised.

"The freezer," she repeated, snapping her long, slender fingers. "Great idea!"

She glanced around as if trying to identify which item in the huge kitchen might fall into the category of "freezer." After a few seconds, she located the two stainless steel behemoths, then made a beeline toward them.

As she floated by, I finally caught sight of her face.

She was remarkably beautiful, with delicate, perfectly symmetrical features: robin's-egg-blue eyes, a tiny nose, perfectly formed, bowlike lips, and cheekbones as sharp as that ice she was in search of. As if she hadn't gotten much more than her share in the beauty department, she also had a long mane of silky blond hair. In her case, the color looked genuine.

It only took half a second for me to recognize her. She was Gretchen Gruen, the German supermodel that Federico had mentioned would be one of the guests here tonight. As difficult as it was to believe, she was even more breathtaking in person than she was in the advertisements and magazine spreads I'd seen her in—even the way she was dressed today, in a totally nondescript outfit.

"Ice!" she cried, sounding both triumphant and surprised. She must have realized how ridiculous this little episode had been, because she turned to me and said, "I'm used to finding ice in a bucket."

One that was brought by room service, no doubt, I thought. Aloud, I said, "Would you like me to help you find a glass?"

Her perfectly sculpted eyebrows knit together for a second or two before she said, "*Danke*, but I'm not thirsty."

"Then why did you need ice?" I asked.

"For the disgusting bags under my eyes!" she cried. To prove just how monstrous she looked, she leaned forward so I could inspect her face. If I squinted, I could see that the skin under her left eye curved slightly more than the skin under her right eye. Maybe a millimeter or two.

"I have to look my best for Omar's party!" she exclaimed. "After all, he helped make me who I am."

I suddenly remembered something I'd read in a magazine, probably while sitting in a doctor's waiting room. According to the story, Gretchen Gruen had been working at a pretzel factory in a small industrial town in Bavaria when, one Saturday evening, she went to a local beer garden. Omar DeVane had been there, too. He was chugging down a few brewskis when she strolled in, arm in arm with two of her best pals. Omar spotted her across the crowded room filled with lederhosen-bedecked Germans and burst out, "That's the face of my future!"

At least, that was the rags-to-riches story she told in interviews. Who knew what the truth was?

Gretchen held the single ice cube against one eye and flashed me her ten-million-dollar smile. It was bright enough to illuminate an entire BMW factory.

"Now I have to go upstairs and make myself beautiful," she told me before turning and dashing off.

That shouldn't be too hard, I thought. And meanwhile, I have to pretend I'm someone who really knows how to put on an ice cream extravaganza for seventy-five sophisticated people from all over the world, each one wearing an outfit that probably cost more than my truck.

But deep down, I had a feeling that Emma had been right about there being plenty of leftovers at the end of the evening. These people were not going to turn out to be big ice cream eaters. Not when the women here tonight would probably average a size 2.

I had been totally blown over by Omar's mansion from the moment the four of us had pulled up in front of it. Yet my first reaction paled compared to how impressed I was when I had finally got a look at the main part of the house, where tonight's event was being held.

As Emma and I walked out of the kitchen and into the room that Federico had instructed us would serve as ice cream central for the evening, we both gasped. I nearly dropped my tray of dainty crystal ice cream dishes. Federico had pulled them out of a Louis-Something cabinet as soon as he'd spotted the glass tulip dishes I'd brought along to use. He'd practically shuddered at the sight of them.

"Wow," Emma said under her breath.

"My thoughts exactly," I agreed.

The party space was basically a glass-enclosed sunroom. But it was on a scale unlike anything I'd ever seen before. In fact, it reminded me of something you'd find in a French château. Three of the walls were made entirely of glass, and its high, peaked ceiling was punctuated with skylights. Aside from two pairs of French doors that led outside, the glass walls were lined with lush greenery housed in gigantic ceramic pots.

Directly outside was a modest-sized sculpture garden enclosed by a dense hedge that probably stood ten feet tall. I'm not exactly a sculpture aficionado, but I'd spent enough time in New York's art museums to recognize a Calder, a Henry Moore, and—one of my favorites because of her playful use of color—a Niki de Saint Phalle. When it came to private art collections, Omar DeVane was apparently someone who could give John D. Rockefeller a run for his money.

As if the space itself wasn't like something out of the pages of an architecture magazine, for tonight's event it had been decorated to look like a fairyland. Countless strings of tiny twinkling white lights were draped along the windows. They were also strewn along the edges of the buffet tables, which were covered in pale blue linen tablecloths. Tremendous bouquets of fragrant flowers, some three or even four feet high, were positioned in corners and on tables.

In the back corner, the members of a string quartet were taking their places. The two men, the cellist and one of the violinists, wore tuxedos. The two women, a violist and the other violinist, were dressed in cream-colored evening gowns made of a shimmery fabric.

Meanwhile, a team of bartenders was setting up in one of the smaller rooms off the main space. Not only was there was huge selection of wines that I was certain were considerably better than the stuff I generally indulged in, but every top-shelf brand of liquor was also lined up.

Then there was the champagne. I had a feeling that tonight's supply had raised the gross national product of France by a huge percentage.

I wasn't the only one who was impressed.

"Whoa, Kate, this place is totally chill," Ethan said breathlessly, stopping in his tracks as soon as he walked into the sunroom. "It reminds me of the parties they used to have at that French castle—Versailles?"

"I know it," I replied, nodding. "I've even been there. Have you?"

"Not yet," he said. "But I've read a lot about it. A couple of weeks ago I read *The Count of Monte Cristo*, which was totally awesome. You know, the novel by that French dude, Alexandre Dumas?"

"I know that dude, too." I handed him a tray of chocolate and vanilla mini ice cream sandwiches. "Here. Pretend you're a footman in the royal court and pass these around."

Even though I was acting calm, the butterflies in my stomach had made a sudden reappearance. I was glad that just then Willow sailed into the sunroom carrying a tray piled high with ice cream cupcakes.

"Do you think my measly little Ice Cream Incidentals are good enough for this place?" I asked her anxiously.

"Of course they are!" Willow insisted. "They're perfect! In fact, look how nicely the pastel colors of the ice cream complement the tablecloths. Strawberry, peach, blueberry, mint . . . they couldn't look any better even if we'd planned it." She set down her tray and glanced around. "You did good, Kate. As usual."

I felt like hugging her. Instead, I got busy setting up the white ceramic fondue pot that I would be using to serve the fudge sauce. The thick molten chocolate was hot, since I'd just warmed it up on the fancy stove in Omar's kitchen, but not *too* hot. I placed the pot over a can of Sterno, which is one of caterers' favorite inventions of all times. Sterno is literally canned heat, a can of alcohol that's been specially treated so that it burns right in the can. It's ideal for keeping food warm while you're serving it.

Once I'd gotten the flame just right, carefully adjusting it so it would keep the luscious fudge sauce hot without burning it, I headed back to the kitchen to pick up another tray of ice cream goodies.

As I was on my way, I passed by a room that I'd glanced at earlier, concluding that it must be Omar's home office. The door was only partially closed, and from inside I heard two men talking loudly. Arguing, in fact.

"You have no idea of the genius behind Omar's vision," I heard someone who definitely sounded like Federico say. Even if I'd been unable to recognize the voice, the accent was unmistakable.

"Okay, I get that Omar's a genius," someone else shot back. I didn't recognize his voice, but I certainly knew a New York accent when I heard one. And this man, whoever he was, definitely sounded like a native of Brooklyn or Queens. "But just because he's a genius doesn't mean he's got unlimited money to do whatever the hell he wants. I mean, really: constructing entire rooms on trucks and parading them through the streets of New York as a way of showing off the furniture he designed?"

"I'm telling you, the launch of his new home design line is going to move him to an entirely new level," Federico insisted. "The world has been waiting for the Omar at Home collection for years, whether they know it or not. For heaven's sake, his Omar chair is going to revolutionize the way people sit!"

"How can I possibly have a constructive conversation with someone who actually believes that?" the New Yorker replied.

"What I believe in is *Omar!*" Federico insisted, his voice filled with indignation. "And if you don't, then maybe you shouldn't even be on his payroll!"

"You must be forgetting the fact that Omar and I go back to before you were out of diapers," New York Guy said.

"You're so old that you're probably back *in* them!" was Federico's retort.

I gasped, certainly not meaning to make my presence known but so caught off guard by what Federico had just said that somehow all the air in my chest had come rushing out before I could stop it.

It wasn't a loud gasp, but it turned out to be loud enough that both men heard me. Two seconds later, they were both standing in the doorway, staring at me with furious expressions.

"You're listening in on a private conversation?" Federico accused.

"No!" I insisted. "I mean, I didn't mean to. It's just that the two of you are talking so loudly that it's impossible not to hear you."

"Are you even supposed to be back here?" the New York accent guy said. I saw that he was dressed in an expensive-looking, meticulously tailored dark business suit and a boring striped tie. His dark, graying hair was definitely thinning, but what was left of it was well-cut and carefully groomed, giving him a decidedly corporate look that somehow seemed out of place here.

While he wasn't what I'd consider old—somewhere in his forties, if I had to guess—he definitely wasn't one of the glamorous fashion folk I'd expected to see here tonight.

"As a matter of fact," I said calmly, "I *am* supposed to be back here. I'm one of the caterers. And passing through this hallway happens to be the most efficient way to get from the kitchen to the party area."

"Gotcha," the New Yorker said. He glanced at Federico warily. "So I guess this isn't the best time and place to be having this conversation. But it's still one that you and I need to have."

Federico folded his arms across his chest and stared at the businessman defiantly. "I'm not going to budge on this," he declared. "And neither is Omar."

They spent another few seconds glaring at each other, then stalked out of the room: Federico first, the other man right behind him.

But while Federico took off as fast as his long skinny legs could take him, which was pretty darn fast, the other man stayed behind.

"Sorry you had to hear that," he said, looking a bit embarrassed. "We had no idea anyone else was back here."

"No problem," I assured him.

"Mitchell Shriver," he said, reaching over to shake my hand. "I'm Omar DeVane's business manager."

"I'm Kate McKay," I told him. "I'm in business, too. The ice cream business. I own an ice cream parlor over in Wolfert's Roost called Lickety Splits. But I also cater parties, which I what I'm doing tonight."

"I see." For a few seconds, his hazel eyes clouded over, as if he didn't see at all. Then they brightened. I could practically see the light bulb that had apparently just flashed on in his head. "Hey, if you're ever interested in franchising, I might be able to help you with that. That's one of the things I do: take a little guy and help turn him—or her—into a big guy."

"Thanks, but I'm pretty happy being a little guy right now," I assured him. I was about to turn away when a question popped out of my mouth: "Have you really known Omar his entire life?"

"Just about," he replied. Chuckling, he added, "Believe it or not, he and I grew up together. He used to dream about becoming a fashion designer, and I wanted to be a surgeon." He shrugged. "Instead, I operate on people's finances."

I got the feeling he'd used that line before.

"I should probably get back to work," I said. "It was nice meeting you. Enjoy the party!"

"Thanks," he said. "I'll be sure to check out your ice cream." With a wink, he said, "And I'll let you know if I think that little shop of yours should go nationwide."

I was back in the sunroom, arranging ice cream cupcakes in neat rows and creating a pattern with their different-colored tops, when I felt someone clutch my arm.

"Kate," Willow whispered, "do you know who that is?"

I turned to see the person she was looking at. Standing a few feet away from us was a slim woman, about five-foot-eight. Her bronze-colored hair was in a perfect flip, and her makeup was flawless. She was wearing a white evening gown that flowed over her slender silhouette in an extremely flattering way.

Somehow, the woman simply exuded elegance. Self-confidence, too.

Given that white dress, I knew there would be no chocolate ice cream in her future. Vanilla, maybe.

"She looks familiar," I said. A couple of seconds later it came to me. "Oh, my. That's Pippa Somers, isn't it? The editor of *Flair*! Federico mentioned on the phone that she'd be here."

Willow nodded. "I'm actually more of a fashionista than you think. I mean, it's not as if deciding what color yoga pants to buy is as involved as I get. But she's so famous that even people who don't care at all about what they put on their bodies know who she is!"

It was true. Pippa Somers was often in the news.

While most magazine editors were nothing more than names to their readers—if their readers even bothered to pay attention to something like that—Pippa Somers was as much of a celebrity as the fashion designers whose clothes filled *Flair*'s pages, the models who showed them off, and the celebrities and other prominent women who wore them. She invariably had a front-row seat at every important fashion show.

She was also a presence at the Cannes Film Festival in France, the Academy Awards in Hollywood, and every other red-carpet event worth covering on *Entertainment Tonight*. Her name and face often appeared in gossip columns with reports on who she dined with at which restaurant or which Broadway play she had just been seen emerging from. Thanks to her fame, she was someone who had the ability to make or break any individual who crossed her path.

"I certainly know who she is," I told Willow. "In fact, I even saw an exhibit of her personal collection of clothing. It was at the Metropolitan Museum of Art a couple of years ago." That exhibit had prompted me to make a beeline for Bloomingdale's, convinced that my own wardrobe needed a serious overhaul.

But as exciting as it was to spot Pippa Somers, I had yet to set eyes on our host for the evening.

The room suddenly felt supercharged, as if someone had opened a window and instead of letting in cool air had let in a bolt of lightning.

Omar had arrived, slipping into the crowded room without the least bit of fanfare.

I immediately recognized him, since I was a fan of the design competition television show on which he served as a judge. In fact, Grams and I hadn't missed a single show during the entire spring season. She was constantly marveling over the talent and technical abilities of the competitors. I, meanwhile, was always amazed at how quickly the contestants could turn a few yards of fabric into something that people could actually wear.

Like everyone else at the party, Omar was dressed in clothing that looked incredibly expensive and well-designed. He was wearing an off-white suit with a turquoise shirt and a bright red tie splattered with turquoise polka dots. Because he was chubby and on the short side, he didn't have the elegant look that so many of his guests had. And somehow he gave off a vibe of being friendly and approachable.

The eyeglasses that were perched on his nose helped create that feeling. They were fun: perfectly round with purple frames. The side pieces had purple and turquoise stripes.

This was a man who didn't take himself too seriously. I liked him immediately.

In addition to coming across as a regular guy who hadn't let his abundance of both talent and good luck go to his head, Omar also had a certain presence. Somehow you just knew he was someone special.

"Those glasses are brand-new," I heard Federico tell the exceedingly thin woman standing next to him. His voice was filled with pride as he added, "They're from Omar's fall collection of eyewear. They come in an entire rainbow of colors! Several shapes, too."

I half-expected him to whip out his order pad and see how many units she was interested in buying. But Omar had just held up his hands, motioning that he was about to speak. The entire group immediately grew hushed.

"Good evening, everyone!" he said, clasping his hands in front of him. "I'd like to thank all of you for coming tonight. I know that most of you live in Manhattan—and that, astonishingly, some of you actually took the train to get here!"

A ripple of laughter erupted.

"I'd also like to thank all the people who have been working so hard to make tonight's party a success," Omar went on. "Federico, of course. My loyal, tireless, infinitely creative assistant. Where would I be without Federico?"

Federico beamed, clearing enjoying all the attention. He blew a kiss at Omar, and a few people applauded.

"And Mitchell, of course," Omar said. "The yin to my yang. For every new idea I come up with, I need someone to tell me whether or not I can afford to make it happen."

Mitchell, standing toward the back, gave an awkward wave. I got the feeling that, unlike Federico, he was someone who preferred to stay in the background.

"Gretchen Gruen—where are you, Gretchen?" Omar held his hands up to his forehead, shielding his eyes from imaginary sunshine as he scanned the crowd. "Ah, there you are, as lovely as always. I could not be here today if it weren't for you."

Gretchen emerged from the crowd. Her black jeans and T-shirt had been replaced by a strapless black evening gown. It hugged her slender frame but had a slit off to one side that went almost up to her waist.

"Most of all," he went on, his eyes growing moist, "I must single out Pippa. Pippa Somers, one of the most important— no, let me amend that to *the* most important figure in the world of fashion today. And I literally mean the world. Paris, London, New York, Milan . . . and yes, even Tokyo. When it comes to being a real star, no one outshines our beloved Pippa."

Omar held out his arm. "Pippa, please come up. Let me give you a hug."

As she grew near, Omar choked out the words, "Thank you, Pippa, for making me who I am today."

With that, he gave her a big bear hug.

"Love you, Omar!" Pippa cooed, hugging him back.

"Love you more!" Omar replied.

The crowd went wild, shrieking and applauding as if he'd just announced that a free Mercedes was waiting outside for each guest as a party favor.

Once Pippa had stepped away, vanishing back into the crowd, Omar began speaking again.

"I'd also like to thank some of the less-known people who helped make tonight happen. Marissa, my housekeeper, who does a truly amazing job. She is the queen of organization. Marissa, are you here?"

Apparently she was not. But the crowd gave her a weak round of applause anyway.

"And a big thank you to the hardworking people who provided the delicious goodies we'll all be devouring tonight," Omar said. "I'm especially grateful to Kate McKay, the owner of the Lickety Splits Ice Cream Shoppe in Wolfert's Roost. Kate is enabling all of you to join me in gobbling up as much of my favorite food as possible. Let's hear it for Kate, her staff, and hot fudge sundaes!"

As the group applauded me, I could feel my cheeks growing pink. Like Mitchell, I gave an awkward wave, although I had an ice cream scoop in my hand as I did.

"Now no more forcing my captive guests to listen to their windbag of a host," Omar concluded. "Enjoy the evening—and I personally give each one of you my permission to eat as much ice cream as you possibly can!"

For the next two hours, my team and I worked nonstop. While there were a few super-skinny people who steered clear of the ice cream, most of them women, there were plenty who were happy to take their cue from Omar and totally gorge on it.

Willow and I stood side by side at the table, doing an assembly-line kind of thing. She scooped whatever flavors of ice cream each person individually requested, then handed me the huge bowl so I could douse it with hot fudge. The guests then gleefully helped themselves to whatever mix-ins they wanted to add. Nuts and M&Ms proved to be the most popular. Sprinkles, not so much. I was surprised that this crowd seemed to care more about taste and texture than appearance.

I was just as surprised by how much ice cream this crowd put away. Rich or poor, thin or not so thin, fashion-conscious or part of the sweats-and-sneakers crowd, hardly anyone can resist ice cream.

This group's excitement over the opportunity to indulge in my sweet, creamy confections reinforced something I'd come to understand only after I'd opened Lickety Splits. And that was that by making and selling ice cream, I was doing much more than living out a longtime fantasy. I was providing people with the ultimate comfort food, one that was unique in its ability to serve as a treat, a reward, a celebration, a way to feel better on a bad day—or a way to simply enjoy life.

When I finally paused to take a deep breath and glance at my watch, I was shocked to see that my stint here was nearly over. It was only then that I realized how physically tired I was: my legs, from standing; my arms and hands, from stirring and scooping hot fudge.

But I was also exhilarated. The evening had been a real success. I'd held my own tonight, even in this posh environment. And while I'd assumed that this crowd would turn out to be a whole lot tougher than either the five-year-olds or the forty-year-olds I'd done parties for recently, in the end they turned out to be just like them: people who really loved ice cream.

In fact, I was contemplating the sweet, creamy treat's universal appeal and its infallible ability to bring people together when I suddenly heard a scream.

So did everyone else in the room. We all froze, bringing the festivities to an immediate halt. The music stopped, people stopped chattering mid-sentence, and a horrible hush came over the entire room.

A few seconds later Marissa came running into the room, her face twisted into a stricken expression.

"It's Omar!" she cried. "He's dead!"

She let out a choking sound, then uttered three words that instantly dropped the temperature in the room by at least fifty degrees.

"He's been *murdered*!"

Chapter 3

As for the hot fudge sundae, Clarence Clifton
Brown, who owned C. C. Brown's Ice Cream
Shop on Hollywood Boulevard in Los Angeles,
California, is credited with inventing it in 1906.
His idea was to combine something hot and
something cold to create a unique dessert.
Needless to say, it was a great success.

—*from pralinesownmade.com/blog/the-history-of-*
the-hot-fudge-sundae/androadsideamerica.com

It suddenly felt as if time had stopped.
No one spoke. No one moved. It was as if no one breathed,
either, as we all struggled to comprehend the words Marissa
had just screamed.

And then, as if a director had called "Action!" everyone
seemed to be in motion.

People began chattering away, the noise level rising to a
deafening level. Some voices were tinged with panic, others
with fury. But the atmosphere became one of total chaos.

Despite the noise, I caught snippets of conversation.

"What happened?"

"How was he killed?"

"Who could have done such a horrible thing?"

"What are we supposed to do now? I've never been in a
situation like this before!"

And perhaps the most heartbreaking: "Omar? Who could possibly have wanted Omar dead? He was the sweetest person in the world!"

And then, through all the confusion, a single voice broke through.

"Please, everyone. Let's stay calm!"

The voice was female, colored by a British accent. Pippa Somers had fought her way through the crowd until she'd reached the same spot in which Omar had been standing at the start of the evening.

"There's no need to panic," she went on, her clipped way of speaking making her sound even more like someone in charge. "I called 911, and the authorities are on their way. In the meantime, they have asked that no one leave the premises and that no one touch anything. So on their behalf I'm asking that you stay where you are until the police get here."

"How was he killed?" a man called out.

Pippa looked stricken for a few seconds. And then, with her usual grace, she replied, "According to Marissa, it appears that he was strangled. With his own necktie."

Killed with his own necktie? I thought. The red one with the turquoise polka dots? A tie that he designed *himself*?

The irony was excruciatingly painful.

The next few minutes were nothing short of surreal. Here I stood in a room full of people who were dressed in their finest, sipping cocktails and eating ice cream in an incredibly elegant house. We were surrounded by fragrant bouquets of flowers, trays of champagne, even a chamber music group. Yet something unthinkable had just happened. And somehow the idea that everyone in this room had come together to be part of a glamorous event made what was going on even more horrifying, if that was possible.

For what seemed like an excruciatingly long time, we were on hold, wondering what would come next as we desperately tried to process what had happened.

And then the atmosphere shifted once again. Only another minute or two passed before people started talking again. At first they spoke softly, but before long their voices returned to the same near-deafening level as before.

The one thing no one was doing was eating. I noticed that a few people headed straight for the bar, as if they needed fortification. But most of the guests stayed in the same spot, honoring Pippa's request that no one move.

I was tempted to start bringing the tubs of ice cream into the kitchen—and more importantly, putting them into the freezer. But I remembered Pippa's other directive: that no one touch anything.

So I had no choice but to stand by and watch the bountiful spread of ice cream a few feet away from me soften. What remained in the tubs of Classic Tahitian Vanilla, Chocolate Almond Fudge, Peanut Butter on the Playground, and Cappuccino Crunch was becoming visibly mushy. My beautiful Ice Cream Incidentals were sagging pitifully, the chocolate cookies on the top and bottom of the mini ice cream sandwiches converging against an amorphous glob of ice cream. The ice cream cupcakes were starting to list to one side.

As for my Heavenly Hot Fudge Sauce, still perched above cans of Sterno that by this point were barely flickering, it was quickly taking on the consistency of mud.

But I was concerned about something much more important than the decline of my lovely display of ice cream treats. Frantically I scanned the crowd, searching for my niece. Before I managed to spot her, I heard her voice right behind me.

"Aunt Kate?"

"Emma!" I cried, turning and instinctively giving her a hug. "Are you all right?"

"I'm okay," she replied in a shaky, scared-little-girl voice.

"I'm so sorry you had to be subjected to this," I told her, overcome with guilt. "I wish I could send you home, but you heard what Pippa said: the police want everyone to stay."

Willow appeared then, her expression one of great relief. "Oh, good, I found you both."

Ethan followed a few seconds later. Somehow, it just felt right for the four of us to be together. Especially since none of us knew another soul in the room.

"I'm in shock!" Willow commented. "Omar seemed like such a nice man . . . It's so hard to take this in."

Ethan nodded in agreement. "I feel like I'm in a movie or something."

Suddenly the mood in the room shifted once again. I immediately realized why.

Someone new had come into the room. A tall, lean man who gave off an air of authority. His dark blond hair was cut as short as possible, and he was dressed in an ill-fitting suit that gave him the distinction of being the least stylish person in the room. Even Marissa's maid's uniform looked better designed.

As he strode across the room, he surveyed the crowd, his expression serious and his eyes hard.

My mouth became dry, and my stomach felt uncomfortably tight.

"Who *is* that?" one of the guests standing behind me muttered.

I knew exactly who it was. I'd met up with Detective Stoltz before.

And my previous interactions with him had been anything but favorable. After all, the man had actually believed that I was someone who was capable of committing murder.

And here I was again, smack in the middle of a crime scene.

"If I could have everyone's attention, please," he began, immediately taking charge. "I'm Detective Stoltz from the Wolfert's Roost Police Department. That gentleman over there in the doorway is Officer Bonano. As I believe most of you already know, a few minutes ago Omar DeVane was killed in what looks like a homicide. The room in which Mr. DeVane died is now a crime scene. Therefore, it is off-limits. The medical examiner is on his way, and other members of the police department are currently on-site, gathering evidence. In the meantime, I cannot state strongly enough that no one is permitted to go into that room.

"In addition, no one is allowed to leave this room until further notice. I'm going to ask all of you to be patient as Officer Bonano takes down contact information for everyone who's here. We need this information in case we have any follow-up questions during our investigation.

"In the meantime," Detective Stoltz went on, "I'll be setting up a spot where I can speak with each of you, one at a time. What I'd like to do first is identify the individuals who were closest to the victim. I'm referring to other people who reside in the house, Omar DeVane's employees, other close associates . . ."

I knew I'd be low on that list. And I was glad.

Still, the tightness in my stomach continued to gnaw at me as I waited with Emma and the rest of my entourage. As for the ice cream, I'd stopped worrying about its future. Instead, I was worrying about how horrific the cleanup was going to be.

Standing around in that room, waiting, was so excruciating that I was actually relieved when it was finally my turn to be questioned.

I was approached by Officer Bonano—who, back in high school, was known simply as Pete Bonano. In those days, he was even better known for his skill as a football player than he was for his chocolate brown eyes, his curly dark brown hair, his chubby cheeks, and his friendly grin. I could see that he still possessed those last characteristics, aside from his smile, which at the moment was nowhere in sight.

"Ms. McKay?" he said, looking a bit sheepish. "Detective Stoltz would like to speak with you next."

It's *me*, Pete! I felt like screaming. Remember all those English classes we took together, with me sitting in the front row and raising my hand every time the teacher asked a question and you sitting in back, throwing spitballs at your buddies?

But I remained silent as I followed the fellow who over the years had traded a football uniform for a police officer's uniform.

Detective Stoltz was holed up in a small room off the kitchen. He sat behind a table that at the moment was serving as a desk. A lone wooden chair was positioned opposite him. I wondered if he'd deliberately sought out the least comfortable chair in the house for the people he was questioning to sit in.

"Ms. McKay, we meet again," Detective Stoltz greeted me dryly. He motioned for me to sit in the wooden chair. The seat was even harder than I'd expected. "You seem to be someone who has a way of putting herself in the path of murder."

"I wouldn't go that far," I protested. "It's just coincidence that I'm here tonight. The same way it was last time—"

Detective Stoltz simply stared at me, making me think of the way insects are pinned to a board. I did my best to refrain from squirming.

I also shut up. I figured that even though I had absolutely nothing to hide, there was no point in volunteering any information unless he asked for it.

"So what brought you to Mr. DeVane's house tonight?" Detective Stoltz asked.

"Hot fudge sundaes," I replied. But I quickly realized that a more detailed answer was required. "Mr. DeVane's assistant, Federico, called me a couple of weeks ago and asked me to set up a hot fudge sundae station at tonight's party. Ap-

parently hot fudge sundaes are—I mean, were—Omar De-
Vane's favorite food."

The detective's laser-like gaze remained fixed on me. I had
a feeling that his ability to stare at people like that was one of
the main reasons the man had been qualified to become a
homicide detective.

"Had you ever met Mr. DeVane before tonight?" Detective
Stoltz asked.

"No," I replied. "Never." I was tempted to mention that I
had once owned an Omar DeVane purse, complete with a big
gold ODV insignia. That was back when I lived a fast-paced
life in the city, a time of my life when accessories actually
mattered. Too much information, I quickly decided.

"So you had no relationship at all with the deceased?" he
persisted.

"None whatsoever."

"I thought that was the case," he said.

I wasn't sure if I should be insulted.

"I think I have what I need," the detective announced
crisply. "Thank you for your time, Ms. McKay. You are no
longer required to remain on the premises."

"Thank you," I said.

I stood up and headed for the door, then suddenly turned
back.

"Detective Stoltz?" I said. "I just want to say that I really
hope you find out who's behind this. I didn't know Omar De-
Vane, but he seemed like a genuinely fine person."

"Thank you again," the detective replied, still businesslike.
"That will be all."

It was past midnight by the time I pulled the truck into my
driveway with Emma sitting beside me. As soon as I turned
off the engine, we were shrouded by the darkness of a moon-
less night.

I glanced over at my niece, who had been silent during the entire ride home. At the moment, she looked about as lively and as energetic as a rag doll. An extremely exhausted rag doll.

It was only then that I realized that I, too, was completely worn out. Not just physically, but also mentally and emotionally. I supposed I'd been in shock throughout the evening, yet now that I was home, that feeling was wearing off fast.

That was the thing about home. You could be your real self.

And the three-story Victorian at 59 Sugar Maple Way was definitely home.

I'd lived in this house since I was five years old. That was when my dad had passed away. That traumatic event had been life-changing for many reasons, one of which was that shortly afterward, my mother, my two sisters, and I moved in with Grams. My sister Julie was twelve then, and Nina was ten.

While making a move like that could have been jarring, I had actually welcomed it. I'd been visiting my grandmother there for as long as I could remember, and I had only positive feelings about it.

That was largely because of my grandmother, of course. But the house itself had always felt as warm and welcoming as the woman who'd thrown open the front door every time we drove up, wearing a huge smile and more often than not bearing a big plate of freshly baked cookies or a new picture book or a set of paper dolls.

And what a house it was.

It had been built in the late 1880s, which I've always considered one of America's most romantic periods. True, women had yet to get the vote, and they were pretty much hampered by the social norms of the day, not to mention—ugh!—corsets. Still, the people who lived then must have felt they were witnessing the dawn of the modern age. After all, it was a time of great innovation, with telephones and electric light bulbs and ballpoint pens making their first appearances.

The bright yellow house was outfitted with the most delightful features of houses built during that era. There were curved bay windows on both sides of the front door running almost to the top of the first floor. Charming gingerbread trim lined the eaves. Jutting out of the top was a turret. The cone-shaped roof had always made the turret look like a gigantic ice cream cone, at least to me.

But my favorite feature by far was the magnificent porch that ran along the entire front. When I was growing up, that porch had been the perfect place for wiling away the lazy hours of a long summer day, reading or daydreaming or giggling with my sisters. A few months earlier, it had gotten a new addition: a wooden ramp that ran alongside the steps to make it easier for Grams to get in and out of the house.

Of course, a house that old had its downside. Every square inch of character meant another square inch of an aging building that needed more and more upkeep with each year that passed. And with Grams able to do less and less, not to mention the high cost of repairs, the house looked a little— well, rough around the edges.

The entire front porch sagged. It also creaked so loudly that we were never surprised when someone knocked on the front door or rang the bell since the aging floorboards had already told us that someone had arrived. The whole house was sorely in need of a paint job, since the yellow paint was chipping off in spots. The wood of the window frames was laced with cracks. Replacing them was another big job that would have to get done at some point.

Now that it was summer, stubby crabgrass covered the front yard. At least it created the appearance of a solid mass of green, close enough to a lawn that I could live with it.

The house definitely needed a facelift. Yet the disrepair wasn't what I focused on. Instead, I noticed all the personal touches that Grams and the rest of us who lived there had added over the years.

With summer at its height, the flowerpots that Grams had lined up along the banister were filled with a profusion of brightly colored annuals. Even in the darkness, I could make out their vibrant petals, wonderful reds and pinks and purples.

Behind the raucous display of flowers sat three rocking chairs. From my perspective, the fact that they didn't match only increased their charm. One was white wicker, one was covered with peeling blue paint, and one was natural wood. Each of them sported a needlepoint pillow that Grams had made. The pillow on the wooden rocker, the one with the sunflowers on it, was my favorite. The splash of yellow was the first thing my eye went to every time I walked up the front steps.

Whenever I looked at that house, what I saw was all the love that had always resided there, and still did.

As I unlocked the front door, I automatically wiped my feet on the welcome mat that was another one of Grams's personal touches. It was adorned with the black silhouette of a cat and the words "Wipe Your Paws." My niece was right behind me, teetering like an extra in a zombie movie.

We had barely stepped into the house before Digger launched into such a warm greeting you'd have thought we'd been gone for months. His tail was swinging back and forth at full speed, and he leaped up and down as if he was spring-loaded, as usual totally unable to control his ecstasy over our return. The furry ball of energy has a lot of terrier in him, which means he has the face of a teddy bear and the personality of a Tasmanian devil.

"Hey, Digger!" I whispered, crouching down to give him a hug and a serious ear-scratching. "How's my favorite doggie?"

Chloe also drifted into the front hallway, looking a bit dazed, as if she'd just woken up. The feline counterpart to our resident canine wasn't about to let a mere dog get all the attention.

As Emma reached down to pet her, she nearly fell over from fatigue.

"Why don't you go straight to bed?" I suggested, concerned that my niece had gone through such a terrible experience.

"Good idea," she mumbled, already heading straight for her room. "G'night, Kate."

I tiptoed farther inside the house. A light was on in the living room, but I knew that even if Grams had gone to bed, she would have left it on for Emma and me.

"Hello?" I called softly.

"I'm in here, Katydid," Grams called back.

So she *was* awake. I was tired enough that the idea of going straight to bed the way Emma did sounded pretty appealing. But I wanted to fills Grams in on what had happened that evening.

I stepped into the living room, with Digger and Chloe still underfoot. To me, this was the homiest, most welcoming room in the house. I loved everything about it: the stone fireplace, the dark red velvet couch with gold carved feet, the two incredibly comfortable armchairs. True, the furnishings were old-fashioned and somewhat threadbare. But that only made them fit into the house itself, reflecting its character and its feeling that it had been providing shelter for a long, long time.

Grams sat nestled amidst the row of throw cushions that lined the back of the couch. She had crafted each and every one of them during an intense needlepoint phase. Draped behind them was an afghan that she had crocheted back in the nineteen-seventies, using a color combination that was apparently quite popular then: orange, lime green, and gold. Those colors made me kind of glad that I'd missed that decade entirely.

She was resting her feet on another one of her handcrafted masterpieces, a footstool with a picture of a house surrounded by a kelly green lawn. She'd made it during her rug-hooking phase, during which she never tired of putting on a big grin and announcing, "Guess what! I'm a hooker!"

Even though it was late, she was working away on her current project, a quilt for Emma's bed. She was bent over it, her face half-hidden by her gray hair, which she wore in a neat, sharply cut pageboy. The cheerful patchwork, the Ohio Star pattern in the bright reds and purples Emma had requested, lay across her lap.

She stopped working as I walked into the room and looked up at me expectantly.

"How did it go?" she asked, her eyes bright. "I couldn't go to sleep without hearing how the evening went!"

She read the expression on my face before I had a chance to answer. "My goodness!" she cried. "What happened, Katydid?"

I sank into one of the comfortable overstuffed chairs. With my hands lying limply in my lap and my shoulders slumped, I told her about the events of the evening.

"Oh, my!" she cried when I was finished. "What a terrible thing! I can't imagine how you must be feeling right now."

And then another thought occurred to her. "Where's Emma?" she asked. "How is she coping with this?"

"She went off to bed," I said.

"And you should do the same," Grams said. "You must be exhausted. Go get some sleep."

She was right; I was exhausted. As for whether or not I'd actually be able to sleep, that was another matter entirely.

Chapter 4

The Good Humor company started in 1920 in
Youngstown, Ohio, when confectioner Harry Burt
created a chocolate coating compatible with ice
cream. His daughter was the first to try it. Her
verdict? It tasted great but was too messy to eat.
Burt's son suggested freezing the sticks used for
their Jolly Boy Suckers (Burt's earlier invention)
into the ice cream to make a handle, and things
took off from there.

—http://www.goodhumor.com/article

It was nearly three a.m. by the time I dozed off. Even then,
my sleep was fitful and plagued by nightmares.

So it was no surprise that when I jerked awake on Sunday
morning, I felt dazed. It was as if some supernatural being
had snuck into my room in the middle of the night and
coated my brain in cobwebs.

Even so, I dragged myself out of bed. After all, I had a
business to run.

Yet it wasn't only my sense of duty that got me out of bed,
tiptoeing past Grams and Emma's closed doors as I headed to
the kitchen. I figured that throwing myself into my work was
the best thing I could do to distract myself from the unsettled
feelings that continued to haunt me.

I filled a mug with freshly brewed coffee, as grateful as I was every morning for the miracle of caffeine. Clutching it, I stepped outside onto the front porch. I could already see that it was turning out to be the perfect day for day-trippers: low to mid eighties, low humidity, not a cloud in the sky aside from a few puffy white ones that looked as if they were there solely to break up the monotony of the endless pale blue. It was such a gorgeous day that I decided to leave my truck home and walk into town.

A half hour later, I was strolling along quiet residential streets lined with towering, leaf-laden trees. I found myself looking forward to my usual low-key Sunday morning. While tourists from New York City and every other place imaginable swarm into town on both days of the weekend, they generally don't become much of a presence until close to noon.

In fact, on Sundays, most of the shops in town don't open until eleven, even those that cater to the visitors rather than the locals. The restaurants are closed until lunchtime, aside from the Hudson Roasters Coffee Company and Toastie's (which is the absolute best place around to get amazing break-fast food like banana and Nutella pancakes sprinkled with chopped hazelnuts or bacon, cheese, avocado, and tomato omelets that are so light and fluffy they practically float off the plate).

All in all, Sunday morning is one of my favorite times. There's something uniquely peaceful about it. The air waft-ing off the Hudson River is remarkably fresh and clear, and the whole world feels silent and still.

As I strolled toward town, I was already lost in a world of heavy cream and sugar. I was busily plotting which flavor-of-the-day to conjure up. Lately I'd been playing around with the concept of combining favorite snack foods to make a groundbreaking new flavor. One idea was caramel ice cream dotted with pieces of pretzel, popcorn, and potato chips. The salt that was in the three add-ins, I figured, would be a fabulous complement to the caramel. I was thinking of calling it something along the lines of Frat Party—or maybe Couch Potato's Dream.

Then again, I didn't have any pretzels, popcorn, or potato chips on hand. As I turned the corner at the main intersection in town, I was racking my brain, trying to figure out how I could find high-quality versions so early on a Sunday morning.

As I turned the corner of the downtown area's main intersection, onto Hudson Street, I let out a yelp.

"What on *earth*—?" I cried.

Rather than the deserted downtown I'd been expecting, Hudson Street was abuzz.

Cars and trucks had already filled all the good parking spaces, and dozens of people were crowding the sidewalks. But they weren't just strolling around. They were setting up cameras or scribbling in notebooks or talking on cell phones. Two or three of them were stopping the few pedestrians who strolled by, trying to engage them in conversation.

Five seconds later, I noticed that some of the trucks bore the logos of TV and radio stations. Not only local stations, either.

There were stations from New York City that I recognized. WCBS, WNBC, WABC. But there were cable stations, as well, including CNN and several others. There were even some from cities as far away as Philadelphia and Boston.

It took me about two seconds to figure out that they weren't here in Wolfert's Roost because word had traveled about the sensational ice cream at Lickety Splits. They were here because of Omar DeVane's murder.

It took me another two seconds to realize that I shouldn't have been the least bit surprised. In fact, I was amazed I hadn't expected something like this. After all, Omar was world-famous and ridiculously wealthy, someone who had a presence in the closets of a large percentage of the world's women.

I wove through the crowd, taking care not to knock over any cameras. Or reporters. I had just turned on the lights in my shop and was putting on my black-and-white-checked apron when Willow dashed in. As was typical, she was dressed in an outfit completely befitting of a yoga instructor. Comfy pants, knit shirt that showed off her slim silhouette, and sneakers. She looked ready to drop to a Downward-Facing Dog position at a moment's notice.

It was still early, but Willow was an early riser by nature. She didn't even mind teaching a couple of classes at Heart, Mind & Soul on Sunday mornings, starting at 7:30. Somehow, people who are into healthy living seem to enjoy getting up with the birds and the sun and the trash-haulers.

"How were your classes?" I asked, tying a loopy bow at my back.

"Fine, I guess," she replied. "At least I hope so. I'm so distracted that I'm not even sure." She frowned, meanwhile running her hand through her short, pale blond hair. "What about you? How are you doing?"

"I'm fine," I assured her. "I was about to make a batch of ice cream. I wanted to experiment with the sweet-salty thing—seeing if I could keep pretzels and potato chips and popcorn from getting too soggy—but I don't know if I can get good-quality junk food on a Sunday morning. So instead I'm thinking of going with a new flavor I'd call Chocolate Explosion. I'm thinking dark chocolate ice cream with three kinds of chocolate chunks: white, milk, and semisweet . . ."

"Are you sure you're okay, Kate?" Willow persisted. "I mean, what happened last night was kind of a big deal."

I realized then that she was probably right: that I was undoubtedly more upset than I was aware of. But I wasn't feeling it. Maybe I was still in shock.

"I could hardly sleep last night," she said. "And today I feel like I don't know what to do with myself."

"I do," I replied. "You can help me make ice cream."

Most of the time, I was crazed and Willow was calm. But today I was the one who took charge. I led her into the back of the shop, handed her an apron and a sharp knife, and said, "Start cutting up these bars of chocolate."

An hour and a half later, as I was lowering a huge tub of my freshly made Chocolate Explosion ice cream into the display case, Ethan and Emma burst into the shop. Emma's eyes were shining, and her cheeks were flushed the bright pink of a strawberry ice cream cone. As usual, I could barely see Ethan's eyes at all.

"This town is positively *crawling* with reporters!" Emma said, glued to the window. "Have you looked outside, Kate? Wolfert's Roost is going to be *famous!*"

"So it seems," Willow replied calmly. "But do we want it to be famous as a spot where an infamous murder occurred?"

She certainly had a point. Of course, I'd heard that expression about how there was no such thing as bad publicity. Believe me, it was a saying that those of us who worked in public relations joked about constantly. But I'd never really believed it. There were too many people—places, too—that had had their reputations ruined by exactly that.

But Emma and Ethan were as excited as if it was Christmas morning—and they'd both been very, very good that year.

By that point, it was time to open. Emma and I stood behind the counter, ready for what I hoped would be a busy day ahead. Willow and Ethan, meanwhile, made themselves comfortable at one of the round tables, both of them absorbed in their phones.

Yet even though it was past eleven, my usual opening time,

and even though the OPEN sign on the front door was displayed for all to see, by one o'clock not a single soul had wandered into the shop.

"Now that's ironic," Emma said, standing with her elbows resting on the glass countertop and her chin in her hands. "Even though Wolfert's Roost is packed with people today, not one of them seems the least bit interested in eating ice cream."

"It's early," Willow pointed out, glancing up from whatever was on her screen. "Aren't things always slow until mid-afternoon?"

Ethan nodded, sending his straight black bangs swaying. "Totally," he said. "My mom always taught me not to eat dessert until after I'd had my lunch."

"Your mother must not have known about Peanut Butter on the Playground," I muttered. "It's got swirls of real peanut butter and jelly in it. If that isn't a stand-in for lunch, I don't know what is."

Emma turned to me, her cheeks flushed. "Kate, since things are so quiet here, would you mind if I went outside for a while? This is the most exciting thing that's happened in this town, like, ever! I want to see if there's anyone out there I recognize!"

"Sure," I said. "There's no reason to spend the afternoon here in the shop when there's nothing going on."

"Thanks!" she replied, already tearing off her apron. "Oooh, maybe we'll see that cute TV reporter who covers hurricanes and tornadoes. He looks so sexy with his hair wet!"

She and Ethan scurried off, ready to enjoy Wolfert's Roost's moment in the spotlight.

As for me, my mood was becoming droopier and droopier.

"Don't reporters like ice cream?" I moaned to Willow.

"Sure they do," she replied. "They're famous for always wanting to get a scoop."

"Ha, ha," I said sullenly. Then I brightened. "I know: I should put out a big sign that says, 'Get your scoop here!'"

Willow laughed. "Not a bad idea." She rose from the table and packed away her phone. "I'm going to run over to Hudson Roasters and get myself some coffee. Want anything, Kate?"

"I'm good," I assured her, even though I wasn't anything even close to good.

She'd barely left before the door opened and someone walked in.

"Finally," I mumbled.

Standing up straighter and brushing away a few stray strands of hair that had come loose from my ponytail, I smiled at the customer. He was in his thirties, I guessed, with slicked-back black hair and a Johnny Depp–style facial thing going on, sort of a mini beard with a dot mid-chin that brought the word "hipster" to mind. The button-down shirt and neatly pressed khakis he was wearing made him look more dressed up than the usual day-tripper. But I figured he might have just gone to church—or that maybe he was a local businessperson himself. I actually settled on the latter theory, since he was carrying a pad of paper.

"Welcome to Lickety Splits," I greeted him. "What can I get you?"

"Great little shop you've got here," he said, squinting at the menu hanging on the wall behind me. "Cool flavors. Honey Lavender ice cream? Peanut Butter on the Playground? Seriously? Those sound like something I'd be more likely to find in one of Brooklyn's trendier neighborhoods than up here in the sticks."

I found myself growing defensive. I didn't know if he was genuinely surprised or if he was simply incapable of hiding his inherent snobbery. I was tempted to say something like,

"Believe it or not, we have electricity and flush toilets 'up here,' too!"

But because I am a responsible, mature, professional businessperson, I simply said, "Thanks. Would you like to sample any of our flavors?"

"You know what? I think I'll take a vanilla cone," he said. "Small."

"Coming right up," I said.

I grabbed the scoop and was tempted to dish out the smallest "small" the world has ever seen. But I remembered the thing about being responsible and mature and gave him the small size I routinely served.

As I handed it to him, he said, "Gotta love the basics, right?"

"My Classic Tahitian Vanilla takes the concept of vanilla to an entirely new level," I informed him. "Taste it. You'll see."

He stuck his tongue into the softball-sized scoop as tentatively as if I'd just given him a blob of mud-in-a-cone and dared him to try it.

"Hey," he said, his face lighting up "this is really good."

" 'Good' is what we do here," I informed him. "Cash or credit?"

"Are you the owner of this place?" he asked as he handed over a credit card. I was accustomed to people using plastic even for small purchases, but somehow this particular guy doing it annoyed the heck out of me.

"Owner, manager, ice cream chef, bookkeeper, custodian, you name it," I replied.

"How long have you been in business?" he asked

"Since the beginning of June," I said as I ran his card. "Which means Lickety Splits has been open for about six weeks."

"So you're new to the area," he observed.

"Yes and no," I said. "I grew up in Wolfert's Roost. I left

for college, then came back a few months ago for personal reasons." I handed him back his card.

"Well, you've certainly mastered the art of ice cream," he said. By this point, he was positively devouring his cone. Practically pushing it into his face, as if he couldn't get enough of my Classic Tahitian Vanilla. I couldn't help smiling. This phenomenon was something I'd seen before.

"Thanks," I said. I was starting to like him a bit better. Or at least dislike him a bit less.

"So I understand this cute little town of yours didn't always have such a cute little name," he said chattily. I got the impression he intended to eat his entire ice cream cone while standing in that exact same spot.

"That's right," I said. I was back to disliking him. In fact, I was beginning to wish he'd leave. Or at least eat his ice cream cone while sitting at one of the tables. In silence.

"But you apparently know all about it already," I said evenly. "And I bet you also know the original name."

He smiled smugly. "Modderplaatz. Which, in Dutch, means 'muddy place.' That may have seemed like a good name in 1699, when this little piece of heaven on earth was founded. But apparently a decade or two ago, some genius in town decided the place would be more attractive to tourists if they came up with a different name. Something that sounded less like—well, like a Dutch word that means 'muddy place.'"

"If you were as thorough in your research as you should have been," I said crisply, sounding like everyone's least favorite high school teacher, "you would have learned that the town's new name came from the title of a story collection of the great writer Washington Irving, who lived in the Hudson Valley. You know who he is, don't you? 'The Legend of Sleepy Hollow'? 'Rip Van Winkle'? Maybe you read those famous stories in your freshman English class? Freshman year of high school, I mean?"

He just smirked.

"Anyway," I went on, jutting my chin out even farther, if that was possible, "Washington Irving named one of his story collections *Wolfert's Roost, and Miscellanies*. The name came from a real person named Wolfert Acker. But you probably didn't know any of that."

"Nope," he replied. "And I didn't know that Wolfert Acker lived in Irvington, not that far from here, during the colonial period. Or that he was an important guy in government, working as an adviser to Peter Stuyvesant, the head of New Netherland, later known as New York. I also didn't know that Acker's place was called Wolfert's Roost, which is Dutch for 'Wolfert's Rest.' "

If I'd disliked this guy before, I now disliked him even more. Even though he'd clearly done his research.

I checked the door, wishing another customer would come in so I could get away from this guy. No such luck.

"So what about this Omar DeVane thing?" he said.

He was certainly a chatty fellow. "Terrible," I said. "The whole town is shaken up by what happened."

"I bet," he said. "But honestly, was the guy well-liked around here? I mean, weren't the locals put off by all the folks from New York City who were moving up to the Hudson Valley? After all, those city people have been flocking here because of the region's quaintness, but what they're doing is changing the very character of the place, aren't they? Ruining it, in other words?"

"You're asking an awful lot of questions," I said. And then the wheels in my head that had been turning slowly suddenly picked up speed. Super-cool facial hair, pad of paper, questions . . . "You're a reporter, aren't you?"

He nodded. "Jason Littleton. I write for the *Tattletale*."

I noted that he told me the name of his publication with pride. But the *Tattletale* was one of those trashy newspapers you can't help noticing when you're in line at the supermarket, steaming over the fact that the person in front of you has at least two dozen items when the sign clearly says, 12 ITEMS OR LESS. It's one of those papers that proclaims ridiculous things like "Kim Kardashian Gets Butt Reduction Surgery!" or "Kanye West Tells Taylor Swift He's Sorry!"

I found myself wishing I'd followed my first instinct and skimped on his cone.

Instead I decided to help him write his headline.

"Actually, the residents of the Hudson Valley are happy to share our beautiful area with anyone who wants to enjoy it," I told him. "And Omar DeVane was a good neighbor. For example, rather than using a caterer from New York for his party last night, he hired local companies, including mine."

The reporter's eyes lit up. "So you were *there* last night?"

I instantly felt cornered. I found this man so distasteful that the last thing I wanted to do was give him any information. Especially since that was what he wanted most. In fact, I suspected it was the very reason he'd come into my shop in the first place: to pump some of the locals.

"I was there," I said evenly.

Jason leaned forward. "How about giving me a quote? Maybe something about what went on there last night at Omar's wild party . . . ?"

"Omar's party wasn't wild!" I cried. "For goodness' sake, it was a bunch of lovely, well-dressed people getting together to celebrate an incredibly accomplished man . . ."

"Lovely?" Jason repeated. "Seems to me one of them wasn't so lovely." Leaning in even closer, he said, "Any idea who that might have been?"

"No," I replied coldly. "No idea at all."

"Let me ask you one last thing," he said. "Think they'll ever get to the bottom of this? Figure out who really killed the great fashion designer Omar DeVane?"

My mouth dropped open. It had never even occurred to me that that wouldn't happen. While Detective Stoltz may not have been my favorite person in the world, I had no doubts about his ability to successfully investigate a murder.

I suddenly found myself feeling uncomfortable. Was it even a possibility that Omar DeVane's murderer wouldn't be caught?

"I'm sure that, in the end, justice will be served," I said, sounding ridiculously prim.

"Maybe," he said with an unctuous smile. "But from my perspective, I hope they take a long, long time to find the killer. That way, the *Tattletale* will get a few weeks' worth of crowd-pleasing headlines out of this little caper.

"I can see them now," he went on, his eyes narrowing. " 'Fashion Designer's Killer Still Not Hemmed In.' " He waved one hand through the air, as if he was highlighting the imaginary headlines. "Or better yet, 'Omar DeVane's Murderer Still At Large. Or Extra Large.' Hey, here's one more: 'Fashion Mogul's Murder Investigation Is Anything But Seamless.' "

I was not the least bit amused by his attempts at being witty. The last thing I wanted was for Wolfert's Roost to remain in the news week after week, unable to shake off its brand-new identity as the scene of a high-profile murder.

I was relieved that the door suddenly swung open. Three giggling girls around thirteen or fourteen years old spilled into the shop.

"Ice cream!" one of them yelled. "We need ice cream!"

The other two let out shrieks of laughter that were guaranteed to make the rest of us feel bad that we weren't in on the inside joke. Or maybe relieved.

"If you'll excuse me," I said to the reporter, "I have other customers to take care of."

"Sure," he said with a crisp nod of his head. "We were done here anyway."

As I watched him sashay out of the store, I hoped the steam coming out of my ears wouldn't melt the ice cream.

Chapter 5

Reuben Mattus, who founded Häagen-Dazs in 1960
with his wife, Rose, invented the company's name
because he wanted something that sounded Danish.
He meant the name to be a tribute to the Danes'
exemplary treatment of their country's Jewish
residents during World War II. The Danish language
has neither an umlaut (ä) nor a digraph (zs).

—*Wikipedia.org*

"What did I miss?" Willow asked when she came back to the shop a few minutes later. In her hand was a paper cup of joe that was nearly the size of a bucket of popcorn. No wonder the woman had so much energy.

"Not much," I replied. "Just a slimy reporter in search of that scoop you were talking about." Grimacing, I added, "He was apparently hoping for a tidbit that was as sleazy as he was."

Before she had a chance to ask me for more details, Emma and Ethan burst in.

"It's *crazy* out there!" Emma cried. "I can't believe how many reporters and TV people there are in town!"

"I'd been hoping there'd be some big ice cream eaters in that crowd," I commented woefully. "But so far it doesn't look that way."

"Things might turn around," Willow said, as encouraging as always. "It's getting hotter every minute."

Ethan, meanwhile, was glued to the window. "It looks like Wolfert's Roost becoming media central isn't the only interesting thing that's going on today," he observed. "Check out the shop across the street."

Emma was the first to join him. "Oh, look!" she cried. "A couple of guys just hung up a sign!"

"Finally," Willow commented. "We won't be kept in suspense any longer."

"*Please* don't be an ice cream store," I said under my breath as I joined them at the window.

A small knot formed in my stomach as I watched two men lift a big sign into place. But the knot dissolved as soon as I read it. The new business in town was about as far away from an ice cream shop as you can get.

"Hudson Valley Adventure Tours," Emma read. Frowning, she added, "I wonder what that's all about."

She'd barely gotten the words out before the two men climbed down the ladder and we got our answer. Printed on the sign, right below the shop's name, were the words KAYAKING, CANOEING, TUBING, HIKING, BIKING, ROCK CLIMBING, SPELUNKING.

"A tour company," Willow said. "That's a great idea! This is such a fabulous area for outdoor activities. Not only for visitors, either. We locals can benefit from something like this, too."

"Whoa, sounds mega-cool!" Ethan observed with his characteristic eloquence. "I'd like to do a bunch of those trips. Hey, I wonder if they do bungee jumping! I'm dying to try that!"

"Me, too!" Emma agreed, her eyes wide. "Bungee jumping sounds totally awesome!"

I was about to assure Emma that no matter how awesome bungee-jumping sounded, as long as her mother had her entrusted in my care she wasn't about to try it. But then the door of Hudson Valley Adventure Tours flew open.

A man strode out of the shop, someone I didn't think I'd seen before. If I'd seen him, I was pretty sure I'd have remembered.

My initial impression was that the Vikings had landed. Or at least one Viking. He had thick, curly blond hair, just shaggy enough to give him a rugged, outdoorsy look. He was at least six feet tall. Yet while he was lanky, his brick-red T-shirt, printed in black letters with the words HUDSON VALLEY ADVENTURE TOURS, was tight enough to reveal an awe-inspiring set of muscles. Chest, shoulders, biceps, triceps . . . the whole deal.

He was exactly the kind of guy you'd want to accompany you on a spelunking adventure.

Or maybe some other kind of adventure.

I was so busy admiring him that it took me a few moments to grasp that he was headed in our direction.

"Hey, that guy is on his way over," Ethan said, reading my mind. "That's so cool. I can ask him about bungee jumping."

I noticed that, behind me, Willow was running her fingers through her short hair, as if she wanted to be sure it was in place. Apparently she, too, had noticed our new neighbor's unusual level of hotness. I half-expected her to pinch her cheeks to put some color in them, Scarlett O'Hara–style.

I realized that finding the four of us standing side by side, staring out the window of Lickety Splits and watching his every move, might not be the best way to make the acquaintance of our newest neighbor. I also realized that the last thing I needed was a crush on the guy who ran the shop right across the street from mine. The only thing more unwelcome was the prospect of the people around me teasing me about it.

"Let's get back to work," I said. "We don't want him to know we've been gawking at him."

"Wow," Willow said breathlessly. "He's really a hunk."

"Think so?" I replied loftily. "I hadn't noticed."

Willow cast me a strange look, giving me the feeling that she noticed that I'd noticed.

And once he strode into Lickety Splits, I noticed something else: that he was even better-looking close up.

"Hey!" he greeted the four of us with a big grin. Wouldn't you know it, he also had a perfect set of gleaming white teeth. And eyes that were a remarkable shade of green. Not fake-looking like Federico's, either. This was the real deal.

We all responded with a hello or another "Hey."

"I thought I'd introduce myself, since I'm the new kid on the block," he said. Turning to face me, he said, "I'm Brody Lundgren. I just opened up a shop across the street."

"Welcome," I said.

"Thanks," he said, his smile widening to reveal even more perfect teeth.

The man positively exuded healthiness. Animal sexiness, too.

I got the feeling that by this point Emma had noticed as well.

"It's *so* nice to meet you," she cooed, draping herself across the table like one of the barmaids in a Western. "We can't *wait* to hear all about this new business of yours!"

Brody shrugged. "There's not much to tell. I've always loved being outdoors. Kayaking, swimming, camping, mountaineering . . . I grew up doing all that stuff and loving it. So I decided to find a way to make those activities available to everybody. And the Hudson Valley is the perfect place to enjoy them. This part of the country has everything: mountains, rivers, forests . . . Besides arranging tours, I also plan to sell clothes and footwear and whatever supplies people may need. Kayaks, tents, whatever."

"What a wonderful idea," Willow cooed. She was looking at Brody the same way I'd seen people gaze at one of my Bananafana Splits.

"Are you from around here?" Emma asked. In addition to her unnatural posture, she was now batting her eyelashes as if she were playing a siren in a silent movie.

Fortunately, Brody seemed oblivious. "Actually," he replied, "I was born in Washington."

"Washington, D.C.?" Willow asked.

Brody chuckled. "Everybody on the East Coast assumes the same thing. By now I should have learned to be more specific. I'm from Washington State. I was born in Seattle. When I was seven my family moved to Oregon. A little town near the Columbia River Gorge. Do you know anything about that area?"

All four of us shook our heads.

"It's a great place," he explained. His green eyes grew dreamy as he added, "It's kind of like this area, but on an even grander scale. Big mountains nearby for rock climbing, tremendous cliffs along the Columbia River for spelunking, rapids to ride and caves to explore . . . I grew up with two younger brothers and parents who loved being outdoors as much as we kids did. Every spare minute the five of us had, we spent outside. Hiking, fishing, skiing and snowshoeing in the winter . . ."

"Sounds like nirvana," Ethan said wistfully. "The state of mind, not the group."

Ethan, a secret spelunker? And here I'd thought the only exercise he ever got was plugging his iPhone into the wall to recharge it.

"It is Nirvana," Brody agreed. "At least, it is to me."

"So how come you left?" Willow asked.

Brody grinned. "The love of a good woman. My fiancée moved back east to try making it as a dancer on Broadway."

"So you're married?" Willow asked. She was deflating so quickly I could practically feel a breeze.

"Nope," Brody said. His smile turned rueful. "Wouldn't

you know it, the relationship fizzled as soon as we got here. The fact that she had to live in the city to take classes and go to auditions sure didn't help. I'm not a city guy. Never have been, and never will be."

He shrugged. "Since I'd already relocated to New York State, I decided to see if there was an area nearby where I could start a business doing what I love most. You know, someplace where there were enough people to support it. And a place where I could find good employees, too, people who are as comfortable in a cave or on a mountain as I am. I figured I'd lead some tours myself but that I'd mostly hire local people to be guides. It also seemed to make sense to sell and rent equipment. Anyway, I did some research about where would be a good place to base my business, and, well, here I am."

"Here you are," Willow repeated dreamily.

"And what about you?" Brody asked.

You'd have thought he was addressing all four of us. Instead, he seemed to be looking directly at me.

I assumed it was because I was the only one wearing the Lickety Splits apron, which gave me official status. "I opened this shop at the start of the summer," I told him. "Back in June. Before that, I worked in public relations and lived in the city."

Almost apologetically, I added, "Unlike you, I loved it. But I grew up here in Wolfert's Roost, and my grandmother, who pretty much raised me, suddenly needed help. So I came back, moved in with Grams, opened a business I'd always fantasized about, and, well, here *I* am."

"It sounds like you and I have a lot in common," Brody observed.

Ignoring his comment, I continued, "Willow, here, who happens to be my best friend, has a story that's just like yours and mine. She teaches yoga here in town. It's been her passion since college. Emma is my niece. She's staying with my grandmother and me for a while. And Ethan . . . well, he's her friend. He's from around here, too."

Brody acknowledged each one of them with a nod, then turned back to me.

"So do you live in town?" he asked.

"Yup," I replied. "Less than half a mile from here. Do you know Sugar Maple Way?"

"I do," he said. "It's a few blocks away from where I'm renting a place. I pass it all the time. That's your street?"

I nodded. "I live in the yellow Victorian with the wonderful porch." I couldn't help adding, "It's the house that looks as if it needs a little yard work."

His expression suddenly grew earnest.

"So what's this I've been hearing about a murder?" he asked. "Is that just some crazy rumor, or is it actually true?"

"I'm afraid it's true," I said.

I filled him in on what I knew. I also assured him that today wasn't a typical Sunday in Wolfert's Roost. After all, I didn't want him to think he'd made a mistake in opening his business here. Not on his very first day.

"Well, keep me posted if you hear anything about this murder business," he said. "I should probably get back to the shop. I was going to have an opening-day sale, but it doesn't look as if any one of us is going to see much action today."

Glancing at the four of us, he said, "Honestly, feel free to stop over any time. I'll show you around my new place. I'm really proud of it. This is a big deal for me."

"We'll do that," Ethan said, nodding vigorously. "We can talk about bungee jumping."

"Definitely, bro." The two of them did one of those obnoxious guy handshakes, the one that makes it look like they're arm-wrestling.

Then he nodded at Willow and Emma, saying, "Great meeting you both."

I was starting to feel a little slighted. But then he came

right up to where I was standing and leaned forward so that his face was only a few inches away from mine. His eyes were positively boring into mine.

With a smile that would have put James Franco to shame, he added, "And I'm sure I'll be seeing *you* again soon."

I told myself that the chill that ran over me was simply because Willow was deflating again.

As he sailed out of the shop, the four of us remained silent for a few seconds.

"Whoa," Emma finally said with a loud sigh. "Is he hot or what?" She was shaking one hand as if it had just touched a hot stove. Or perhaps wandered somewhere else where it was likely to get into trouble.

"He's even more of a hunk up close than he is from across the street," Willow said wistfully, sinking into a chair.

"He's a very nice-looking guy," I said, doing my best to sound neutral. "In fact," I added, turning to Willow, "he strikes me as someone who'd be perfect for you. He's athletic, he loves nature and doing outdoorsy things . . ."

Willow rolled her eyes. "Right. Except there's one small problem."

"What's that?" I asked.

"It was *you* he couldn't keep his eyes off!" she replied.

I was about to scoff when Emma piped up, "She's right, Kate. That guy Brody was checking you out practically the whole time he was here. He looked like he'd just stumbled upon the most spectacular flavor of ice cream in the world."

"Yeah," Ethan agreed, nodding so that his mass of black bangs bobbed up and down. "The dude is totally into you."

"You guys!" I wailed. "You're all nuts."

Still, I could feel my face turning the color of the raspberries I put in my Berry Blizzard ice cream. Which only made the smug looks they were all exchanging all the more embarrassing.

I could feel my cheeks growing even redder when the door of the shop opened and in strode Jake Pratt.

Jake Pratt, who owned and operated the Juniper Hill Organic Dairy on the edge of town, the source of the milk and cream that I regularly used to work my culinary magic. Jake Pratt, who had startlingly blue eyes whose color was made even more pronounced by the robin's-egg-blue shirt he was wearing with jeans.

Jake Pratt, with whom I have what might be called a "history."

"Good morning, ladies," he greeted Emma and me. Glancing over at Ethan, he asked, "How's it going, Ethan?"

"Hi, Jake," I said, keeping my eyes down so he wouldn't see how flustered I was by his unexpected appearance. Especially at that particular moment.

My muddled state got even worse when Jake casually asked, "Who was that?" He gestured toward the street behind him with his thumb.

"The owner of the shop that just opened across the street," Emma replied.

"Which is going to be totally awesome," Ethan said. "The dude's opening a shop that sells adventure."

"What does that mean?" Jake asked, looking startled.

"It means he arranges expeditions for people who want to enjoy the Hudson Valley's natural beauty," I explained. "Kayaking, rock climbing, hiking, all those outdoor activities that granola bars were invented for."

Jake nodded. "Cool. We could use something like that."

"I bet Kate could," Emma said with a smirk.

I glared at her.

"I thought Kate was more of an indoor type," Jake commented.

Emma smiled sweetly. "There are also all kinds of *indoor* adventures—"

"This was fun," Willow interrupted, rising from her seat, "but I'm heading out."

I cast her a look of gratitude. A change of subject was exactly what was needed.

"I've got a few classes scheduled for later this afternoon," she went on, "and I really need to clean the studio before people start arriving." She wrinkled her nose. "The last thing I want is for my clients' yoga mats to start picking up dust bunnies."

"I gotta get going, too," Ethan said. Holding up his tattered novel, he added, "I've almost made it to the halfway point."

"And I should get back to work," Emma said with a sigh.

"You can take a few hours off," I told her. Glancing toward the window with a frown, I said, "I don't think I'm going to be very busy today. You might as well enjoy this beautiful day."

"Great!" she said, her face lighting up. "In that case, I'm going to go ask Brody about bungee jumping."

I opened my mouth to protest. But my niece must have read my mind. Before I had a chance to say a word, she said, "Just to find out more about it, Kate. Don't worry, I'm not going to do anything crazy. At least, not without your permission."

All of a sudden, Lickety Splits was empty. Except for Jake and me, of course.

"Pretty wild, isn't it?" he said. "What's going on out there, I mean?"

"Insane," I ageed. "Omar DeVane's murder is putting Wolfert's Roost on the map. And not in a good way."

His expression grew earnest. "Are you okay? I mean, you were there last night, weren't you? At the guy's house?"

I nodded. "It was kind of surreal," I said. "One minute, a

houseful of glamorous people were enjoying a lovely evening, and then all of a sudden—"

I didn't finish my sentence. There was no need to.

"I bet you were pretty shaken up," Jake said. Frowning, he added, "Emma and Ethan were there, too, weren't they?"

"Yes," I said. "Willow, too."

"How are they all doing?" Jake asked.

"Everyone is fine," I assured him. "We were all upset, of course. But aside from the shock, it's not as if any of us actually knew the man."

"True," Jake agreed. "I just hope Detective Stoltz doesn't start bothering you. After all, you do have a way of being in the wrong place at the wrong time."

"I think Stoltz realizes that I was only an innocent bystander," I assured him.

"Good. But if you ever need a lawyer, don't forget that that's what I used to be before I became a dairy magnate." Glancing out the window, he said, "I just hope they find the killer soon. I hate what this is doing to Wolfert's Roost."

"Me, too," I agreed, glancing at my display cases filled with lovely vats of ice cream. "Want some ice cream? It looks so lonely, sitting there with no one to eat it."

Jake grinned. "That's definitely something I can help you with."

For him, I filled a large cup with Strawberry Banana Blast—strawberry ice cream studded with chocolate-covered strawberries and chunks of chocolate-covered bananas. For me, it was Cappuccino Crunch, my personal version of breakfast.

"Have some berries and bananas," I told him, joining him at the table where he'd sat down. "Fruit is good for you."

He didn't waste any time before digging in. I was starting to wonder if there was some other reason he'd stopped by—other than to ask how my 'Cream Team and I had weathered the events of the night before—when he said with unnatural casualness, "So-o-o, there's this Spanish movie I was thinking of going to see." He kept his eyes fixed on the beautiful bevy of berries in front of him. "It's by that director whose name I can never pronounce. Anyway, it's playing at the Rhinebeck Cinema all week. I wondered if you might like to join me."

I was glad I'd just shoveled a golf-ball-sized glob of Cappuccino Crunch into my mouth since I needed time to think.

Was Jake asking me for a date? Or was he simply looking for someone to go to the movie with, perhaps someone who would be able to teach him how to pronounce Pedro Almodóvar's name?

When it came to Jake, I still wasn't sure.

I also wasn't sure whether I wanted it to be a date.

Which is why I was surprised when I heard these unexpected words pop out of my mouth: "Sure. That sounds great."

After all, it's only a movie, I told myself. A chance to do something fun.

By late afternoon, the news crews had vanished.

I stood at the window, watching the photographers and videographers packing their cameras back into black canvas bags and the reporters climbing into their cars and taking off.

Suddenly, Wolfert's Roost was a ghost town.

When Emma drifted back to the shop, ready to work, she froze as soon as she walked in.

"Really?" she cried. "There's literally no one here?"

I cast her a woeful look. "Apparently this is another example of how crime doesn't pay."

My cleverness was wasted on her. "Do you want me to stand outside and hand out free samples? Maybe that would help get customers in here."

I shook my head. "I can see the sidewalk perfectly from here. And the problem isn't that no one's coming in. The problem is that no one is even out there! Now that the media folks are gone, we might as well roll up the sidewalks."

I sighed. "In fact, you might as well take the rest of the day off. I'll stay, just in case something changes. But there's certainly no reason for both of us to hang around here."

After she left and I was debating whether or not to allow myself to eat even more ice cream, I heard the door open. I glanced up excitedly.

But I realized immediately that the two women coming into my shop weren't customers.

Selma Silver and Palma Lanciani were the owners of Stitchin' Time, the quilting shop a few doors down. The two women had opened their store back in the 1990s, when Wolfert's Roost was still called Modderplaatz. Back in those days, their only customers were local women who loved cutting up fabric and then sewing it back together again, albeit in very different ways. Grams had been one of their regulars since the start.

But since then, word had spread. For a modest-sized store, it offered an amazing selection of fabrics. Bright splashy batiks, solids in every shade imaginable, and hundreds of novelty fabrics. Even though I was about as handy with a needle and thread as Digger, I loved going in there with Grams and examining the bolts of material printed with skiers or puppies or flowers or polka dots. I couldn't imagine how anyone could ever make a choice.

Then again, I felt the same way about ice cream.

The shop also carried a huge selection of notions. Thread in every color, an endless selection of needles and hoops and scissors and rotary cutters, pincushions shaped like hearts or little houses or even donuts. Then there were all the items whose purpose was a complete mystery to me.

But the reason that Stitchin' Time had become so incredibly successful was its two proprietors. Both Selma and Palma were expert quilters. They were remarkably patient, too. The two women were happy to spend as much time as was required to talk their customers through whatever quilting challenges they happened to be facing. I knew this because I'd seen them give Grams a tutorial in a technique called Stack-'n'-Whack. The effect of stacking and whacking fabric, it turns out, is astounding patterns that remind me of a kaleidoscope.

Their topnotch web site had also helped the store thrive. Palma's grandson, a tech wiz who now lived in Silicon Valley, had created an interactive feature that allowed shoppers to choose fabrics, pick a pattern, and instantly see exactly how the project would look when it was finished. It was no surprise that orders came pouring in.

Usually, Selma and Palma dressed in fabulous garments they had handcrafted themselves, like a jacket made from a hundred pieces of fabric stitched together in a star pattern or a vest made from holiday-themed fabric with pumpkins or hearts or Christmas trees.

Today was no exception. Palma was wearing mom jeans, a cream-colored T-shirt, and a short vest with a summertime theme. The background was smears of blue that looked as if they'd been applied with watercolor. And appliquéd along the edge were beach umbrellas, suns, starfish, and, I was glad to see, ice cream cones. Her nearly waist-length gray braid was tied at the end with the same watery blue fabric.

Selma wore a solid green sundress with a jacket made of a hundred square patches in a hundred different shades of green. Somehow, they all seemed to blend together perfectly. I noticed that she was also wearing earrings that were two tiny spools of thread, dangling from below her short white pageboy. One earring was purple, and the other was royal blue, which added to their charm.

But while every other time I'd seen them they'd exuded cheerfulness, today they both looked positively glum.

"How's business?" Selma demanded as she strode up to the display counter.

"What Selma means is," Palma interjected, "is it as bad for you as it is for us?"

Selma nodded hard, making the spools of thread dangling from her ears dance. "This town is infested with journalists, photographers, and film crews today," she grumbled. "The one thing that isn't here is tourists."

Palma nodded. "It's August!" she cried. "Tourists should be *flocking* to Wolfert's Roost!"

"You weren't here last summer," Palma went on, "but we had such a parking problem in town, especially on weekends, that the Chamber of Commerce formed a special committee to look into putting in another public parking lot."

"They were talking about putting it behind Let It Brie," Selma said, referring to the gourmet cheese shop a few doors down on Hudson Street.

Palma peered outside at the nearly deserted street and let out a long, loud sigh. "We don't exactly have a parking problem today, do we?"

"And who knows how long this will go on?" Selma said. "It could be days."

"It could be weeks," Palma added, nodding.

"It could be months!" Selma cried. "The bottom line is that no one's going to want to come to our town for a fun and relaxing day as long as this horrible murder is in the news."

Palma and Selma continued to complain, but I'd stopped listening. Instead, I kept hearing the *Tattletale* reporter's words echoing inside my head. He had said he hoped it would take "a long, long time" to find Omar DeVane's murderer.

And it was certainly true that a murder investigation could take a while. It was equally true that Lickety Splits was still new enough that a major drop in business—for months, weeks, or even days—could be devastating.

It could even be fatal.

I suddenly felt chilled to the bone, a feeling that had nothing to do with the frostiness of the display freezer I was standing in front of.

It was at that moment that I made a decision. I was going to do everything I could to find out who had killed Omar DeVane—not only for me and the future of Lickety Splits, but for the good of the entire town.

Chapter 6

"Cream Ice," as it was called, appeared regularly
at the table of King Charles I of England during
the 17th century.

—*http://www.idfa.org/news-views/media-kits/
ice-cream/the-history-of-ice-cream*

On Monday morning, downtown Wolfert's Roost was as
quiet as it had been late on Sunday afternoon after the
news crews had dispersed.

That wasn't surprising, since that's the way Monday mornings always are. It happens to be one of the main reasons I
enjoy the start of a new week. Hudson Street seems reborn. It
feels fresh and clean and ready to jump right into the new
week after the craziness of Sunday's crush of day-trippers.

I followed my usual Monday-morning routine. As I unlocked the front door of Lickety Splits, I spotted Carrie
Porter, the owner of Petal Pushers, unpacking her van. Today,
like on most other Mondays, I stood in my doorway for a
minute or two, watching her cart armloads of flowers into
her shop: long-stemmed roses in half a dozen different colors, brilliant orange tiger lilies, purple hyacinths, and clusters
of vibrant blossoms whose names I didn't know. The morning breeze was just right, and I got a whiff of what heaven
surely must smell like.

Several of the other shops along Hudson Street were getting deliveries, too. A small white van was parked in front of Toastie's, and a young man was unloading crates of produce. I could practically taste one of Big Moe's crispy Belgian waffles smothered with fresh strawberries, sliced bananas, and whipped cream.

Other shopkeepers were cranking the handles of their awnings. That included Brody Lundgren, who I noticed was doing exactly that at his shop across the street. All along Wolfert's Roost's main drag, lights were being turned on, doors were being propped open with doorstops, and CLOSED signs were flipped over in shop windows so that they now read OPEN.

Yet while Monday morning usually makes me feel as if I'm making a fresh start, today I sensed a feeling of doom hanging over Wolfert's Roost. It reminded me of the dark gray clouds that gather in the late-summer sky, a warning that violent thunderstorms are on their way. True, that time of year was almost upon us. But today's oppressiveness had nothing to do with the weather.

My determination to get to the bottom of Omar DeVane's murder was stronger than ever.

I'd been so keyed up the night before that it had taken me forever to fall asleep. My mind had churned out one scenario after another, each centered on how I could figure out who had killed the famous fashion designer.

And I'd come up with a great first step. One that had to be accomplished that very morning.

Which was why my heart was pounding a little harder than usual as I whipped up two fresh batches of ice cream. One was a standard at Lickety Splits: Hawaiian Coconut, made with fresh coconut and big chunks of crunchy macadamia nuts. One lick and you found yourself transported to a sandy, palm-tree-lined beach on Maui. The other was a cinnamon-and-vanilla concoction I planned to call Snickerdoodledoodle. Cinnamon wasn't a flavor I associated with summer, but then again, I reasoned it was refreshing enough that it was appropriate year-round.

To be perfectly honest, I had no idea if I would even *have* any customers today. But I wanted to be ready if I did.

While my ice cream maker was churning away, spinning straw into gold—actually, cream, sugar, and other yummy ingredients like the fresh coconut I'd chopped up myself and fragrant cinnamon from Sri Lanka—I did what any respectable amateur sleuth would do to kick off an investigation.

I Googled "Omar DeVane."

Wow.

A full page of listings came up. And the row of numbers along the bottom promised many more. But I figured that was to be expected with someone so well-known.

I started with Wikipedia.

His biography was surprisingly brief. Formal, too. It consisted of little more than a string of bare facts. Omar had been born in New York City. His father was an extremely successful businessman, and his mother was a fund-raiser for a charitable organization. He attended the best schools, culminating with a year studying design in Paris and another learning the business in Milan.

Then came the launch of his boutique on Madison Avenue, ODV DesignWorld. Soon after it opened, his fashions had been featured in *Flair*. Then, a string of runway shows all over the world, industry awards, and expansion into one new area after another, each accomplishment increasing his fame. His fortune, too.

Next I clicked on his web site. And even though I already knew that Omar was a serious player in the world of fashion, it bowled me over.

What struck me immediately was the way it exuded good taste. The home page was quietly dignified, radiating sophistication and luxury. A soft shade of pale blue served as a background for the brand's familiar font: the gold initials ODV swirled together in a curlicue font.

The only other printing on the page was a gold bar along the top. It invited me to explore ten different areas: Women's, Men's, Children's, Handbags, Shoes, Jewelry, Eyewear, Accessories, Gifts, and Home. That last category, I assumed, included—or was slated to include—Omar's new furniture designs, the launch of which I'd overheard Mitchell and Federico arguing about.

I clicked around and learned that the Women's category included dresses, sportswear, bathing suits, lingerie, and coats. Men's offered everything from T-shirts to tuxedos. As for the Accessories category, it covered a wide assortment of items, ranging from scarves to iPhone cases to wallets.

In other words, Omar's company had been involved in pretty much every imaginable aspect of fashion.

I was impressed by how the man had managed to turn his creativity into such a large and successful business. Then again, he'd had Mitchell Shriver to help. I got the sense he was the brains behind the business aspects of the operation. And Omar had had Federico as well, a man who clearly had a unique sense of style.

And no doubt Gretchen Gruen, one of the most famous faces of his brand, had played a large part in Omar's enterprise. She wasn't only beautiful; she was one of those unique individuals who positively glowed. Pippa Somers, too, had played a key role in Omar's life, providing ongoing support for both the man and his products.

Was it possible that one of them had killed him?

I realized that I'd only encountered a small part of Omar's entourage. After all, there had been seventy-five guests at Saturday night's event.

Yet I suspected that those four—Federico, Mitchell,

Gretchen, and Pippa—were the people who had been closest to Omar. They were four individuals who had the most to gain—or lose—from whatever went on in his life.

So even if none of them had had any reason to want him dead, I had a strong feeling that they knew enough about Omar and his fashion empire to help me figure out who had.

I was lowering the freshly made tub of Hawaiian Coconut ice cream into the display case when Emma came bursting into the shop.

"Good morning, Kate!" she greeted me. "It sure felt great to sleep in this morning. And Grams made a fresh batch of peach muffins for breakfast. Yum!"

All I'd had was some leftover coffee, heated up in the microwave.

But before I had a chance to feel too sorry for myself, Emma reached into the purple backpack she almost always had with her, since she never liked to be more than three feet away from her laptop. She pulled out two oversized muffins, wrapped in paper towels. When she handed them to me, I discovered that they were still warm.

Grinning, Emma said, "No one, including you, Kate, can live on ice cream alone!"

Once I'd fortified myself with one of the muffins, I updated Emma on a few details concerning the shop.

"And now I'll be off," I told her. "I'm leaving you in charge this morning."

"Fine," she said, tying a black-and-white-checked Lickety Splits apron around her waist. "Hopefully we'll have some real, live customers. Where are you going?"

"I'm just running some errands," I told her.

I wasn't quite ready to tell her about my real mission for the morning: following in the footsteps of my childhood idol, Nancy Drew.

*   *   *

This time, as I turned into the driveway of Omar DeVane's estate, I was prepared for the mind-boggling display of wealth I knew I was about to be confronted with.

What I wasn't prepared for, however, was the heaviness that hung over Greenaway, the same feeling I'd sensed downtown.

At least, that was the way it seemed to me.

Even though the sun was shining, even though a brand-new day was just getting under way, I could practically see a dark cloud hanging over the huge stone mansion that loomed in front of me.

The man had had everything. International fame and respect, the opportunity to work in a glamorous field he clearly loved, a ridiculous amount of money, and, perhaps most important, a long list of similarly successful, sophisticated friends who truly seemed to like and admire him.

I wondered if he would have been willing to trade in all of it for a few more years.

Still, I tried to find solace in the fact that Omar had truly enjoyed his life, rather than simply mourning the ugly and abrupt way in which it had ended. I also reminded myself that I needed to put aside the flood of emotion that was engulfing me and instead focus on the reason I was here.

I parked near the back door, reminding myself with amusement that Federico had referred to it as the "servants' entrance." This time, I was actually pleased that I'd be able to get into Omar's house without much fanfare. After all, the main reason I'd come here today was to do a little spying. And I figured that the best spies were the ones who could blend into the background.

I knocked on the back door. A few seconds later, Marissa answered.

As soon as I saw her face, all the emotions I'd been fighting off swooped over me once again. Her eyes were swollen and rimmed in red, which explained the tremendous wad of crumpled tissues bulging out of her apron pocket. Her black hair was pulled back into a bun, just as it had been on Saturday evening. But so many strands had come loose that it was clear that her appearance was the last thing she was thinking about.

In addition to these obvious changes, her entire demeanor was different. Her shoulders were slumped, her facial features sagged, and she seemed to be surrounded by the same cloud that I was sure I'd seen hanging over the house.

She really cared about him, I thought. Marissa was much more than Omar's housekeeper.

"I don't know if you remember me," I started to explain. "I'm Kate McKay from the Lickety Splits Ice Cream Shoppe—"

"Of course I know who you are," Marissa said, opening the door wider. "Come on in, Kate."

As I followed her into the kitchen, I launched into the little speech I'd prepared as I'd driven over. "I'm sorry to bother you at such a terrible time, but I'm afraid that in the chaos of Saturday night, I forgot a few things. Some serving platters, a couple of trays . . ."

Marissa waved her hand in the air. "Just look around and take whatever is yours."

"Thank you," I said. I really had left some things behind, although nearly all of the items had been picked up in local thrift shops. They'd only cost a few dollars apiece and were completely expendable.

"You should probably check the sunroom, too," Marissa suggested. "I tried to clean everything up, but there's a good chance I left some things behind." With an apologetic smile, she added, "As you can imagine, I've been a bit distracted over the past couple of days."

"I'm sure," I said sympathetically. "How are you holding up?"

"It's hard," she replied with a shrug. "But I've found it

helpful that a few of Omar's friends are staying around. He always liked to have a house full of people, especially during the summer. His guests had been planning to stay all week, and I didn't see any reason to ask them to leave." She bit her lip. "Of course, that's not a decision that would be up to me, anyway."

I wondered whose decision it would be but didn't ask.

"I'm pretty sure these plates are yours," Marissa said, abruptly changing the subject. She pointed at two of the platters I'd brought along for serving my Ice Cream Incidentals. "I washed them and put them aside, figuring you might come back for them."

"Thank you," I said. "I'll check the sunroom now."

I just assumed I'd find it empty. So I let out a yelp of surprise when I walked in and found Gretchen Gruen draped across an upholstered lounge chair. She was idly filing her perfectly polished nails with a silver nail file. But aside from the minimal effort she was exerting, she lay perfectly still, looking as if she were posing for a photograph.

And it wasn't only because of the way she'd positioned herself. It was also because she was wearing an outfit that would have looked great on a magazine cover: loose-fitting black pants, a flowing white silk blouse with a low-cut V-neck, and glittery gold sandals. Her jewelry accented her ensemble perfectly: a gold necklace consisting of a thick chain and a pendant shaped like a flattened donut, simple gold hoop earrings, and a similarly simple gold bangle bracelet.

Her makeup was subtle, applied so perfectly that she didn't appear to be wearing any. It was almost possible to believe that her cheeks really were tinged with just the right amount of color and her eyelashes truly were that dark and that long. Her pale blond hair hung loose, as if it hadn't been styled. But there was enough height to it and enough of a swirl along the bottom that I suspected that that particular effect had required plenty of time, effort, and product.

I decided she must always look this well put-together. Habit, perhaps. Or maybe it was because she was so frequently photographed by the prying paparazzi who followed her wherever she went. She probably figured that she might as well look good in the photos they were inevitably going to splash all over the tabloids.

As soon as she spotted me, she slipped the nail file into her pants pocket. I wondered if she felt a little guilty about being caught engaged in an act of vanity in the midst of such a tragedy.

"*Acht*, the ice cream lady!" she greeted me. "I'm afraid I have forgotten your name."

"Kate McKay," I told her.

"And I am Gretchen Gruen," she replied.

I simply nodded, acting as if I didn't already know that. Me and just about everyone else in the world who had access to a computer, a newsstand, or a TV.

"I see that you've decided to stay on here at Omar's," I observed, hoping to engage her in conversation.

Her eyes filled with tears. "I don't know what else to do with myself," she said. "I am so very sad. It is fortunate that I have the next few days off. I need some time to process what has happened. To understand it, to try to find a way for it to make sense."

She shook her head slowly. "Omar—he was everything to me. He was like a father, a brother, a friend . . . Not only did he help me so much in my career, but also in every other part of my life."

"I'm sure that you're devastated," I said.

"Did you know that he discovered me?" she said. "I was nothing. A nobody, working in a spaetzle factory in a small town near Munich—"

"Spaetzle?" I interrupted without thinking. I was pretty sure that I'd read it was a pretzel factory.

"*Ja*," Gretchen replied. "It is what you call egg noodles."

Spaetzle, pretzel . . . I could see how that piece of history had become altered over the years.

"So I was working in that factory," Gretchen went on, "and then, one day, there was Omar DeVane. In an instant, my entire life changed. I owe him everything. Everything!"

"I can't imagine what you're going through," I said sympathetically. "I—"

I'd suddenly gotten that creepy feeling that comes over you when you realize that someone is watching you. It's as if you can feel their eyes burning into your skin.

I turned quickly, just in time to see a familiar face in the doorway. A face that vanished less than a second after I laid eyes on it.

Federico.

He'd been spying on us.

Or, more likely, he'd been spying on *me*.

My mind raced as I debated what to do. Pretend I hadn't noticed . . . or call him on it.

"Federico!" I called, even before I'd actually decided. "How nice to see you again!"

Not, I thought. Then I reminded myself that I wasn't here to socialize, that in fact I'd come back to Omar's mansion to do a little spying of my own.

But since I'd spoken to him, he had no choice but to come out of his hiding place.

He looked completely different from the way he'd looked the night of the party. His hair was disheveled, and his chin was covered with dark blond stubble. His eyes were not only free of makeup, they were rimmed in red. The irises were also considerably less green than they'd been the last time I'd seen him. As for his trendy togs of Saturday night, they had been replaced by a pair of nondescript khaki pants and a plain white T-shirt that revealed just how thin he was.

Yet despite the dramatic change in his appearance, his manner was exactly the same.

"Ms. McKay," he said formally, peering at me with great disdain. "What brings you back here?"

I braced myself for the usual cliché comparing me to one of those bad pennies that keeps turning up. Fortunately, I was spared it, perhaps because Federico was from Italy and therefore wasn't familiar with the saying.

"With all the chaos of Saturday night," I explained in an even voice, "I left behind some of my supplies. A few pans, some trays, a bunch of paper goods . . ." For some reason, I couldn't help making my imaginary list even longer than it had been before. "I'm usually pretty organized, but, well, Saturday night was anything but usual."

"I see," he said, his tone softening. "That's not surprising. A lot of us weren't ourselves on Saturday night."

I noticed then that Federico's expression had transformed. Instead of haughty, he looked sincerely distraught. His eyes became shiny, too, as they welled up with tears.

I immediately felt terrible for all the awful things I'd ever thought about him.

"How are you holding up?" I asked him quietly.

"Not well," he replied, choking out the words. "I'm still trying to comprehend that this horrible thing has really happened. I keep telling myself that Omar isn't gone, he was simply called into the city unexpectedly or he's in Paris getting ready for a show or . . . or . . ." His face crumpled. "None of it seems to work, though."

I instinctively reached over and put my hand on his arm. "Federico, I can't imagine how tough this must be on you. I know you were one of the people who was closest to Omar."

"This is tough on all of us," a male voice boomed from behind me. "But that doesn't mean we don't have a job to do."

Mitchell Shriver had come striding into the room. As I glanced over my shoulder, I saw that, unlike Federico and Marissa, he looked exactly the same as he'd looked Saturday night. He was dressed in a drab business suit, possibly the same one he'd been wearing then. His necktie was certainly similar. His hair was neatly combed, and he was freshly shaven. As for his eyes, the look in them was stone-cold.

"We had all day yesterday to moon around," Mitchell went on. "We need to move on."

"My heavens, you're heartless," Federico said, spitting out his words. "We all loved and respected Omar. The fact that you can just jump back into a business-as-usual mode . . ."

"That's because Omar *was* his business," Mitchell shot back. "He would have wanted the people who were close to him to take the same care with the empire he was so proud of that he would."

As if to illustrate his point, he held up the stack of manila folders he was holding. "Federico, you really need to pull yourself together so we can go over some of these files. There are things that need to be done right away. Legal decisions, business decisions . . . for goodness' sake, have you seen what's going on with the price of ODV's stock today?"

The look that Federico flashed at Mitchell was icy enough to freeze ten gallons of ice cream. On a hot summer's day. At high noon.

"Omar wasn't *just* his business," Federico insisted. "He was also a warm, caring, ridiculously creative *genius* of a man." His face became distorted with grief once again as he added, "And I miss him. I will *always* miss him."

"I will, too," Mitchell said, sounding as if he wasn't going to miss him at all. "But this is no time to be sentimental. There are certain things we need to deal with immediately. And, unfortunately, I need your help with them."

"Fine," Federico said loftily, angrily tossing his head. "Maybe doing things *your* way will help give me something else to focus on besides how badly my heart has been broken."

The two men left, Federico looking as if he were on the verge of tears and Mitchell looking the same way he seemed to look all the time.

I turned back to Marissa. "Goodness," I said, "I don't mean to be a gossip, but how did those two ever manage to work side by side with Omar? They act like children fighting over a toy!"

She shrugged. "They're always like this," she said. "Omar had a theory about their difficult relationship. He thought it was because they were basically so different. Mitchell was all numbers and business, while Federico was all about creativity."

She sighed. "But I think there was more to their rivalry." With a little smile, she noted, "They've always been so competitive because each wanted Omar to like him best."

That certainly made sense. In fact, from what I could see, everyone in Omar's circle had wanted him to like them best.

And they, in turn, all seemed to be totally devoted to him.

Yet something about his entourage gnawed away at me. Not only because of their personalities, but also because of the way they interacted with each other. I could feel a strong undercurrent just by being in that household.

And it was an undercurrent that I sensed had been powerful enough to set off an electrical fire.

Chapter 7

In Ancient Rome special wells were used to store
ice and snow which slaves brought down from the
mountains to luxurious villas. Among the ruins of
Pompeii there are traces which lead us to believe
that some shops specialized in selling crushed ice
(from Vesuvius) sweetened with honey.

—*http://www.expo2015.org/magazine/en/economy/
a-short-history-of-ice-cream-from-ancient-roman-
snow-to-love-with-a-heart-of-cream.html*

As I drove back to Wolfert's Roost, I found myself growing increasingly discouraged. The task I'd set out for myself was going to be even more challenging than I'd thought. And it wasn't only because of my limited access to Omar DeVane's house—and his life.

Even more, I could see that it wasn't going to be easy getting past the façades that the people around him were clearly used to hiding behind.

It was late morning by the time I pulled into town. I decided that rather than heading straight to Lickety Splits, I'd take advantage of Emma's ability to run the store on her own and stop off at home. Taking time out for a quick lunch would undoubtedly be good for my morale as well as my blood sugar level.

As I walked into the front hallway of 59 Sugar Maple Way, I automatically called "Hello!" I just assumed that Grams would be around. Her car wasn't in the driveway, but I figured it was in the garage. I expected to find her puttering in the kitchen or working on one of her craft projects in the living room. But no one was home except for Digger and Chloe.

"Hey, Digger!" I cried, crouching down so I could give the feisty terrier mix a suitable greeting. As usual, that included neck scratching, ear scratching, tummy scratching, and an embarrassing amount of baby talk.

"Whooza cutest doggie? Whooza *best* doggie?"

In response to this ridiculous lovefest, Chloe trotted over. For a few moments, she seemed to forget she was a cat. She also wanted to say hello, which she did by rubbing against me while meowing loudly, as if to say, Where's *my* neck scratching? Where's *my* ear scratching? I was only too happy to oblige.

"Okay, you two," I demanded. "Where's Grams?"

As if on cue, I heard the front door open behind me. Standing in the doorway was the woman I'd been looking for.

"Katydid!" she cried. "What are you doing home in the middle of the day?"

Her tone sounded almost—well, critical. I would have thought I was reading something into it if she wasn't also wearing a strange expression. She was acting as if she'd been caught doing something she wasn't supposed to be doing.

There was something else that got my attention: she was considerably more dressed up than I would have expected for someone going to the post office or the supermarket. Like me, Grams likes to wear super-comfy clothes. Sweat pants, loose shirts, sneakers.

Yet she was wearing a pastel-colored paisley blouse and her "good" dark blue pants, a pair she generally reserved for dinner at one of our area's nicer restaurants. She even had a string of pearls around her neck. Her gray hair, which as usual was in a gentle pageboy, was neatly combed. And unless the late-afternoon light was playing tricks with me, she was wearing makeup: a swipe of blush, a hint of eye shadow, and lipstick.

"I just stopped off to grab a quick lunch," I replied. Looking her up and down, I added, "And what have you been up to? An early date?"

I meant my comment as a joke. Instead, she immediately turned beet red. "Don't be ridiculous!" she countered. "I was simply out doing some . . . errands."

Errands? In your best pants, your best jewelry, and more makeup than I've seen you wear since the neighborhood New Year's Eve party the Hillermans threw in 1999?

My detective skills led me to think of another strong possibility: that she had gone to a doctor's appointment she didn't want me to know about.

But Grams clearly didn't want to tell me any more than she already had, so I didn't push it.

That didn't mean I wasn't worried.

Even so, all I said was, "Any chance I can interest you in a grilled-cheese-and-tomato sandwich?"

I headed back to Lickety Splits as soon as I'd fortified myself with one of those sandwiches, a tall glass of iced tea, and a few minutes of Grams's company. But I shouldn't have bothered.

Business was that bad.

"We might as well call it a day," I told Emma at the end of a long, quiet afternoon. A total of three customers had wandered in. "If I wipe down this counter one more time, I'm going to wear out the glass."

She looked as bored as I felt. But she replied, "It's barely six o'clock!"

"I know," I said. "But even if some of the local folks suddenly develop an overwhelming craving for ice cream, it's not likely that there'd be enough customers over the next few hours to cover even the cost of the electric bill." I began clamping lids on the tops of the giant tubs of ice cream lined up in the display case.

"Whatever you say," Emma said. She jumped right in and started helping.

"I suppose you'll go hang out with Ethan for the rest of the evening," I commented.

She stiffened. "A quiet evening at home sounds pretty good right now," she said without making eye contact.

My radar told me something was going on. But my common sense told me to leave it alone.

First Grams, now Emma . . . all of a sudden, it seemed as if there were just too many mysteries swirling around me.

"I totally agree," I said cheerfully. "Hanging out with you and Grams tonight sounds great, even if we just watch TV or play cards."

It turned out that Emma, Grams, and I had a wonderful time making dinner together, something we hadn't done in a while. Coordinating the schedules of three very busy, very independent women meant that sitting down together for a meal had become unusual. Actually preparing that meal together, doing more laughing than chopping, grating, and stirring, was even more of a rarity.

Afterward, instead of Emma disappearing into her room— or as had become more and more usual, going off with Ethan—she joined her great-grandmother and me in the living room. I was glad to see that she'd brought a sketch pad and a fistful of drawing pencils with her. Much better than that computer she was usually lugging around, at least as far as I was concerned.

As usual, Grams was working on a craft project. She was laboring over the quilt she was making for Emma, carefully hand-sewing around each patch. The bold shades of purple and red, neatly forming the repeating pattern of the Ohio Star, cascaded around her like a magnificent wizard's cape.

Emma flopped into one of the upholstered chairs and immediately became absorbed in her drawing. Meanwhile, Grams sewed away happily.

Digger was lying in front of the fireplace, chewing apart one of those shapeless rawhide things that really, really hurts if you have the bad luck to step on one barefoot. Chloe was curled up in a chair, just watching us. Sometimes I felt that cats were actually creatures from another planet, sent here to spy on us earthlings.

Still, the entire scene was wonderfully cozy. In fact, I decided to join our extraterrestrial pussycat by indulging in something I'd been doing very little of lately: like her, I just sat. And enjoyed the moment, which was about as blissful and serene as life gets.

When the floorboards on the front porch creaked and the doorbell rang, the three of us exchanged surprised looks.

"Could that be Ethan?" I asked Emma.

"I doubt it," she replied curtly.

O-kay, I thought. So my theory about a lovers' quarrel was correct.

"Are you expecting anyone, Grams?" I asked.

"No, but sooner or later, one of us has to go answer the door," she replied. She started setting aside her project, but I jumped up.

"I'll get it," I said.

By that point, I had a hunch that it might be Jake. Sure enough, when I opened the door, there he was.

"Hey, Kate," he greeted me, his face lighting up. "I thought I might find you here. I drove by Lickety Splits, but it was closed."

I made a face. "No use staying open when there aren't any customers."

"Still feeling the fallout from Omar DeVane's murder, huh?" he asked. "That's tough."

"Come on in," I told him, moving aside. "You're in luck. You've got all three of us here tonight."

"I *am* in luck," he said, grinning as he strode into the living room.

"Jake!" Grams cried. "It's so nice to see you!"

"Hi, Mrs. Whitman," he greeted her. "Hey, Emma."

Grams was instantly all aflutter. "It's *so* nice that you dropped by," she cooed, sounding like Amanda Wingfield in *The Glass Menagerie*, entertaining a gentleman caller. "Can I get you a cold drink?"

I glared at her, wishing she'd rein in her embarrassingly obvious desire to pair me off with a man simply because he'd already played that role a million years ago.

"Or how about some ice cream?" Emma suggested. "It's always a good time for ice cream."

It was clear that Emma was also doing her best to play matchmaker.

The living room was starting to feel just a little too crowded.

"Ice cream sounds like a great idea," I said. Sounding as sweet as a scoop of chocolate marshmallow ice cream dotted with meringue, I suggested, "Why don't you go get us some, Emma? Grams, why don't you help her?"

Grams and Emma both took the hint. They popped up out of their seats—well, Grams didn't exactly pop—and headed into the kitchen.

It looked as if Jake and I would have at least a couple of minutes to ourselves.

"So how have you been?" Jake asked. "Have you heard anything more from Detective Stoltz?"

"Nope," I replied. "I have a feeling I'm not very high on

his list of suspects this time around. Actually, I don't think I'm on it at all."

"That's a relief," Jake said. "I sure hope they get to the bottom of this soon. All the bad press Wolfert's Roost is getting is hurting everybody. Even the dairy had an unusually quiet day today—"

When the doorbell rang again, I jumped.

"Maybe that's Stoltz," I said, instantly filled with dread. "As in 'speak of the devil.' "

But it wasn't Detective Stoltz I found standing on the doorstep once I opened the door. It was Brody.

"Hey!" I cried, surprised. In fact, I immediately added, "What a surprise!"

"Hey, yourself," he replied with a wide grin. "I hope you don't mind me stopping by like this, but I wanted to see how you were doing. I noticed that you closed early today. I assumed it was because business was so slow. It's been the same with me, although I figured it would take me a while to get things going even under the best of circumstances. Anyway, are you holding up okay?"

"I'm doing fine," I replied. I sounded calm enough, but my mind was racing. After all, Jake was sitting in the living room. And now, here was Brody.

But Brody isn't anyone, I told myself. I mean, not to me. He's no one aside from another merchant in town, a merchant who I've become friends with. Not even friends. Acquaintances. Barely.

Yet Willow and Emma's teasing words about how he couldn't take his eyes off me or some such nonsense were echoing in my head.

I told myself I was reading too much into this. There was nothing wrong with a friendly visit from the gentleman who ran the shop across the street from mine.

With or without Jake Pratt sitting on my couch.

"Why don't you come in?" I said to Brody. "We were just about to have some ice cream."

His grin widened. "Ice cream sounds perfect. It's really hot out there. This is a heck of an August we're having."

My plan was to walk Brody into the living room, introduce him to Jake, and then retreat to the kitchen to instruct my team of ice cream scoopers to bring in one more serving. But as the two of us strolled over to Jake, the tension in the air immediately became as thick as whipped cream.

It may have been hot outside, but it was even hotter in here.

"Hey," Jake greeted him, eyeing the newcomer warily.

"Hey," Brody returned. His tone was breezy, but I picked up on the fact that he was sizing up Jake in the exact same way Jake was sizing him up.

"Jake, this is Brody Lundgren. You just missed meeting him yesterday. Brody is the owner of the new outdoor shop that opened across the street from Lickety Splits."

I was trying to sound matter-of-fact, but even I could hear the strain in my voice. Somehow I felt as if I was standing in the middle of the ring of a cockfight, introducing the two contenders.

"And Brody, this is Jake Pratt." I paused, not sure how to describe Jake and my relationship with him. Finally, what I came up with was, "Jake and I have known each other since high school."

They both mumbled another round of "Heys," still eyeing each other warily.

When Emma chose that moment to walk in, I felt like hugging her. It wouldn't have been possible, though, since she was clutching a tray with four ice cream dishes. Each one contained a scoop of Pistachio Almond and a scoop of Chocolate Almond Fudge.

"Here's our ice cream!" I cried inanely. "I consider this combination my own personal tribute to the almond."

"I hope everyone likes—oh, hello, Brody!" Emma said. Her entire posture changed. Instead of Waitress, she was back to being Saloon Girl.

"Hello, Emma," Brody replied warmly. "Nice to see you again."

"Nice to see you, too—"

"Emma, thank you so much for bringing in the ice cream," I interrupted. "But we'll need one more dish. So why don't you hand those out and I'll go get some for myself?"

"I can do it," Emma said.

"No, really. I insist."

With that, I dashed out of the room, seeking refuge in the kitchen. I wished I could crawl into the freezer and spend the rest of the evening in hiding.

I found Grams wiping splatters of melted ice cream off the counter.

"Did I hear the doorbell again?" she asked.

"We have another guest," I told her. "Brody Lundgren, who just opened the shop across the street from mine. He arranges adventure tours."

"How nice that he's joined us for the evening!" Grams said.

You only think that because you haven't seen the two alpha males pounding their chests in the living room, I thought.

"Come meet him," I added, figuring that the more people in the room, the more distractions there would be.

As Grams and I returned to the living room, I saw that Jake was still sitting on the couch, while Brody had taken a seat way on the other side of the room. Emma, meanwhile, was sitting in the space between them, chattering away.

"So I figured I'd take a year off before I decide what to do next," she was saying cheerfully. "I'm hoping that having some time to myself, time to just *think*, will give me a better idea of what direction I want to go off in. And being able to live with Grams and Kate, two of my absolute favorite people in the world, is totally awesome. I've been working at Lickety Splits, which means I can be a help to Kate, and I'm doing some chores around the house to make things easier for Grams. Kate, too, since she's got plenty to do with the shop . . ."

Brody stood up when Grams walked in. "Good evening, ma'am," he said.

"Oh, heavens, you don't have to get up," Grams said, waving her hand in the air. But the bright shade of pink of her cheeks made it clear that she was impressed. "I'm Caroline Whitman, Kate's grandmother. And Emma's great-grandmother!"

"I prefer to call you Grams," Emma interjected. " 'Great-Grams' would be too complicated."

"I'm Brody Lundgren." He crossed the room to shake her hand. "It's a pleasure to meet you."

Jake just glowered.

"Now if you young people don't mind," Grams continued, "I'm going to take my ice cream into my bedroom so I can watch TV. I don't mean to be rude, but I just remembered that there's a television program on right about now that I hate to miss. It's one of those cooking shows. I believe they're demonstrating a Grand Marnier soufflé tonight!"

She trotted off to watch what I suspected was an imaginary cooking show. That left the four of us sitting together in a cloud of awkwardness. An uncomfortable silence hovered in the room for what seemed like forever but was probably more like five or ten seconds.

Thank goodness, we each had a dish of ice cream in front of us. At least we could pretend we were so absorbed in eating that we couldn't possibly carry on a conversation.

"Wow, this is really good," Brody commented as he shoveled in a big spoonful of Chocolate Almond Fudge. I noticed that he was one of those people who eats all of one flavor before embarking on the second flavor. Me, I like to skip around.

"Of course it's good," Jake shot back. "Kate is a master. Everything she makes is incredible."

Brody grinned. "In that case, I'm glad my shop is located right across the street from hers!"

Score one point for Brody, I thought. Not that there was any need to keep score.

"I hope I don't get fat," Brody added. "This stuff is addictive."

"Maybe you'll have to limit the amount of time you spend at Lickety Splits," Jake countered. "Besides, won't you be out hiking and rock climbing most of the time?"

"Actually, I plan to hire local people to be guides. I've already put up ads on a couple of web sites." Brody studied Jake for a second or two, then said, "If you know anybody who's in good shape and is well-coordinated, send them my way."

Ooooh. That one hurt. A second point for Brody.

"What is it you do, again?" Brody asked.

"I run an organic dairy," Jake replied tartly.

"Ah," Brody said dismissively. "Cows."

Before Jake had a chance to come up with a retort, Brody turned to me.

"So-o-o," he said. "Why ice cream?"

I shrugged. "A few reasons. One reason is that I love it. And it's a passion my dad and I shared, ever since I was a little girl. He passed away when I was pretty young, which is when my mother brought my two sisters and me here to live in my grandmother's house.

"And in more practical terms," I went on, "I was looking for a way to make a living. Preferably one that didn't involve going to an office every day. I enjoyed that lifestyle well enough while I was living in the city, but now that I'm up here, I wanted to do something different." Another shrug. "And Lickety Splits seemed like the way to go."

"Very cool," Brody said, nodding. "Just like me. Find something you really love, and make it the center of your life."

"I actually enjoy the dairy business," Jake interjected. But he sounded anything but convincing.

"I just had a great idea!" Emma suddenly exclaimed, setting her empty ice cream dish on a table. "Let's play a game!"

Jake cast her a wary look. "I don't really play games."

"I like video games," Brody offered.

Jake's expression instantly changed to one of disdain. Which annoyed me. I had yet to meet a man in his thirties who wasn't now, or hadn't at one point, been a video game addict, or at least an aficionado. I suspected that he was no exception.

"Then let's play a game that isn't a real game," Emma said brightly. "Let's play Trivial Pursuit!"

"I really don't think—" Jake protested.

"I'm not sure—" Brody said at the same time.

But Emma wasn't taking no for an answer. She'd already pulled the Trivial Pursuit box off the shelf where it was stacked up with a few other classic board games that dated back to my childhood.

I realized immediately that her idea was a brainstorm. Answering questions about trivial matters was so much easier than dealing with the complicated matters at hand.

"We'll form two teams," Emma announced. "Brody, you can be on my team. Jake and Kate, you'll be the other team.

"That way," she added, "each team has a female, who's likely to be better at the Entertainment questions, and a male, who will no doubt be better at the Sports questions."

"That's sexist," I mumbled, even though I suspected there was some truth to her analysis.

She ignored the looks of dismay on Jake and Brody's faces as she opened the board in the middle of the coffee table and picked out one of the colorful wheels for each team. Next, she divided the question cards into two separate piles, placing one at each end so we could all reach them easily.

"Who goes first?" Emma asked brightly. She reminded me of a kindergarten teacher, focusing all her energy on infusing the room with enthusiasm.

When none of us expressed the least bit of interest in that particular issue, she said, "You know what? My team will go first, since playing was my idea. We'll be orange."

She threw the dice, got a three, and moved her small plastic wheel to a green space. "Green is Science and Nature," she said. "Kate, pick a card and ask my team a question."

I did as I was told. "Which plant takes away sunburn pain?"

"That's easy," Emma replied. "Aloe. Brody, are you okay with that answer?"

"Sure," he said. "It's something I use all the time. Of course, I'm usually pretty careful about using sunblock. I wear a sun hat, too, since my coloring is so fair."

"Then maybe you shouldn't spend so much time outdoors," Jake muttered.

"Aloe is correct!" I cried, doing my best game show host impersonation. "Emma, your team gets to go again."

After inserting a green wedge into her team's wheel, Emma threw the dice again and moved to an orange space.

"Sports," she declared. "Question, please."

Dutifully I picked up another card. "Who was the last professional ice hockey player who played the game without wearing a helmet?"

Emma looked at Brody. "I told you we needed a guy on each team to answer the Sports questions. Brody?"

He shook his head. "I have no idea."

Jake was grinning.

"Craig MacTavish," I read the answer from the card.

"That's a tough one, unless you happen to be a serious hockey fan," Brody grumbled.

"I would have gotten it," Jake insisted. "And I'm not that big a fan."

"How would you have known that?" Brody challenged.

"Everybody knows that," Jake shot back. "He's Canadian. He played for the Boston Bruins, the Philadelphia Flyers, the New York Rangers . . . a couple of other teams, too, including a Canadian one. And everyone knows that one of the things he's famous for is being the last NHL player to play without a helmet, back in the late seventies."

"I didn't know that," Emma commented. "Obviously."

The two men just glared at each other.

The rest of the night proceeded in pretty much the same way. Emma and I were playing Trivial Pursuit, while Jake and Brody were playing an entirely different game.

The only part of the evening that could have qualified as even remotely fun was when a question about the Kardashians came up. It turned out that none of us could name more than two members of a family famous for its mega amounts of money, makeup, and melodrama.

By the time the clock struck ten, we still didn't have a winner.

"It's getting late," Emma announced abruptly. "Even though we haven't finished the game, I've got to get to bed. Those of us who work in the fast-paced ice cream industry have to get up with the birds. Good night, everybody!"

As she skittered off, Jake stood up. "And those of us in the milk industry have to get up with the cows," he added. He glanced over at Brody. "Can I give you a lift home?"

At first, I was startled by the generosity of his offer. But then I realized he had an ulterior motive: preventing Brody from staying behind, which would leave the two of us alone together.

His ploy didn't work. "Thanks, but I drove here," Brody replied.

But he, too, stood up to leave.

"So, Kate," Jake said in a voice I thought was unnecessarily loud, "I'll be seeing you tomorrow night. The movie we're seeing starts at seven, so why don't I swing by to pick you up around six-fifteen? That way we won't have to rush."

Brody looked shocked. I actually felt sorry for the guy. But I simply mumbled, "Sounds good."

By that point, I could hardly wait for this excruciating evening to end. But as I was shepherding the two men out the door, Jake suddenly said, "Hey, I don't have my phone. It must have fallen out of my pocket. I'd better go look for it."

He headed back into the house. Brody, meanwhile, had no choice but to head out. After all, he couldn't every well claim that he, too, had lost his phone.

When I went back into the house, I found Jake standing in the living room. He wasn't even pretending to look for a lost phone.

"So what's up with that guy?" he demanded.

"You mean Brody?" I said. "Nothing. He's just a friend. Not even. He's merely another friendly shopkeeper."

"Hmph," Jake replied. He looked anything but convinced.

As I climbed into bed a half hour later, I expected to feel agitated about the tense evening. Instead, I was surprised that I felt as if I was floating.

I realized it was actually fun having two men vying for my affections.

Especially since they were both—to use an ice cream term—utterly delicious.

The problem was that with men, as with ice cream, no matter how many delectable possibilities there were, in the end you had to make a choice.

Chapter 8

In January 2017, the town of Nashville,
Michigan, working with the local Moo-ville
Creamery, broke the Guinness World Record for
the longest ice cream sundae. The Nashville
sundae contained 864 gallons of ice cream,
36 gallons of chocolate syrup, 56 gallons of
strawberries, 172 cans of whipped cream, and
7,200 Michigan-grown cherries. It was 3,656 feet
long and weighed over 5,400 pounds.

—*https://www.upi.com/Odd_News/2017/01/09/*
Michigan-town-scoops-ice-cream-record-with-
3656-foot-long-sundae/5271483972139/

I slept well that night, reveling in my new role as femme fatale. Even though I wasn't sure how I felt about either Jake or Brody—or even whether I wanted a man in my life at all—it felt great being pursued by not one but two suitors.

I was in such a good mood, in fact, that I decided to indulge my creative side and try out a brand-new flavor of ice cream that I'd been unable to stop thinking about: Pear with Blue Cheese.

Yes, I know it sounds weird. But since those two foods go together so beautifully—the sharp tanginess of the blue cheese playing off the sweetness of the pear—I couldn't wait to see how such a satisfying combination would translate into ice cream.

So first thing on Tuesday morning, before heading into Lickety Splits, I made a quick run to the closest farm stand, which opened when the sun came up. I picked up a big basket of organic pears that looked so luscious and smelled so sweet it was all I could do to keep from devouring them on the spot.

Next, I pulled up in front of Let It Brie, the cheese shop a few doors down from Lickety Splits. Even though it was still early, its proprietor, Elton Hayes, was already bustling about his store, fussing with a display of Stilton. The setup he was constructing consisted not only of a tower of cheese, but also cute little Tudor houses, tiny trees, and miniature farm animals, all of it meant to recreate the quaint English town where the cheese was made.

Elton, a sweet, slightly paunchy man who at forty has already lost most of his hair, was only too happy to sell me a generous slab of a ripe blue cheese. He was even more excited than I was that it was about to be turned into ice cream.

Sure enough, I came up with a winning flavor. Not only was it delicious, thanks to the interplay of the two opposing yet strangely complementary flavors, but there was also the delectably creamy texture that came from the ice cream itself. As soon as I nervously tried my first spoonful, I knew I'd created something that was going to sell like hot cakes—which got me thinking that Hot Cakes might make a fabulous flavor, too. (The flavor of butter with a hint of maple, and perhaps even some bits of actual pancake . . . ? Maybe even toss in a few blueberries . . . ?)

By the time I'd put the freshly made tub of Pear with Blue Cheese into the display case in the front of the shop, Emma came shuffling in.

While I was still energized by the great night's sleep I'd had, my niece didn't seem to have had a particularly pleasant night at all.

Emma's strong sense of responsibility includes near-compulsiveness about being on time. In fact, she considers it a personal failing if she's late for anything at all. So when she showed up twenty minutes later than usual, I was more surprised than annoyed.

I also suspected there was a good reason.

The expression on her face told me I was right.

Her blue-streaked hair, which she usually wore styled a certain way to make it look calculatedly disheveled, was mussed up way more than it was supposed to be. And her clothes, which were often mismatched but still gave off an air of having been chosen with the utmost care, looked like an afterthought. Jeans and a plain T-shirt simply weren't her style.

Her entire demeanor broadcasted the fact that something was wrong.

My hunch was that one of two things was behind her distress. One possibility was that she'd had another one of her ongoing arguments with her parents about her future—more specifically, her decision to postpone making any concrete plans about said future anytime soon. But I suspected that by now her father had gotten used to the idea of his only offspring taking a year off. As for her mother, my sister Julie, I expected that veering off the straightest and narrowest path imaginable was something she'd never get used to.

The other likely reason for Emma's distressed state was something related to Ethan.

I was betting on that one.

"Everything okay, Em?" I asked breezily as she came in, her shoulders slumped in a way that brought to mind the heaviness of the Abominable Snowman.

I half-expected her to brush me off, insisting that everything was fine. Instead, she dropped into one of the pink chairs at the small marble table closest to the front of the shop, tossed her backpack onto the floor beside her, and moaned, "I need ice cream. *Now.* I was up until three last night. In fact, you'd better make that a double."

Even though I was startled, I did my best to act matter-of-fact. "Coming right up. Would I be correct in assuming that Cappuccino Crunch is the order of the day?"

"What else?" she replied.

There's good reason why I consider Cappuccino Crunch the breakfast of champions. After all, it contains real espresso—meaning real caffeine. The presence of that wonder drug, combined with a hefty dose of sugar, makes it enough to give Red Bull a run for its money when it comes to jump-starting a person's day.

Emma, being a blood relative, clearly felt the same way.

I scooped up an extra-large portion for my niece. Then, deciding that I might need some help myself to prepare for the conversation we were apparently about to have, I scooped myself a smaller portion. Then I added a little Heavenly Hot Fudge Sauce to each. It just felt like the right thing to do.

I sat down next to my niece and focused on my delectable dish of ice cream. I didn't press her. Instead, I waited for her to volunteer to talk about whatever was causing her distress. I watched silently as she shoveled spoonful after spoonful of ice cream into her mouth, moving so fast I doubted she was truly appreciating its meltaway creaminess, its perfect level of sweetness, the smooth taste of the Italian coffee I brew to make it, and the barely perceptible hint of cinnamon that I consider to be the true secret of its irresistible lusciousness.

"Men," Emma finally muttered.

Ah. So I'd been right.

"By 'men,'" I said, keeping my tone casual and my eyes on my spoon, "I assume you mean Ethan."

"That's the one I'm referring to." With a deep sigh, Emma said, "Why do they always have to complicate things?"

A question women have been asking each other ever since

Eve offered Adam a bite of her apple—and he said, "That looks like a Macintosh. Don't you have any Granny Smiths?"

I decided it was safe for me to be a little more proactive. "What, exactly, is Ethan complicating?" I asked.

"The rest of the summer," she spat back, keeping her eyes fixed on her dish of ice cream. Or what was left of it. Which I was impressed to see was very little.

"What about the rest of the summer?" I prompted.

"I've been assuming that the end part would be just like the beginning," Emma replied. "Which meant me working here, helping you out and saving some money and basically giving me some structure in my life. And Ethan working at the dairy. And in between, the two of us spending as much time together as we could."

I remained silent. I had a feeling I was about to find out the specifics of whatever complication Ethan had thrown into this idyllic-sounding plan.

"And then, completely out of *nowhere*, Ethan decided he wants to spend the rest of the summer bumming around Europe," Emma announced.

"Whoa!" I exclaimed. "That's a pretty ambitious plan. Not to mention an extremely expensive one."

Emma didn't seem to have heard me.

"He brought it up for the first time a few nights ago," she said, still speaking to her ice cream dish. "He said it was only an idea he was thinking about. He told me that travel and change of place impart new vigor to the mind."

"Ethan said that?" I asked, surprised.

"Actually, it was Seneca who said that," she replied.

"Seneca?" I repeated.

"You know, the Roman philosopher?" Emma said. "Ethan quotes people like that all the time."

"Ah, yes. *That* Seneca." I was thinking that maybe the lad deserved more credit than I'd been giving him.

"But Ethan is always coming up with nutty schemes," she

went on. "I figured this was going to turn out to be nothing more than one more of those."

"What nutty schemes are those?" I asked, trying to sound only minimally interested.

"Oh, you know," she replied with a wave of her hand. "Opening a store that specializes in tie-dyed products. Going to acupuncture school. Creating an app for people who share a passion for reptiles."

Of course, I thought. *Those* ideas.

"What's the story with Ethan, anyway?" I asked casually. "Is he going back to school in the fall? Or does he plan to work at the dairy for a while . . . ?" In other words, I thought, what are your gentleman caller's long-term prospects?

"He's doing the same thing I'm doing," Emma replied. "He started working for Jake part-time last winter, during his senior year of high school. But now that he's graduated, he wants to take some time off to figure out who he is. He's really into reading. And thinking. Yeah, he spends a lot of time just thinking. But he also wants to experience life, which is how this travel thing came up in the first place."

"Got it," I said. Despite the two young lovers' conflict, I was finding that the more I learned about Ethan, the better I liked him.

"Anyway, last night, right after I get into bed, Ethan starts texting me," Emma said. "He says he's all excited about some web site he just found out about that helps people find really cheap flights at the last minute. And he announces that he's got a friend who's spending the summer in Amsterdam and has a floor he can sleep on for free. He says that for all the other places he's been thinking about going to—Prague, Paris, Berlin, Hvar—there's Airbnb. He figures somebody is bound to have a couch he can crash on for, like, hardly any money at all."

That didn't exactly sound like my idea of a European tour,

especially the part about Hvar, since I had no idea where Hvar was. Or why anyone would want to visit a place with a name that has an H and a V right next to each other. But I could see that for someone with an extremely limited budget, a back that's less demanding than mine, and enough imagination to think up the idea of an app for reptile lovers, it could hold a certain appeal.

"It sounds as if Ethan has given this trip some serious thought," I interjected, trying to sound noncommittal.

"But that's not even the most complicated part!" Emma wailed. "He wants me to go *with* him!"

My mouth dropped open. That, I had to admit, I hadn't seen coming.

I was shocked.

And the idea of losing my number-one employee was the least of it. The thought of Emma traveling around Europe without a plan, scrounging around for a couch to sleep on in a city whose residents spoke Dutch or Czech or one of the many other languages my niece didn't speak a word of, not to mention whatever language was spoken in Hvar, was nothing short of terrifying.

It's not that I didn't love the idea of travel. I'd traveled quite a bit during the time I worked in public relations and had the luxury of a steady income. But I was one of those stuffy people who liked to have a detailed itinerary, hotel reservations, and at least two credit cards before I got on a plane that would whisk me a few thousand miles away.

"Of course, the trip Ethan wants to take sounds amazing," Emma went on. My horror over the idea of sleeping on a floor instantly made me feel like an old-timer. "I'd love to visit all of those cities. Or even one of them. I mean, seeing Amsterdam in August? How great would that be?

"But the timing is terrible!" she wailed. "I'm just not sure I want to drop everything and follow Ethan to Europe."

Using her spoon to make little circles in the bottom of her ice cream dish, she continued, "It's so sudden, for one thing. He's talking about going soon. Like this weekend. But I've been totally enjoying myself all summer, and I don't want to give all that up. Working at the shop is really fun. I like everything about it: chatting with the customers, being around all this lovely ice cream, thinking up crazy new flavors and then watching people try them and actually like them . . .

"Besides," Emma added, "me taking off like that for a couple of weeks wouldn't be fair to you! I made a commitment to help you in the shop. How would you find someone to fill in for me with only a few days' notice? And, of course, it's *summer*, your busiest time of the year . . ."

I glanced around my empty shop. Okay, so there wasn't a soul in sight. But that didn't mean things wouldn't pick up again as soon as Omar DeVane's murder was solved. I was clinging to the hope that once the story became old news, visitors would flock back to Wolfert's Roost again.

And I was still hopeful that would happen *soon*.

Emma let out another loud sigh, this one even more soulful. "Anyway, Ethan and I were up late, having a huge fight about this."

"Really?" I said. "I didn't hear you."

"That's because we were texting the whole time," she said glumly.

That was a much better way of fighting, I thought, than yelling angry words at each other. Having arguments using only the written word was clearly one of the greatest advantages of living in the digital age.

"So now Ethan is acting as if the fact that I'm not ready to just jump up and follow him to Europe means I don't really care about him," Emma said. "He's taking it so personally. And it actually has very little to do with our relationship. It's more about being practical."

Then came the moment I'd been dreading. Emma fixed her mournful eyes on me and cried, "Aunt Kate, tell me what I should do!"

I was suddenly reminded that my strong, independent, funny niece was, in fact, only eighteen years old. Barely out of childhood. Still technically a teenager. And a long way from feeling able to make important decisions without the input of someone she trusted.

Not to say that I didn't feel the same way myself, at least some of the time.

Even so, I got the feeling this was one she had to handle on her own.

"Emma," I told her, "I can't make this decision for you. This is something you have to figure out yourself."

"Really?" Emma said woefully. "I was kind of hoping you'd say, 'Emma, you can't possibly leave me in the lurch! You promised you'd work for me, and I desperately need you in the shop!' Or else, 'Go for it, Emma! How could you possibly turn down a fabulous trip like that?'"

"Which one of those things did you *wish* I'd say?" I asked gently, trying to be helpful.

She frowned. "I'm not sure. But either way, I was hoping you'd make the decision for me." Brightening, she added, "And if you insisted that I stay, that would help keep Ethan from blaming me."

I shook my head. "I'm not going to do that, Emma. You're on your own with this."

To emphasize my point, I stood up and said, "I've got to get busy. I haven't given up hope that a few brave day-trippers will find their way to Wolfert's Roost today. And I want to be able to offer them my usual array of fabulous flavors. Speaking of which, I was thinking about soaking raspberries in raspberry-flavored balsamic vinegar and then combining them with lemon ice cream. I think the combination of the tartness of the vinegar and the lemons would be a lovely complement to the sweetness of the ice cream. The raspberries, too, of course. Tart and sweet, two qualities that kind of bounce off each other in a surprising yet pleasing way . . . How does that strike you?"

Emma's eyes grew as big as the aforementioned lemons.

"In that case," I said, "why don't you run out to the organic farm stand right now and pick up some lemons and raspberries?"

"I'm on it," she replied, already jumping up and heading toward the door.

I had a feeling she wasn't simply being a cooperative employee. I figured that just like me, she couldn't wait to taste this new concoction.

Besides, there are few substances better suited to drowning one's miseries than ice cream.

Long before the grand opening of Lickety Splits, I'd developed what some people might call a business plan. Me, I liked to think of it as a philosophy. I wanted my shop to offer three basic types of ice cream flavors.

The first was the classics. These were the flavors people expected, like vanilla, chocolate, and strawberry. But my goal was to make each one the absolutely finest version anyone had ever tasted. My strawberry ice cream would be chock-full of fresh strawberries, my vanilla would use only the best-quality vanilla from Tahiti, and my chocolate would be made with the richest, most flavorful chocolate I could fine.

The second type would be more adventurous. This was where my Hawaiian Coconut fit in. Peanut Butter on the Playground was another example. I wanted anyone who tasted my peanut butter and jelly ice cream, made with freshly ground peanuts and just-sweet-enough grape jelly, to be transported back to the most idyllic moments of their childhood.

The third type was the most fun—and the most creative. I was excited by the ice cream revolution that was erupting all around me. Suddenly it seemed as if there was no limit to the ingredients that could be combined with cream and sugar to invent new, never-seen-before flavors. Pear with Blue Cheese, Banana Walnut Bread Pudding, the lemon ice cream with raspberry balsamic vinegar concoction that I'd just suggested to Emma . . . I literally lay awake nights, dreaming up new ways to tickle the palate. If only there were more hours in the day, more room in the display case, and more customers to gobble up my tasty offerings!

In fact, as I stood behind the counter of my once-again-empty shop later that morning, I was still thinking about that last one, the combination of tart lemon and equally tart raspberry. I was so lost in thought that I jumped when the door opened.

A customer had finally come in.

I realized immediately that it wasn't just any customer. Or maybe it wasn't a customer at all.

It was Pippa Somers.

"Good morning," she greeted me regally, her elegant British accent making it sound as if she was reciting Shakespeare.

Even though it was still early, Pippa looked ready to be photographed for the cover of her international fashion magazine. As always, her bronze-colored hair was styled into the perfect flip that had become her signature. While on most women the retro style would have seemed dated, somehow she elevated it to new heights of sophistication. She was wearing a simple yet elegantly styled cream-colored sleeveless top with a pair of meticulously tailored pants made from the same fabric. Silk, I guessed, given the flattering way it draped along the minimal curves of her slender frame.

On her feet was a pair of brown suede sandals with a million straps, the style that wraps around the ankle and up the calf, bringing to mind Roman gladiators. Fashionably dressed Roman gladiators. And her jewelry positively screamed minimalism: shimmering pearl earrings and a fine gold chain necklace dotted with more pearls.

She was also wearing an oversized pair of sunglasses. I'd seen her wear similar sunglasses in hundreds of photos. Whether she made that a habit to try to keep people from recognizing her or to make sure they recognized her, I couldn't say.

"Good morning, Ms. Somers," I replied without thinking.

She reacted with surprise. "Do we know each other?" she asked, sliding her sunglasses upward and letting them rest on top of her head.

I could feel my cheeks turning red. "I know who you are because of . . . who you are," I stuttered. "And I was at Omar DeVane's party Saturday night. I was the caterer who supplied the ice cream."

"Of course," Pippa replied. "I thought you looked familiar."

I doubted that someone like her ever bothered to notice someone like a caterer. But I appreciated her politeness.

"The ice cream was fabulous," she remarked. "Which is why I made a point of remembering the name of your shop."

"I suppose that's why you're here," I joked. "You obviously want more."

"Yes and no," she replied. She pulled her sunglasses down and chewed the end of one earpiece, meanwhile glancing around the store appraisingly. "I actually stopped by to see if you'd be interested in catering another event. Something I'm planning for this coming weekend. Sunday afternoon, starting at around four o'clock."

"I'd have to check my calendar, but I believe I'm available," I said. "In the city?"

"No, it would be close by," she replied. "I have a weekend place that's not far from here."

For some reason, I was strangely pleased by that. It was as if the fact that one more prominent New Yorker—a fashionable, world-renowned one, no less—had chosen the area I called home as the place to spend her down time reflected positively on this corner of the world I loved so much.

"Interestingly," Pippa went on, "it was Omar who convinced me that I should buy a weekend retreat here in the Hudson Valley." She sighed, meanwhile gazing off into the distance.

I had a feeling that what she was actually doing was gazing into the past. I discovered I was right when she wistfully said, "Omar loved his home here so much. He talked about it all the time." With a little laugh, she added, "It was as if he were Henry Hudson himself, the way he carried on about how beautiful this part of the country was. You'd think he was the one who'd discovered it!

"But in a way, he was," she said. "He did discover it. He was the first of our group of friends to get a house here. We'd all heard about the Hudson Valley, of course. Living in New York City, how could you not? But since most of us aren't from this area originally, we weren't as familiar with it as he was. It's always seemed easier to get a place out on eastern Long Island, in the Hamptons."

"Is Omar a native New Yorker?" I asked, even though I already knew he was. Thank you, Wikipedia.

"Yes, he is," Pippa said. "He grew up on the Upper East Side. That's one of New York's chicest areas, you know."

Yes, I knew. I had lived there myself, although my address had been Upper enough and East enough that the rents were relatively reasonable, at least by New York City standards.

"He bought Greenaway—his 'Hudson hideaway,' as he liked to refer to it—a few years ago," Pippa explained. "And he was enraptured by it. The way he talked about it impressed all of us. Finally, I came up here one weekend and saw for myself how lovely it was. I didn't waste any time before I found myself a real estate agent. A few weeks later, I, too, had a Hudson hideaway.

"Which is why I'm here," she said, as if the time for raving about this part of the country had ended and it was now time to get down to business. "Since I have a home here, it's the perfect place for Omar's memorial service. And I was hoping you'd be part of it."

She looked at me expectantly, as if waiting for me to reply.

But I hardly knew the man, I thought, puzzled.

Then I realized she wasn't referring to *me*. She was referring to Lickety Splits. And its ability to make a party special by including ice cream on the menu.

"Of course," I said. "Let me just check my schedule . . ." I made a big deal about consulting my phone, frowning as if I were trying to read through the many upcoming commitments on my calendar. In truth, I was checking to see if I'd gotten any new e-mails, which I hadn't. "Ah. It happens that I'm free on Sunday. I'd be happy to cater your event."

"Excellent," she said. "Since hot fudge sundaes were Omar's favorite food, I thought it was imperative that ice cream play a large part in his memorial service."

The corners of her mouth drooped, just a millimeter or two. But half a second later, she was back to her usual poised self.

"I was quite impressed with what you did the other night," Pippa went on. "Not only the ice cream itself, which was utterly delicious. But the way you managed to make everything run so smoothly. You certainly have a way with the catering business. So I'd be happy to leave all the details in your hands."

"Of course," I told her. "Let's start with how many people you'll be expecting."

"About two hundred," she replied without even stopping to think. "Or perhaps as many as three hundred."

I gasped. Three hundred people! I couldn't even picture how many that was. I tried to picture three hundred ice cream spoons. And couldn't.

And then another thought occurred to me.

"Do you have enough room for that many guests?" I asked.

She smiled. "Why don't you come over to my house later this week—shall we say Thursday? That way you can see the space for yourself. Late morning, at around eleven, would be best. Perhaps then you could share your thoughts on how we might pull this off."

She stared off into space again for a few seconds before adding, "Usually I have my people work out all the details for something like this. But since Omar and I were such close friends, I prefer to make all the arrangements myself."

She looked back at me. "With help from experts like you, of course."

If Pippa was using flattery to win me over, it was totally working. Not that I wasn't inclined to do the very best job I possibly could with any catering gig I got.

But this one was extra-special, and would enable me to add a little glamour to my life as I hobnobbed with the elite players of the fashion world once again. Even more importantly, I hoped that being part of the memorial service would also help me with my investigation of Omar's murder.

After Pippa left, I couldn't wait to do what anyone else would do upon suddenly finding herself in the employ of one of the best-known, most influential figures in the fashion world.

I Googled her.

"Do you mind if I borrow your computer?" I asked Emma as soon as she came bounding into Lickety Splits, her arms wrapped around two big baskets. One was filled with ripe red raspberries and the other with bright yellow lemons. She looked as if she were posing for an oil painting by one of the Dutch masters. Except for the blue streaks in her hair, of course. "I could use my phone, but doing research is so much easier with a real screen."

"Be my guest," she said. "Just let me set these down and I'll get it out."

As soon as I settled in at one of the round marble tables with Emma's laptop in front of me, I opened Google and typed in the words "Pippa Somers."

Several photos came up. Not surprisingly, in each one Pippa was fashionably but conservatively dressed. And in all of them, her bronze-colored hair was perfectly styled in her famous flip. I got the feeling that whoever did her hair every morning used a special device, something the size and shape of a soup can, so that it always looked exactly the same.

I studied the photos more carefully. Pippa Somers sitting in the front row next to Heidi Klum at Paris Fashion Week. Pippa Somers whispering to Stella McCartney at Milan Fashion Week. Pippa Somers attending fashion week in countless other glamorous cities throughout the world, including London, Berlin, Florence, and Brisbane. Pippa on the arm of Michael Kors at the annual fashion extravaganza at the Costume Institute at the Metropolitan Museum of Art in New York City, an event that was known as the Met Gala.

The woman certainly got around.

But I already knew that. There was nothing new here. So I kept clicking.

I learned that her annual salary as the editor of *Flair* was three million dollars a year. I also discovered that the Queen of England had awarded her a damehood, the female equivalent of a knighthood.

On Wikipedia, I learned that Pippa had been born and raised in London, the only child of a wealthy couple. Her father worked in the City, London's version of Wall Street.

Her mother ran three boutiques in London with a high-end clientele.

After graduating from Oxford University, Pippa began working at various fashion magazines. A standout from the start, she quickly landed a position at the British edition of *Flair*. She did such a good job of distinguishing herself that, when she was barely out of her twenties, the media company that owned *Flair* moved her to New York. In an amazingly short time, she took over the editorship of the magazine's American version.

In addition to her business sense and her fashion acumen, Pippa Somers was known for her charitable work, her love of animals, and—the thing that most interested me—supporting young designers. Omar DeVane was named as an example, but so were a dozen others. Most of them were well known enough that I'd heard of them, even if I couldn't afford to buy their clothes.

But as I read on, I learned that the media star was almost as well known for her dark side as she was for her fashion sense. Various sources had characterized her as "cold," "calculating," "merciless," and "vengeful." Her hard-driving personality, along with her quickness to anger, had earned her the epithet "the Ice Queen."

And that was one of her kinder nicknames.

She had also been called "Pippa the Pulverizer," "Sullen Somers," and "The Pippanator."

I felt a wave of discomfort as I read the disparaging names.

I checked a few more web sites, and they all contained pretty much the same information. Some of the write-ups were kinder, while some were even harsher.

I was about to abandon my search when the last listing on the page caught my eye.

"Feud Between Pippa and Omar Hits a New Low!" screamed a headline.

The appearance of those two names in the same line made me freeze.

My heart was pounding as I clicked on the link. According to the URL, the article had been published by the *Sun,* a British newspaper, fourteen months earlier. I couldn't be certain, but I was fairly sure the *Sun* was one of those gossip-spreading and rumor-creating tabloids that England was famous for.

Which meant that what I was about to read might be true—or it might be fiction. Or it could be an exaggerated version of something that had really happened.

I began reading, my mouth already uncomfortably dry.

"The ongoing dispute between internationally acclaimed fashion designer Omar DeVane and *Flair*'s influential editor-in-chief Pippa Somers reached new lows last night at a high-profile fashion event. The fashion show, held at the Piccadilly Institute, introduced a controversial new designer from Japan, O. O, whose age, physical appearance, and gender remain a secret, wowed London with a runway show that featured the designer's spring collection. The fashions included a three-armed and three-legged pantsuit made of newspaper, a pair of platform shoes made of metal two-Euro coins, and, for the finale, an elegant wedding dress made of paper towels and toilet tissue.

"Despite the outlandishness of the clothes on display, the true highlight of the evening turned out to be a loud argument between DeVane and Somers. The two were sitting in the front row when a discussion they were having during the show became increasingly louder and more heated. Their spat culminated with Somers rising to her feet, opening her purse, taking out a bottle of perfume—several onlookers reported that it was the classic Chanel No. 5—and dumping the contents on DeVane's head. Somers then rushed out of the venue. The runway show continued without interruption.

"Increasing difficulties between DeVane and Somers have been in evidence for the past several years. Yet the two have a long history together, one that until recently has seemingly been only positive. In fact, in interviews DeVane has always credited Somers with helping him launch his career.

"Back in the early 2000s, DeVane opened his own boutique on Madison Avenue and 63rd Street in Manhattan. He quickly made a name for himself, thanks to his creative use of unusual fabrics—for example, an evening gown made of ruby red corduroy, a tailored women's suit made of pink terry cloth, and a sleek black bathing suit trimmed with fake leopard-skin fur.

"But it was reportedly Somers's decision to feature DeVane's designs in *Flair* that made him and his inventive approach to fashion famous. Orders began pouring in, and he was sought out by such retail giants as Macy's, Bloomingdale's, and Nordstrom in the United States and Harrod's and John Lewis in England, to create exclusive lines that would be featured in their stores. The designer quickly expanded into such diverse areas as footwear, jewelry, and handbags. Over time, DeVane moved away from his original concept, which some critics dismissed as 'gimmicky.' Yet he never strayed completely from his signature: incorporating his own unique and sometimes humorous use of surprising materials in every item that bore the famous ODV logo.

"As DeVane's empire grew, he and Somers appeared to remain fast friends. They were seen together at fashion events, charity balls, and film festivals like Cannes and Sundance. However, in recent years, the relationship suffered a dramatic shift. The two fashion powerhouses became increasingly at odds. Explanations for their growing rift vary. Some people claim they've had conflicting ideas about what the relationship between fashion magazines like *Flair* and individual designers should be. Others say there have been problematic financial entanglements between the two. Still others simply attribute their difficulties to differences in their personalities.

"While the reasons for their falling out aren't clear, what is clear is that the bad blood between the two fashion moguls has escalated to such an extreme level that they are no longer able to contain their hostilities while out in public. And if there's one thing that people involved in the fashion industry should avoid, it's airing their dirty laundry in public."

I sat in front of the computer for a long time, thinking. This last piece of news left me reeling.

I certainly hadn't picked up on any hostility between Omar and Pippa. If anything, the opposite was true. They appeared to be the best of friends. On Saturday night, Omar's last night, he had gone out of his way to credit Pippa with helping launch his career, just as he had apparently done all along. And now Pippa was arranging a memorial service for the man, opening her home to hundreds of people.

Yet it was clear that the two of them had a past.

Was it possible that their feud, whatever it had been about, had reared its ugly head again more recently?

And that Pippa Somers's equally ugly tendency to be "merciless" and "vengeful" had, too?

Chapter 9

Ice Pops began in 1923, when Californian Frank
Epperson patented a "frozen ice on a stick."
While he originally called them Eppsicles, he
soon changed their name to Pop's Icle—which
eventually became Popsicle. He made seven
flavors, including cherry, the most popular. They
sold for 5 cents each.

*—http://www.expo2015.org/magazine/en/economy/
a-short-history-of-ice-cream-from-ancient-
roman-snow-to-love-with-a-heart-of-cream.html*

Late Tuesday afternoon, I left the shop in Emma's hands.
As always, I was confident she could handle anything
that came up.

And business continued to be shockingly light. Lickety
Splits' only customers were a smattering of locals who needed a
quick ice cream fix in the form of a cone or a Bananafana Split.
One woman bought a half gallon of Classic Strawberry for a
family barbecue. But when it came to tourists, they were still
avoiding Wolfert's Roost.

As I headed home, I was preoccupied. But for a change, I
wasn't obsessing about how bad business was or Omar De-
Vane or even new ideas for ice cream flavors. I was ruminat-
ing about my date with Jake.

Not that it was a *real* date. It was just . . . a movie. Maybe
with ice cream afterward.

But definitely not anything that would be considered a date in the classic sense. At least that was what I kept telling myself.

Once upon a time, Jake and I were boyfriend and girl-friend. He and I had fallen for each other—hard—back in high school. During our junior and senior year, we were in-separable. That is, whenever he wasn't playing baseball. He was our school's star player, his impressive record culminat-ing in hitting the ball out of the park during the big game against Rhinebeck High, our school's number-one rival.

So it was inevitable that the two of us would go to our se-nior prom together. At least, that was the plan.

Then the big night arrived. I'd spent hours getting dressed, taking a long bubble bath, and fussing endlessly with my hair and makeup. At last it was time to put on the perfect dress, one I'd spent weeks shopping for. The flatteringly cut strap-less gown was the same shade of blue as the sky on a perfect day. I actually gasped when I looked at the final result in the mirror.

But Jake never showed up. Seven o'clock rolled around. Then seven-fifteen, then seven-thirty . . . I'd waited until al-most nine, certain that this couldn't be happening. And then, finally, I'd thrown myself across my bed, crying for hours. Poor Grams did her best to comfort me, but I was beyond being consoled.

After that night, Jake disappeared. For the next fifteen years, I heard nothing. Not an apology, not an explanation, not even a posting on Facebook.

It had been only a few weeks earlier, right after Lickety Splits opened, that I'd finally learned the truth about what had happened that night. The reason Jake had stood me up was that he'd had to rush over to the police station, dressed in his rented tux. His father had been driving drunk—again. But this time he'd been in a car accident in which three peo-ple were injured. One of them had been a little girl.

Yet I still didn't know how I felt about him. Not just because of prom night, either, but also because of his silence during all the years that followed.

Part of me could see things from his perspective, now that I knew the full story. But part of me still couldn't let go.

As I pulled up in front of the house in my red pickup, I was snapped out of my distracted state by the sight of Grams. I spotted her in the driveway, climbing out of the front seat of her Corolla.

I was struck by how slowly she moved. I could see that the simplest movement, like getting out of her car, had become a challenge. I also noticed that, just like the day before, she was dressed nicely. She was wearing her good pants, a pretty flowered blouse, and jewelry.

I jumped out of my truck and dashed over to help her. To ask her a few questions, too.

"Okay, the jig is up," I said sternly as I gave her my arm. "I want to know where you've been sneaking off to, all dressed up like that."

It was all I could do to keep from adding, "young lady." After all, I did sound like a protective parent.

I knew what I was doing bordered on ridiculous. But I really did want an explanation.

Grams sighed. "All right, Katydid, I'll tell you. I didn't want to say anything because it's a little embarrassing."

My eyebrows shot up to my hairline. I could hardly wait to hear what she was going to say next. Was she about to admit that she was having an affair with Doug, our mail carrier? Or that she'd started sneaking off to the nearest casino because of a secret slot-machine addiction?

Or maybe she'd found another ice cream shop somewhere in the Hudson Valley and didn't want me to find out she'd become one of their best customers.

Without making eye contact, Grams said, "I've starting going to the local senior center."

I blinked. To tell you the truth, I was disappointed in her answer.

"A senior center?" I repeated. "That's it?"

With a shrug, she said, "I feel silly. At least, about you finding out. I don't want you to think of me as . . . well, a senior citizen."

"But you *are* a senior citizen!" I replied.

I was perfectly aware of Grams's age. And it seemed to me that once you'd passed the age of seventy, you deserved a title of respect, which is what "senior citizen" was to me. She'd earned it along with whatever bonuses came along with it, including reduced ticket prices at the movies, a guaranteed seat on a bus, and being able to wear bedroom slippers in public if that was what you found the most comfortable.

"Of course I am," she replied. "But that doesn't mean I want *you* to start seeing me that way! I don't want you to think of me as *old*."

The expression on her face was despondent, and her shoulders were slumped. I reached over and hugged her.

"Of course I don't think of you as old," I assured her as I gave her a good, hard squeeze. "You're *Grams*! You're the most solid person in the world for me! You're the one I know I can always count on, the one I know will always love me . . . and the one I'll always love more than anyone else on the planet!"

She hugged me back. "You don't have to love me the *most*," she replied. "Just make sure you keep me on your top-ten list."

"It's a deal," I told her, laughing. "Now tell me about this senior center. What do you do there?"

Her face lit up. "Actually, it's a lot more fun than I thought it'd be. I was getting kind of bored, staying at home. I certainly love all the crafts I do—the knitting, the sewing, the weaving, and everything else—but I've been feeling kind of lonely lately. Like I need to get out there and meet new people. And then I saw an article about the center in the *Daily Roost* and figured I'd give it a try."

"And you like it?" I prompted.

Her smile widened. "I like it a lot. Oh, Katydid, I've met so many interesting people! There's a man there who once competed in the Olympics. In fencing, of all things! And I've gotten to know so many women who are interested in knitting. Probably a dozen lovely ladies. In fact, we've been talking about forming a separate knitting group. And I've been told that once school starts in the fall, children from school bands and choruses in the area will be coming to perform. The first time I went, a representative of a travel company gave a lecture on tour groups geared toward retired people . . . I've already gotten so much out of it, and I've only gone a few times."

Now I was smiling. "Grams, I'm so happy for you. This sounds absolutely perfect. It also sounds as if you're going to be going there regularly from now on."

Instead of agreeing, however, she simply shrugged.

"Maybe," was her mysterious reply. "I'll have to give it a little more time before I decide if it's really for me."

While I was surprised by Grams's surprising response about the long-term prospects of the senior center, I didn't have time to dwell on it. I was too fixated on the evening ahead.

I was strangely anxious about going to the movies with Jake. So I continued to remind myself that even if he was thinking of the evening ahead as a date, I wasn't.

Not when I still couldn't bring myself to let go of the anger I'd harbored for all those years.

So I was relieved that when he came to pick me up, he was simply his normal self. No flowers, no candy, no spiffy shirt or hair gel. Even more important, he didn't appear to be the least bit nervous. He was just acting like, well, like Jake.

"So has business picked up?" he asked as we drove toward Route 9.

"Not really," I replied. "Things in town are still ridiculously quiet." With a sigh, I added, "I'm incredibly upset about how Omar DeVane's murder is affecting not only me, but just about everybody in Wolfert's Roost. Having such a horrible thing happen right under our noses has certainly cast a shadow over everyone who lives here. But it's also turning out to be a total disaster for all the local businesses."

"Yeah, some of my customers were telling me the same thing earlier today," Jake said. "One of them runs a restaurant over in Wappingers Falls. He said things have been pretty quiet there, too."

"So it's not only affecting Wolfert's Roost," I mused. "It's the whole area."

"Seems that way," Jake said.

"Actually," I said casually, making a point of staring out the window, "Omar DeVane's murder is turning out to be so disruptive that I thought I might do some poking around to see if I can find out anything that helps solve the case. You know, talk to some people to try to learn more about the man's life and who might have wanted to get rid of him. I'm sure Detective Stoltz is doing a thorough job, but it's hard not to want to jump in and get involved in something that's having a negative effect on so many people.

"I've already started," I continued. "Yesterday I made up an excuse to go back to Omar's house. I wanted to see if I could find out anything more about the people he kept close to him. And today Pippa Somers, the editor of *Flair* magazine and someone who's known Omar for decades, came into the shop and asked me to cater a big memorial service for him on Sunday. After all, hot fudge sundaes were his favorite food. I'm thinking that might give me a chance to do a little sniffing around, too."

I glanced over at Jake, curious about what his reaction would be. I expected him to be shocked. Or at least to disapprove, launching into a speech on how dangerous it was to get involved in a murder investigation and how I would be better off leaving it to the professionals.

So I was surprised when he said, "In that case, you may be interested in something I heard about today. I was at the bank, waiting in line, and I heard a couple of people talking about a photo shoot at Wilderstein tomorrow."

Wilderstein, whose name in German means "wild stone," was an elegant estate in Rhinebeck that was now a tourist attraction but for over a hundred years had been the home of three generations of the Suckley family. I'd first visited it on a field trip back in the ninth grade. Built by a well-to-do property developer named Thomas Holy Suckley in 1853, the luxurious Queen Anne–style mansion was known for its lush interiors that had been designed by a cousin of Louis Comfort Tiffany and for its round, five-story tower overlooking the Hudson River. It was also famous for its sumptuous gardens, which were designed by Calvert Vaux, best known for designing New York City's Central Park with his partner, Frederick Law Olmsted.

But there was another interesting layer to Wilderstein's history. The last member of the Suckley family to live there, Daisy, was a distant cousin of Franklin D. Roosevelt. In fact, she's credited with giving him his famous Scottie, Fala, as a gift. When Daisy died, a stack of letters from FDR was found, their contents indicating that the two of them might have been more than friends.

"But the really interesting part," Jake went on, "is that the model they're using is that famous one who was at Omar DeVane's party Saturday night. Gretchen Whatever-her-name-is."

"Gretchen Gruen," I said. "Will she be modeling clothes that Omar designed?"

"I don't think so," Jake replied. "At least, not based on what I heard. One of the people said something about this Gretchen person modeling the creations of some hot new designer. She said it would undoubtedly provide a tremendous boost to his career. I didn't catch the designer's name, but it didn't sound as if Omar had anything to do with it."

That was good news, I figured, already plotting how I'd crash the fashion shoot. It meant that Federico wasn't likely to be creeping about Wilderstein during the shoot. Federico of the soft silent soles and the big prying ears.

"Do you know if the photos are for *Flair*?" I asked, wondering if Pippa Somers was likely to be there.

Jake frowned. "I don't think so. They mentioned the name of the magazine, but it definitely wasn't *Flair*."

More good news. That meant Pippa Somers wouldn't be at the shoot, either.

All I needed was an excuse for *me* to be there. And I already had an idea.

"So do you have any theories about who might have killed Omar DeVane?" Jake asked, glancing over at me from the driver's seat.

"Not yet," I told him. "But what I've observed so far is that there are four people in Omar's entourage who seem to have been particularly involved with the man. And they were all at the party Saturday night."

"So you've already put together a list of suspects." There was a teasing glint in Jake's eyes. "You're faster than the folks on *CSI*."

I swatted at him playfully. "I'm just telling you what I've seen so far."

"And who are these people who've made your top-four list?" he asked.

"Omar's assistant, Federico, is at the top," I began. "Then comes Gretchen Gruen. Another person of interest, shall we say, is his business manager, Mitchell Shriver, who's known him since childhood. And the fourth is Pippa Somers, who's pretty much credited with launching his career back in the eighties. But there's apparently been some rockiness in their relationship over the years."

"That's it?" Jake asked.

"Actually," I said thoughtfully, "there is one other person. His housekeeper, Marissa." Quickly, I added, "But I don't consider her a suspect. The only reason I'm even mentioning her is that she seems to have been a fairly big presence in his life." Gazing out the window, I mused, "Besides, I get the feeling that Marissa was genuinely fond of Omar." I thought for a moment, then said, "Of course, that's true of Gretchen, too."

"Maybe they're both just good at acting," Jake noted. "Not that I'm cynical or anything."

I laughed. "True." I thought of mentioning the confusion about the pretzel factory versus the spaetzle factory but decided it was insignificant. After all, *People* magazine, where I'd first read that anecdote, couldn't possibly get one hundred percent of the facts right. Or what was more likely was that some public relations person had felt that pretzels made a better story than spaetzle, perhaps because pretzels were definitely the better-known carbohydrate of the two. Tastier, too, at least in my opinion.

"Federico and Mitchell bicker constantly," I went on, partly because Jake appeared to be genuinely interested and partly because I was thinking out loud. "Honestly, they act like two little kids. I don't know how Omar could stand to have them both around."

"Any theories about what's up with that?" Jake asked.

I hadn't really tried to come up with a reason before, but this seemed like the perfect time to do just that. "Mitchell has apparently known Omar since the two of them were children. They grew up together, which would account for Omar trusting him. At least, that's how Mitchell tells the story."

"And we both know that when it comes to murder investigations, there can be a lot of different versions of the same story," Jake interjected. "We can't assume that anything anyone says is true."

"You're certainly right about that," I said. "As for Federico, he was apparently Omar's right-hand man. But he strikes me as kind of a difficult person, which makes his constant presence in Omar's life more of a puzzle. Why would Omar want to rely on someone who's obviously self-centered and extremely temperamental? But the other side of the coin is that Federico seems to know a lot about style. He looks as if he truly belongs in the world of design. He was probably a real asset to Omar when it came to making decisions about fashion and trends and what would sell."

Thoughtfully I added, "I also wonder if Federico and Omar might have been involved in other ways, aside from business." I let out a deep sigh. "Federico definitely strikes me as someone worth finding out more about."

"Hey, a parking space!" Jake suddenly cried. "Right near the theater, too."

By that point, we'd reached the center of Rhinebeck, a town that's at least as cute as Wolfert's Roost. I was surprised that we'd gotten here so fast. And relieved that we'd arrived without any awkward moments.

While discussing a recent murder wasn't exactly what I considered casual conversation, it had given Jake and me something to talk about. Something that didn't involve *us*, that is.

The movie was absorbing, both the funny parts and the heartbreaking parts. Still, as Jake and I sat together in the dark, I was back to feeling tense. But the only time our hands touched, it was an accident. We happened to make contact in the process of sharing a huge tub of buttery popcorn.

Which reminded me that I really had to try making that Couch Potato's Dream ice cream, the caramel flavor with the popcorn, pretzels, and potato chips.

"That was a terrific movie," I commented as we strolled out of the theater. "Thanks for inviting me."

"Thanks for coming." Glancing at his watch, Jake said, "Hey, it's only nine-thirty. Want to go somewhere for a drink or coffee?"

"How about some ice cream?" I suggested, grinning. "I happen to know where to get the best ice cream in the Hudson Valley. For that matter, the best ice cream in the entire New York metropolitan area."

Jake feigned surprised. "What? You mean it's not the best ice cream in the whole universe?"

"Could be," I said, laughing. "I heard about this one place on Mars that sounds like pretty stiff competition."

"In that case," he said, "I'd be happy to settle for the closer place. I have to be up too early tomorrow to drive us all the way to Mars."

"Then Lickety Splits it is," I said.

When we walked into my ice cream shop, Emma was standing behind the display counter. But she was clearly very bored. Her laptop was set up on the counter, and she was staring at the screen dully.

A guilty look crossed her face as soon as she spotted us.

"Kate!" she cried. "I was just—"

"It's fine," I assured her, glancing around. "I can see that this place isn't exactly bustling. In fact, why don't you go on home? Or wherever you want to go."

"Home," she said quickly. *Too* quickly.

Even Jake seemed to notice. He caught my eye and raised his eyebrows questioningly. I just shrugged.

Once we were alone, he commented, "I thought Emma and Ethan were the new Romeo and Juliet."

"They are," I told him as I headed over to the display case. "But they've had more time together than Romeo and Juliet ever did. Which means it was inevitable that sooner or later some sort of conflict would arise.

"I mean, can you imagine if Romeo and Juliet had gone on to have a long-term relationship?" I continued. "Or even got married? Think about the first time a major holiday came around. Midsummer Night's Eve or something. Romeo would say, 'My mom expects us to go to her house for dinner.' And Juliet would say, 'But your family hates me! Besides, my mother always makes a huge fuss. Midsummer Night's Eve is her favorite holiday, and she always makes her special hedgehog pot roast. She'd be devastated if we didn't go to her house!'"

Jake laughed. "Yeah, you're right. I guess it's impossible for any couple not to have *some* conflicts."

Time to change the subject.

"So what flavors can I dish up for you?" I asked brightly, poised behind the counter with an ice cream scoop in hand. "Perhaps you're in the mood for a Bananafana Split? Or may I suggest a Rootin'-Tootin' Root Beer Float? Or maybe you'd like to go with Lickety Splits' famous Hudson's Hottest Hot Fudge Sundae?"

"Definitely not a hot fudge sundae," Jake said, pretending to shudder. "How about a big scoop of Cherry Cheesecake and . . . let's see, a scoop of Dark Chocolate Hazelnut?"

"Both are excellent choices," I told him, already digging in. "And those two flavors happen to complement each other really well."

For me, I scooped up some Berry Blizzard, which is strawberry ice cream with locally grown organic strawberries, raspberries, and blueberries. I also added two delightful spices, cardamom and cinnamon, to give it extra zing.

Even though the single scoop was generous, it looked lonely. So I added a second scoop: Chocolate Marshmallow.

"Chocolate Marshmallow was one of my dad's favorite flavors," I said as I sat down opposite Jake at one of the round marble tables. "I remember him making me an ice cream cake for my third birthday. It had three layers of ice cream: chocolate marshmallow, vanilla fudge, and chocolate mint chip, which was my favorite at the time. In between he put crushed-up cookies. And there were sprinkles on top, along with candles and this crooked sign he made that said, 'Happy Birthday, Kate!' I still have pictures of it. It was easily the best birthday cake I've ever had."

"You were really close to your dad, weren't you?" Jake said softly. "That's something I remember you talking about when we were younger."

I nodded. "As I was saying the other night, he's one of the main reasons I started Lickety Splits. There were a bunch of other reasons, too, of course. But my father loved ice cream so much that Lickety Splits is kind of a tribute to him."

"That's great," Jake said. "How old were you again when he died? I know you were pretty small . . ."

"I was five."

And I still haven't gotten over it, I thought, feeling my throat thicken and my eyes burn.

"I guess we never really get over losing someone who matters to us," Jake said, almost as if he'd read my mind.

I just shook my head. I was afraid if I tried to speak, I'd end up crying instead.

There was a long silence as we both dug into our ice cream. The cold, creamy chocolate ice cream and the way it contrasted with the stark sweetness of the marshmallow ribbons running through it seemed especially tasty tonight. Somehow, no matter what else was going on, ice cream always made the world seem like a slightly better place.

It was Jake who broke the silence. His voice was strained as he said, "I guess we never really forgive ourselves for hurting the people we care about, either."

I looked up at him. But he was keeping his eyes on his ice cream.

"I still think about that night, you know," he went on, putting his spoon down on the table. "The night of the prom."

I bit my lip. I'd spent fifteen years waiting for the chance to rail at him, to tell him how hurt I'd been that night. But now that I knew the truth about what had happened, I remained silent.

I certainly wasn't about to add to his misery. Not when his feelings about the events of that night apparently remained a demon that continued to hover over him, unwilling to leave him alone.

"It was a long time ago," I said softly. "It's time for us both to put it behind us."

Instinctively I reached over and took his hand.

His eyes met mine. As he squeezed my hand, his expression was apologetic, regretful, and above all, relieved.

"You'd better eat that ice cream before it melts," I said, taking my hand back and trying to change the mood. "If it goes to waste, I'm going to be offended."

He picked up his spoon. Looking at me meaningfully, he said, "The last thing I want, Kate, is to do anything that offends you."

From that point on, we kept the conversation light. It was as if we'd tacitly agreed that we'd both had as much baring of our souls as our still-wobbly relationship could handle. Instead, we ate our ice cream, meanwhile brainstorming about different flavors that might be worth trying. Some of the ideas we came up with were absolutely hilarious. In fact, I laughed so hard at Jake's suggestion of Thanksgiving ice cream—

gravy-flavored ice cream dotted with pieces of turkey, stuffing, sweet potato, and cranberry—that I actually choked on my ice cream, something I'd never known was physically possible.

When he drove me home, he pulled into the driveway and kept the car running. The awkward time was suddenly upon us.

"I'll walk you inside," Jake offered.

"You don't have to," I insisted.

"Hey, chivalry isn't totally dead," he teased. "Besides, it's the least I can do after you fed me all that incredible ice cream."

We were silent as we walked the few steps from the car to the porch, then up the wooden steps. The night sky was un-usually light, thanks to both a nearly full moon and about a million stars. All around us I could hear the crickets chirping, one of my favorite sounds of summer.

And then we found ourselves standing at the front door.

It was the moment I always dreaded. A moment that, for me, anyway, looms over every first date like a gloomy rain cloud.

To kiss or not to kiss?

That's always the question.

With Jake, it was a huge question.

A kiss wasn't just a kiss, after all. And the vibe I was get-ting from Jake was that he was ready to make the move to the romance level. I, however, was not.

So I laid on the friendship stuff, big-time.

"That was really fun!" I said, as cheerful as a camp coun-selor. "Thanks again for inviting me to come along." As I chat-tered away, standing a good three feet away from Jake, I unlocked the front door. Predictably, Digger came dashing out.

I immediately scooped him up.

"Good night, Jake," I said with that same forced cheerful-ness, still grasping the scruffy, squirmy terrier mix in my arms.

Poor Digger. I was using him as a shield.

Of course he didn't mind in the least. Or even notice. He was too busy licking my face, overjoyed that I'd reentered his universe.

As for Jake, he didn't seem quite as happy. In fact, he looked crestfallen.

"Good night, Kate," he replied, already turning away.

I watched him walk back to his car, not sure how I felt. Or at least not sure which one of the mishmash of emotions that was rushing over me was the strongest.

All in all, the evening had turned out to be a lot more intense than I'd expected. It had felt good to have someone to talk to. Someone who had known me for so long that it wasn't necessary to explain things or make excuses or try to be anyone aside from who I really am.

At the same time, I was aware of how very dangerous it felt to make myself so vulnerable.

Especially with Jake.

Chapter 10

"In the 1920s, officials at Ellis Island became
convinced that serving new immigrants ice cream
'was an efficient method for making our future
citizens more at home in their new environment.'
Ice cream was, these immigration officials
believed, the ultimate American experience."

—http://www.ultimatehistoryproject.com/
ice-cream-and-immigrants.html

On Wednesday morning, I awoke with an excited Christmas-
morning fluttering in my stomach. Today was the fashion
shoot at Wilderstein. And if things went the way I hoped, I'd
be getting a behind-the-scenes peek at the glamorous world
of modeling.

Not that I was a complete stranger to going behind the
scenes. When I worked in public relations, my job involved
learning as much as I could about the companies my PR firm
represented.

At one point, we'd had a theater company as a client, and
I was given a backstage tour. My eyes were wide as I took in
rooms full of wigs, racks of costumes sitting in the middle of
the hallway, and the surprisingly tiny, grungy dressing rooms
that even big-name Broadway actors had to use.

We'd represented a candy company, and I visited its factory in Pennsylvania. I was amazed by the sight of Dumpster-

sized containers filled to the top with colorful pieces of sweetness in every color of the rainbow.

Over the years, I'd also gone to a few food shoots—photography sessions for magazine ads for food companies or restaurants—in which the food had to look as irresistible as possible. I'd learned something about the tricks routinely employed by the food stylists, the people who arrange the food before it's photographed.

Ice cream, for example. Because it melts so easily, especially under the hot lights photographers require, food stylists substitute mashed potatoes for ice cream. When it's photographed, it looks just like the real thing. The stylists usually use instant mashed potatoes, dyeing it as they whip it up to make it look like chocolate or strawberry or any other flavor. As for whipped cream, shaving cream is a great substitute.

There are dozens of tricks to enhance the appearance of the foods being photographed. Hairspray or deodorant make it gleam so it's more appetizing. White glue is substituted for milk because it doesn't make other foods like cereal get soggy. Motor oil is used instead of syrup because it's so shiny that it looks better in pictures. And, of course, plastic ice cubes behave much better under hot lights than real ice cubes do.

I'd always found it fun, being an insider. And today I'd be getting a firsthand look at what really went on at a fashion shoot.

That is, if I managed to get myself in the door.

Which remained a big "if." But for now, I was focused on making myself look the part.

Even though I'd decided to use ice cream as an excuse to sneak into the photo shoot, I still wanted to look a little more presentable than usual.

I stood in front of my closet, frowning as I tried to decide what to wear. When I lived in Manhattan, my closet was full of the latest, trendiest clothes that a woman on a budget could buy. Over the years I'd lived in the city, I'd become a regular at the upscale consignment shops on Madison Avenue. Shopping in places like that was always hit or miss. But if you went in often enough, you might find a top-of-the-line Stella McCartney dress or a Calvin Klein jacket for about the same price you'd pay for lesser brands at Marshall's or T. J. Maxx.

Since moving to Wolfert's Roost, however, my "nice" clothes had been pushed to the back of the closet, along with my heels and designer purses. For an ice cream mogul like me, jeans and T-shirts were much more practical.

As I surveyed my big-city clothes, I was surprised to find that I was actually looking forward to dressing up. Especially when I spotted a pair of pants I'd always loved. They were a soft dove gray, made from a fabric that was a silk-and-linen blend. I'd worn them a lot, partly because of the material's fine quality but also because I always thought they made me look pretty darned good—even with the ten or twelve extra pounds I'd put on since high school.

I couldn't wait to put them on and feel, well, *stylish* again. So I stepped into them, pulled them on, and started to zip them up.

And discovered that I couldn't come close to doing so.

Did they shrink? was my first panicked thought. Maybe the dry cleaner messed up somehow?

The telltale stain on the left thigh, a barely noticeable blob, reminded me that I hadn't had these cleaned since the last time I'd worn them.

It wasn't that they'd shrunk. It was that my waistline had expanded.

My stomach clenched, making me feel as if I'd just eaten a scoop of lead ice cream.

I had no choice but to face the fact that despite all the plan-

ning I'd done before opening Lickety Splits, despite all the
flow charts I'd drawn and all the Excel spread sheets I'd laid
out, there was one important detail I'd forgotten to consider.

And that was that eating ice cream day and night, living it
and breathing it and devouring as much of as I wanted any
time I felt like it, was bound to have an effect. A *negative* effect.

Of course, I was aware that eating ice cream at least once
a day—and that's on a bad day—was not the best way for a
person to keep her weight at a consistent level. Especially since
I'd never been a natural string bean the way Willow was.

Yet I'd always managed to strike a balance. Some days I
gorged on ice cream, but other days I was too busy or too
distracted or simply not hungry. All in all, I had managed to
keep my weight from getting out of control.

Now that I ran an ice cream business, spending my days
surrounded by three-gallon vats of Cappuccino Crunch and
Chocolate Fudge Swirl and Pear with Blue Cheese, I was
going to have to do some rethinking.

In the end, I threw on a pair of nondescript black pants
and a loose-fitting, pale blue top that was stretchy enough to
hide all kinds of secrets. I didn't exactly feel fashionable in it,
but I looked nice enough. As an afterthought, I draped a long
silk scarf covered with colorful swirls of blue and purple
around my neck. Surveying my reflection in my full-length
mirror, I decided that I'd created what appeared to be a carefully thought-out outfit.

Even so, as I drove to the photo shoot, I was in a bit of a
funk. Maybe I'd solved my immediate problem by putting together an acceptable ensemble. But that didn't take away the
basic problem I was now confronting.

And then a light bulb flashed on in my head.

I'm hardly the only one who's struggling with those evil
laws of physics or biology or whatever it is that persistently

wants to put weight on us, I thought. Which means that there are lots of people who find themselves having to just say no to ice cream.

Obvious, of course. But what was less obvious, or at least had been up to that moment, was that it wouldn't be a bad idea for Lickety Splits to offer other options.

Lighter options. Options that were less likely to make people unable to zip up their favorite jeans or button the jacket they'd counted on wearing that night.

I decided to look into it right away. And rather than seeing my sudden burst of fleshiness as a curse, I could now consider it inspiration.

A new concept called Lickety Light had just been born.

While I could hardly wait to get to the photo shoot at Wilderstein—or, to be more accurate, to *crash* the photo shoot at Wilderstein—first I had to stop at Lickety Splits to pick up the magic ingredient that was designed to get me in the door. I figured I'd drive over to the shop with Emma, pick up my cold, creamy bribe, and make sure she was settled in before I headed over to Rhinebeck.

My niece shuffled into the kitchen as I was finishing up breakfast. I was about to lay out my plan but changed my mind when I saw the expression on her face. It was clear that her conflict with Ethan over his upcoming grand tour of Europe was still under way.

"You look like you need coffee," I greeted her. "Or, even better, a big scoop of Cappuccino Crunch. I'll set you up as soon as we get to Lickety Splits. A little caffeine and a little sugar and you'll be your old self in no time."

She cast me a mournful look. "Kate, I'm dealing with something that even coffee and sugar can't take care of."

I sighed. "So things are still rocky on the Ethan front?"

"He's impossible!" she wailed. "He expects me to drop everything in my life and just run off to Europe with him! And he can't accept the fact that my reluctance to do that isn't a statement about how much I value him! He's simply not seeing this the same way I am."

Welcome to the world of relationships, I thought cynically.

But I knew better than to get involved. "I'm sure you two will figure this out," I told her.

Given how upset she was, I hoped I wasn't asking too much by leaving her alone in the shop. But I figured the distraction of having to throw herself into her work might cheer her up. Especially since around here, "work" meant dishing out the absolute best food on the entire planet—literally.

I quickly forgot about Emma's little soap opera. I was too focused on my commitment to investigating Omar DeVane's murder—and, I'll admit, a bit giddy over the prospect of going to the fashion shoot.

When I got to Wilderstein, I spotted a big handwritten sign on the front lawn that said, CLOSED TODAY FOR PRIVATE EVENT. I breezed right past it and up the driveway.

The brick-red Queen Anne–style country home, built in the mid-1800s, looked like an illustration in a children's book. I'd always found the three-story house absolutely charming, thanks not only to its famous towering turret but also its various peaked roofs, its multisized and multishaped windows, and its ornate wraparound verandah.

I parked my truck and walked purposely toward the front door. By that point, I was actually starting to believe that I belonged there.

The good news was that there was no security guard or bouncer guarding the entrance. The bad news was that, instead, a young woman holding a clipboard was stationed there. While she was petite enough that she didn't look capable of strong-arming me, she did appear to have been charged with keeping interlopers out.

Fortunately, I was ready, having anticipated that getting myself into the photo shoot was going to take a little creativity. And a little creativity is something I happen to possess.

So not only had I made a point of showing up wearing the best outfit I could put together, I was also carrying two giant tubs of ice cream, one of Chocolate Explosion and one of Berry Blizzard. If there was one thing I'd learned in my first thirty-three years of life, it was that very few people could resist ice cream.

I sashayed over to the woman at the door. "Hi-i-i-i," I greeted her, plastering on my biggest smile. "I'm Kate McKay from the Lickety Splits Ice Cream Shoppe in Wolfert's Roost. I'm here to set up a snack area. I brought everything I need, so if you can tell me where I can find a nice big table . . ."

She glanced at me warily. "I don't know anything about an ice cream delivery," she said.

"That's because it's supposed to be a surprise," I replied, acting like the picture of confidence. "Pippa Somers arranged this. She said something about wanting only the best for Gretchen Gruen."

"Pippa arranged this?" the woman exclaimed, her hard expression melting as fast as a scoop of Chocolate Mint Chip that had been put into a microwave. "How thoughtful of her!"

Amazing what a little name-dropping could accomplish. And fortunately, the irony of the editor of one of the fashion industry's most important magazines sending a gift of ice cream to one of the world's top models went unnoticed.

"You'd better get that ice cream inside before it turns to mush," the woman said. "It's hot out there."

I could practically hear her mouth watering.

"I'm on it," I said, sailing inside.

At least, I'd intended to sail. Instead, as soon as I stepped into the front room, which appeared to be the center of the action, I was confronted by a maze of thick cables and wires and other scary electrical equipment that snaked across the thick Oriental carpets. Huge cameras and oversized lights were positioned throughout the room, a startling contrast to the old-fashioned surroundings: dark wood paneling on the walls and ceiling, ornate stained-glass windows, and an intricately carved wooden fireplace that covered an entire wall. Personally, I'd always found it kind of fussy. But I could certainly understand how it would make an intriguing background for fashion photos.

I stopped the first person I spotted who didn't appear to be completely frazzled, a thin young man wearing a white T-shirt and jeans. But his T-shirt was very chic-looking, while his jeans had been strategically torn in all the right places. It was as if Giorgio Armani had decided to dress James Dean.

"Excuse me, I'm the caterer," I told him. "I need a place to set up."

"Just grab whatever you need," he replied with a shrug. "But we're about to get started, so if I were you I'd keep out of the way."

He took off before I had a chance to ask any more questions. I glanced around the room, which appeared to be a front parlor. I quickly spotted a good-sized antique end table that was relatively free of knickknacks. That table was probably worth as much as Grams's house, but I decided that today it would have to serve a more practical purpose than simply being a work of art. I covered the top with plastic, plunked down the two tubs of ice cream, and headed out to the truck to get the rest of my supplies.

It was on my third and final trip back into the house that I spotted Gretchen. She looked like a page in a magazine come to life. Her makeup was perfect, her hair was arranged in a complicated twist, and she was wearing a short purple dress with sleeves shaped like two cube-shaped cardboard boxes.

"Kate!" she cried, clearly surprised to see me. "*Gott im Himmel*, what are you doing here?"

"Ice cream, of course," I replied with a shrug. "I just set

everything up over there. Please, help yourself. Or I can bring you some—"

"Maybe later," she said with a wave of her hand.

Right, I thought. Like in forty years.

Anxious to engage her in conversation, I said, "I'm actually pretty excited to be here. I've never been to an actual photo shoot before."

"You'll probably be bored silly," she said, sighing. "There's so much waiting around while they adjust the lights and rearrange the furniture and change the pocketbook or the shoes . . ."

"I had no idea it would be such a big production," I commented, gesturing at all the equipment and the masses of people standing around. "Who are all these people, anyway?"

"Crazy, right?" Gretchen replied. "Those women over there work for the magazine, and that group over there by the big camera represents some of the designers whose clothes we're photographing today. Then there are the photographers, their assistants, the lighting people, the hair people, the makeup people . . . and of course the models."

The models were the easiest to pick out, since they were all so thin that I desperately wanted to hand each one a huge dish of ice cream.

"It's not as if the model just throws on the outfit and the photographer starts clicking away," Gretchen went on. "In fact, the most important people at a photo shoot—aside from the photographers and the models, of course—are the hair stylists, the makeup artists, and the clothing stylists."

"How long does it take to put makeup on a model?" I asked. In my life, it took about two minutes to put on some blush and eyeliner and maybe splurge with a little lip gloss.

"Usually a half hour to an hour," Gretchen replied. "But it can take even longer if it's a close-up. And especially when it's a print ad for a cosmetics company."

"And I bet the makeup artists have all kinds of tricks," I

prompted, curious about how photographing beautiful people compared with photographing beautiful food.

"They do," she agreed. "Like putting lip gloss on eyelids to get a real shine. Or putting lipstick on the model's cheeks. Still, a lot of their effort goes into keeping the model's faces from getting too shiny under the hot lights. They're constantly retouching the makeup.

"And getting the right look is crucial," she added. "For a seductive look, like for an evening gown or clothes that are dramatic or extreme, the makeup artist has to put on really heavy makeup. But for an innocent look that goes with something like sportswear, simple makeup works much better. The same goes for the hairstyle."

"What does the clothing stylist do?" I asked. I could tell that we'd found a subject she loved to talk about, and I was hoping to use it to establish as good a rapport with her as I could.

"The stylist's job is to make the clothes as attractive and enticing as possible," Gretchen replied. "And the stylist we're using today, Gabrielle, is one of the best. She always has a style kit with her, and she generally ends up using everything in it."

"What's that?" I asked.

"One of the most important things is a steamer," she explained. "When a model puts on an outfit, there can't be a single wrinkle anywhere. After steaming every garment, Gabrielle goes over it with a stiff brush. That's especially important with suede and velvet. The nap—that's a term that refers to the texture—has to all be going in the same direction. She uses a lint roller, too. There can't be even the tiniest speck anywhere on the fabric. That especially matters with dark clothes."

I didn't mention that I hadn't used an iron since I'd moved out of the city. These days, laying my clothes out flat on the bed while they were still warm from the dryer and smoothing them out was about as good as it got. As for specks on one's clothes, I wasn't going there.

"Gabrielle has also got every type of pin you can imagine in her style kit," Gretchen went on. "She has boxes of safety pins, bobby pins, straight pins . . . She uses them to make the clothes fit the model perfectly. And it's best to put the pins inside the garment. That way, the photographer can snap away, taking pictures from any angle, without stopping to adjust the model's clothes.

"And if pins don't do the job, there are always clips," she continued. "Binder clips work best. And then there's tape. Gabrielle always brings all kinds of tape. Scotch tape, duct tape, double-sided tape. There are lots of uses for tape, like holding the clothes in place. Like keeping shoulder straps from slipping down or keeping plunging necklines from revealing too much . . . Tissue paper is useful, too. It can give volume to puffy sleeves, for example. Or make a collar stick out.

"And there are plenty of other tricks the stylist uses. Like nipple concealers and breast-lift tape . . . Of course, there are more obvious things a fashion stylist does, too," Gretchen noted. "Like making sure the accessories for each outfit are absolutely perfect. The wrong shoes or handbag can ruin a look. And adding the right accessories, like fabulous earrings or a scarf or some textured item like a jacket, can make any garment look amazing."

My head was spinning. And I'd thought photographing food took a lot of patience and creativity!

I couldn't wait to tell Willow about all of this. Emma, too. Even Grams would get a kick out of it. Maybe none of us subscribed to *Flair* or any other fashion magazines, but that didn't mean we were above devouring them while we were in line at the supermarket or waiting in a doctor's office.

But one thought stood out: How were the rest of us supposed to come even close to looking like the beautiful, perfectly put-together women in the magazines if even *they* required so much help?

Before I got too discouraged, I was distracted by a stylist, presumably the legendary Gabrielle, who rushed over with an evening gown draped over her arm. It was absolutely gorgeous, made of flowing silk in a shade of silver that was so pale it bordered on white.

"This one's next," she told Gretchen. "We should be ready to shoot in about five minutes."

"*Danke*, Gabrielle," she replied.

Without a moment's hesitation, Gretchen pulled the purple minidress over her head and wriggled into the gown. The shimmering fabric spilled over her curves like water. Yet when she studied her reflection in the full-length mirror that was propped up in front of a bookshelf, she frowned.

"If I were working with this fabric," she said, "I'd drape it over the shoulder like this, and put a few embellishments here. Nothing too showy, maybe a few rhinestone buttons to add a little sparkle . . ."

I was surprised. I'd assumed that Gretchen simply put on whatever clothes were handed to her and then did her best to make them look good. I'd never even considered the idea that she might have had a creative streak of her own.

I guess my shock showed.

"You don't think I could be a fashion designer?" she challenged.

"Of course you could," I replied. "It just never occurred to me that you were interested in fashion. From a design perspective, I mean."

"I'm *passionate* about designing clothes," she said, still staring into the mirror. Wistfully she added, "One day, I'd love to have my own line of clothing. What I envision is separates that all go together so you can mix and match. Each piece would be exceptionally comfortable and flattering, tops and bottoms that are made of really great fabrics. But I'd want them to be priced so that the average woman could afford them."

"Maybe you'll be the next Omar DeVane," I said.

"Oh, no!" she insisted, looking positively horrified. "I could never be that good. And I'd never want to be seen as one of ODV's competitors, even now that Omar is gone. After all, I owe him so much. If it weren't for that man, I'd still be working at that horrible factory."

"It sounds as if Omar was a really good person," I commented.

"He truly was," she replied. "And I'm not the only person to benefit from Omar's generosity. When I think about all the people who'll be helped by his foundation . . ."

"His foundation?" I repeated, startled. "Omar had a foundation?"

"It was brand-new," Gretchen explained. "He started it a few months ago, so it was just getting off the ground. I'm not surprised that you don't know about it since he never wanted it to get much publicity. Omar was much too modest for that. When it came to his fashion business, he wanted all the exposure he could get. But when it came to his philanthropic activities, he was positively secretive."

"What were his plans for the foundation?" I asked.

She looked at me blankly. "To help people, I suppose. Isn't that what foundations are for?"

Before I had a chance to ask her any more questions, the stylist came back. "It's time, Gretchen," she said. "Dan is ready."

Gretchen flashed me her million-dollar smile. "Got to run," she said. "Thanks for helping me kill some time!"

As I watched her float away, my brain was fixed on this new piece of information. I couldn't help wondering if the fact that Omar had recently started a foundation had something to do with his murder. After all, things that involved money often did.

Of course, it was just as likely that it didn't mean a thing.

"Beautiful! Simply beautiful! You're absolutely amazing. There's no one like you! Now look over here . . ."

I snapped out of my reverie, whirling around to seek out the source of such loud praise. The words were being spoken by the photographer who had just started snapping pictures of Gretchen.

She was standing in front of the elaborate fireplace, posing. But rather than jerking from one position to another, she moved fluidly, almost like a dancer. She was holding the skirt of her gown in both hands, giving the impression that she was totally in love with it. Her eyes had a dreamy look, and her expression was one of pure joy.

I realized that as she stood in front of the camera, Gretchen was transformed into an entirely different person.

I suddenly understood why she was considered one of the top models in the world. She had the ability to make the clothes she was wearing seem like—well, much more than simply clothes. She somehow managed to make it seem as if that gown had the ability to turn the woman who was lucky enough to be wearing it into someone spectacular.

But Gretchen's talent for morphing into someone else also made me uneasy. To me, it meant that she was a very good actress. While she seemed like a golden girl whose beauty had blessed her with a storybook life, there were clearly other layers beneath the surface.

And that meant that if she had a dark side, she was undoubtedly capable of hiding it.

Chapter 11

The most popular flavor of ice cream is vanilla, accounting for 29% of sales. Other popular flavors are chocolate (8.9%), strawberry (5.3%), butter pecan (5.3%), and Neopolitan (4.2).

—*http://www.derinice.com/news/15-most-popular-ice-cream-flavors*

First thing Thursday morning, instead of whipping up an original flavor of ice cream, I tried making something really *really* new.

At least it was new for Lickety Splits.

My heart was pounding and my palms were actually sweating as I dipped a small spoon into the finished batch and tasted it, letting the frosty glob dissolve in my mouth.

Its surprising yet delectable flavor made me moan with pleasure.

I had just created my very first sorbet. Something to mark on my calendar as a cause for celebration for years to come.

And Peach Basil Bliss sorbet was definitely going to be the first item on my brand-new Lickety Light menu. It was only mildly sweet, which allowed the fresh flavor of the real peaches I'd used to come through. The basil added another flavor altogether, a contrast that was the perfect complement to the icy fruitiness.

Emma came rushing in shortly afterward, the dismayed

look on her face telling me she was about to apologize for being three minutes late.

"Kate, I'm so, so sorry!" she cried. "It's Ethan. Again. We were up until two a.m. texting about this Europe thing. And then I was so upset about it that I couldn't fall asleep—"

I waved my hand in the air dismissively. "Emma, we can talk about all that later. At the moment, I have something much more important to tell you about."

A shocked look crossed her face. "Something bad?"

"Something fabulous!" I told her. "Something amazing, something life-changing. Something—well, try this."

Warily she studied the spoonful of the concoction I'd handed her, peach-colored but dotted with tiny bits of dark green. She raised it to her lips, stuck out her tongue to taste it, and then shoved the whole thing into her mouth. For three or four seconds, she kept her eyes closed.

And then, her eyes snapped open, and she smiled dreamily.

"Oh, my," she said, her voice a near-whisper. "Kate, that is everything you said it was. Fabulous, amazing, life-changing . . . You *have* to let me have more!"

"You can have all you want!" I told her, laughing. "As long as you leave a little for the customers!"

"What *is* this?" she demanded as she devoured a few more spoonfuls, acting as if she hadn't been near a morsel of food in days. "It's heavenly!"

"It's sorbet," I said. "Peach sorbet with a hint of basil. I call it Peach Basil Bliss. Somehow the light texture makes me feel, well, blissful."

"What other flavors of sorbet do you plan to make?" she asked eagerly. I wasn't sure if she was asking for the sake of the store or for her own purposes.

"I've got a whole list," I told her. "Watermelon, Coconut Banana, Pink Lemonade . . ."

Emma was nodding enthusiastically. "Each and every one

of those flavors screams summer, too. So does the texture. It's so frosty, and it's amazing the way it magically melts on your tongue."

"I came up with some more exotic ideas, too," I said, glancing at my list. "Strawberry Champagne, Lemon with Raspberry Balsamic Vinegar . . . And those are just the result of fooling around on the Internet for half an hour this morning, looking at what other shops offer. I'm sure that if I dig a little deeper and think a little harder I can come up with all kinds of unusual flavors.

"And the best part—well, aside from the flavor and texture—is that there are lots fewer calories in sorbet than there are in ice cream. It has no fat, either. And while a lot of the recipes I've seen call for more sugar than in ice cream, I tried cutting it down a bit, and it seems to work fine. Of course, I don't think there's anything that's good enough to totally replace ice cream. But for people who want something lighter, this will be part of the new Lickety Light menu."

"Lickety Light!" Emma repeated, savoring the words in the same way she'd savored that first spoonful of Peach Basil Bliss sorbet. "That's so perfect."

Letting out a loud, contented sigh, she added, "Aunt Kate, you are an absolute genius."

I only hoped my customers would feel the same way.

As eleven o'clock drew near, I left Emma in charge of Lickety Splits and headed over to Pippa Somers's house.

The nervousness about my appearance that I'd felt before the photo shoot paled beside my near-panic over the prospect of showing up at the weekend home of the editor-in-chief of *Flair*. I'd had to resist the urge to squeeze in a last-minute shopping spree.

In the end, I'd opted for the same outfit I'd worn the day before: the flowing blue top, the purple and blue scarf, and the black pants. Still, I made a mental note to add a few new items to my wardrobe the very first chance I got.

Since Omar DeVane and Pippa Somers were part of the same social set, I simply assumed that Pippa's house would be a lot like his. After all, she'd told me herself that he had been her inspiration for buying a weekend getaway in the Hudson Valley in the first place.

As I drove up the winding road that led to the address she'd given me, I tried to imagine what the hideaway of one of the most important and influential people in the world of fashion would be like. Elegant, stylish, tasteful . . . I was picturing an English version of Omar's estate, meaning it would have a rose garden, plenty of cobblestones, and perhaps a vine or two crawling up an exterior wall. In other words, I just assumed that Pippa's place would look like a set from a movie based on a Jane Austen novel.

I couldn't have been more wrong.

At the end of the driveway stood an architectural wonder. The modern white building was all sharp angles and offset levels and glass windows that covered entire walls. It was a building that appeared to defy all the laws of engineering.

Not that I know much about engineering. Or anything at all about engineering, to be more accurate. But the place was astonishing enough that it looked as if it deserved to be on the cover of *Architectural Digest*.

I suspected that it had.

After I parked, it took me a couple of minutes to locate the front door. I finally spotted it tucked between a towering sculpture made of tiny silver balls all stuck together and a spiky, six-foot-tall bush that looked as if it was perfectly capable of accompanying the plant from *The Little Shop of Horrors* to an all-you-can-eat-buffet.

As I rang the doorbell, my heart was pounding. I wished I'd taken the time to get my nails done and my eyebrows threaded. Or at least washed my hair.

The door opened, and I found myself face-to-face with a pretty young woman in a black dress and white apron. Her blond hair was pulled back into a neat bun.

She looked about as out of place in this house as a pink flamingo lawn ornament.

"You must be Ms. McKay," she greeted me. She spoke with an accent that sounded Eastern European.

"That's me," I replied, holding up the folder I'd brought along with me as if to prove my identity.

"Please come in," she said, moving aside. "Ms. Somers is expecting you."

I expected the house's interior to be just as distinctive as the exterior. And as I followed the housekeeper, I saw that I was correct. The furniture was ultramodern: an S-shaped swerve of leather that was a chair, a coffee table that appeared to be suspended in midair. The artwork was similarly stark, from the painting that appeared to be nothing more than a blank canvas to the piece of sculpture in one corner that was a series of three-foot metal sticks standing parallel to each other.

But what I didn't expect was that pretty much everything would be white.

The walls were white, the furniture was white, the carpets were white. Even the art, like the blank canvas, was white. A bouquet of white roses stood on a table, their dark green stems practically garish.

You could perform surgery in here, I thought.

I wished I'd brought Emma with me. Given her artistic talents, I would have loved to hear her take on how to inject color into this stark, impersonal backdrop.

The housekeeper walked me into a giant living room. Surprise: more white.

Pippa was perched on the edge of the stark white couch, talking on a cell phone. Her outfit was pale gray, consisting of another pair of perfectly tailored pants and a simple sleeveless top. Still, the contrast of the color of their fine linen fabric against the backdrop of her completely white surroundings was positively startling.

As always, her hair was carefully styled in her signature flip, with not a single strand out of place. Her nails, her eyeliner, her light dusting of blush . . . it all looked exactly the way you'd expect from the world's most famous and influential fashion editor.

I tried not to be rude by listening in, but since she was only a few feet away from me, I couldn't help overhearing.

"Desmond, darling," she was saying sweetly, "I suggest that you remind him that merely showing a swatch of his third-rate made-in-China faux leather in *Flair* would be enough to get him and his dim-witted wife and his ugly children out of Yonkers and into a town that matters, someplace like Chappaqua or Scarsdale or Bedford Hills. Perhaps then he'll see his way to extending the payment date."

She ended her call and smiled at me. "Kate! How nice to see you. Please sit down."

I did as she suggested.

"Thank you so much for coming by," Pippa continued. "I did think it was important for you to see the space." Raising both arms dramatically, she indicated the rooms around her. "Here it is, my own little 'Hudson hideaway.' "

"Your home is lovely," I said politely. But what I was thinking was that we'd better avoid dark-colored ice cream like chocolate and strawberry and even coffee. Vanilla, yes. Butter Pecan, maybe. Meyer Lemon, possibly.

Then I remembered that hot fudge sauce was to be at the core of my ice cream offerings. Involuntarily, I shuddered.

"Before we start, may I offer you anything?" Pippa asked graciously. "Coffee or tea?" Her face lit up. "How about some champagne?"

I automatically glanced at my watch, wanting to make sure that it really was only eleven o'clock in the morning.

"Um, coffee sounds good," I said. I made a mental note not to spill any on the white carpet.

Pippa was already calling to her housekeeper. "Katarina, would you please bring in some coffee for our guest? And some champagne would be lovely, as well. You can bring the bottle that's already open. Thank you so much."

Turning back to me, she commented, "I think starting the day with a glass of champagne is so civilized. Don't you?"

Actually, I'm a Cappuccino Crunch girl, I was tempted to say. But I simply smiled.

Katarina came in almost immediately with a tray. No doubt she had been anticipating Pippa's request. On it was a sleek, modern-looking silver coffeepot with a matching creamer and sugar bowl. Two snow-white linen napkins were neatly folded into triangles that stood up like tiny Himalayas. I sat up straighter, feeling like Lady Mary from Downton Abbey.

The tray also had a champagne flute on it, along with a bottle of the stuff. I noticed that the bottle was half empty.

Katarina poured me some coffee, then filled the champagne glass almost to the top.

"Thank you, Katarina," Pippa said regally. "That will be all for now."

I watched her pick up the slender flute, expecting her to take a teensy sip and then set it down. But by the time the bottom of the glass made contact with the table again, it was half empty.

"Much better," she half-whispered. "I feel more refreshed already."

She smoothed her hair, then asked, "Now, where were we?"

Her words came out sounding a bit fuzzier than before. I realized that this probably wasn't Pippa's first glass of champagne of the day. In fact, given how much was missing from the bottle, I'd guess it was probably her third or fourth.

"I thought I'd begin by running some ideas by you," I said, pulling out the folder containing the notes I'd prepared. "I'll be serving classic hot fudge sundaes, of course, as we discussed. But I thought we could offer a few other options, as well. A couple of more inventive twists on desserts that also incorporate hot fudge.

"One idea is Coconut Balls with hot fudge sauce," I continued. "Those are balls of ice cream—vanilla, for sure, and, uh, possibly lemon—that have been rolled in coconut flakes and topped with hot fudge. Another idea is Donut Sundaes, which consist of warm donuts—chocolate or cinnamon or even just plain—served with a scoop of ice cream and a dollop of hot fudge sauce . . ."

Pippa didn't appear to be listening. "Omar certainly loved his ice cream," she interrupted. She was gazing off into the distance, her eyes shiny and faraway. "He loved a lot of things," she said. "He was one of those people who was in love with life."

"I'm sure you're devastated," I said quietly. "It sounds as if you two were extremely close." Aside from that time you gave him a Chanel No. 5 shampoo, I was tempted to add.

"We *were* close," she said, her voice as dreamy as the look in her eyes. "Omar and I knew each other for a long time. Of course, for someone in my position, maintaining a solid relationship with a designer without getting too personally involved is always a challenge. You must understand that I have to be careful not to show favoritism."

"Still," she noted sadly, "the man was a true genius."

I was dying to find a way to bring up the feud I'd read about online. But there didn't seem a way to do it gracefully.

So instead, I said, "It's nice that so many of Omar's close friends are around to support each other through this. Federico, Mitchell, Gretchen . . .

"I really like Gretchen," I commented, hoping to engage Pippa in conversation about her. "And I must admit, I'm kind of surprised that she's so nice. I would have expected that someone who's that beautiful—not to mention famous and successful—would be a snob. Yet even though she's had such a golden life, she seems sweet."

Pippa cast me a wary look. "That's certainly a lovely sentiment, but I'm afraid you're wrong on both counts."

I blinked.

"The woman hardly had a golden life," she said. "She came from quite humble beginnings."

"I guess working in a factory isn't exactly glamorous," I commented, stirring sugar into my coffee. "Even if the factory makes something fun like pretzels."

I made a point of adding that last line. I had a feeling that Pippa was someone who could clear up the question of whether Gretchen's place of employment at the time Omar "discovered" her was a pretzel factory or a spaetzel factory.

Pippa let out a contemptuous snort. I had no idea that a creature so thin and so stylish was capable of making such a sound.

"Gretchen's 'factory' produced something a lot more 'fun' than pretzels," Pippa said sharply.

Ah. So it *was* spaetzel, I thought. Not that I thought that spaetzel was more fun than pretzels. In fact, between those two foods, I was pretty sure that most people would think—

"How about a flesh factory?" Pippa said, her eyes glittering.

I dropped my spoon. Literally.

"Are you saying that the famous story about Gretchen isn't true?" I asked.

"Not even close," Pippa said dryly. "The real story is that Omar first met her when he was on a business trip in Germany. The men he was meeting with—wool manufacturers, I seem to recall—insisted on taking him out to a strip club. Apparently they didn't get that Omar wasn't into women."

"Gretchen was a *stripper*?" I asked, trying to keep my voice even.

"I think she was actually a pole dancer," Pippa replied matter-of-factly. She paused to finish off the rest of the champagne in her glass. "Strippers are so outdated, don't you think? My impression is that it's all about pole dancing these days. We probably have *The Sopranos* to thank for that."

My image of a young Gretchen Gruen twisting rolls of dough into pretzel shapes, dressed in a Bavarian outfit—dirndl skirt, white apron, ruffled blouse—vanished into thin air. It seems there had been plenty of twisting going on, but it had been of an entirely different nature.

And then an idea popped into my head: Was it possible that Omar had been blackmailing Gretchen about her past?

But I quickly dismissed that thought. After all, sullying her name would only damage his own brand. Why would he want the world to know that the elegant Gretchen Gruen, the face of Omar's fashions and his perfume and all the other luxury products that comprised his fashion empire, had started out writhing around on stage practically naked?

"There's more to her unsavory past," Pippa went on, waving her glass in the air. She stopped, as if suddenly realizing it was empty. She grabbed the champagne bottle, refilled the delicate flute, and took a sip. Then another. Then another.

"Who knows how many of the rumors are true?" she said. "The stories about her being involved with unsavory people, the possibility that perhaps she had done a few other scandalous things besides dancing in a sleazy club . . . We'll never know the whole story. Omar was never able to find out, and in the end, he decided that none of it mattered. All that did matter was how beautiful Gretchen was—and how good her lovely face and body were at selling his designs."

My head was spinning. But I remained silent, hoping that Pippa's inebriated state would cause her to tell me more. I was especially interested in her claim that the second half of my statement about Gretchen was also wrong—that she wasn't "sweet."

So I was disappointed when she said, "But let's get back to what we're here to discuss: Omar's memorial service." Pippa's mouth drooped a bit as she added, "Omar was such a special person that I want to make sure this celebration of his life and his achievements is worthy of the man."

And then her entire face crumpled. She began to cry, gasping for breath as raw sobs choked their way out of her, almost like hiccups. She clasped her hands over her face.

I stayed in my chair, paralyzed. I didn't know what I should do. Rush over and hug her? Say something consoling? Call Katarina for help?

But while I wasn't sure how to react, there was one thing I was quite sure of. And that was that I was witnessing something rare indeed.

And that was the great Pippa Somers showing sincere emotion. A woman who was known all around the world as the ultimate professional, someone who'd been called an Ice Queen and a Pulverizer and even the Pippanator. Allowing herself to break down in front of someone else was clearly completely out of character for the woman.

As I listened to her deep, throaty sobs, I felt like crying myself. The rawness of her sadness truly touched me.

But then it occurred to me that her display of grief could simply be the result of drinking too much champagne.

Or worse, that it was all just an act.

That had been Jake's take on it. Or at least he had raised it as a possibility.

I felt bad for even thinking such a thing. Yet I knew it wouldn't be wise for me to simply ignore what I'd read about the woman online.

As real as Pippa's grief seemed to me, given the fact that the man we were talking about had been murdered, I knew I had to be at least a little bit wary.

After all, she was one of the people who had had the opportunity to kill Omar DeVane. And while it was difficult to believe that this accomplished, well-mannered woman with impeccable taste and flawless hair could possibly be capable of such an act, she *was* known for her vengefulness.

I wanted to know more about Pippa. Gretchen, too. And Federico and Mitchell . . .

I realized I needed to talk to someone who was an insider, someone who had access to Omar's world, but who was also able to be objective about the people who had been closest to him. Someone I could trust. Certainly someone I was pretty sure had nothing to hide.

And I knew exactly who that person was.

Chapter 12

"About 10.3 percent of all the milk produced by
U.S. dairy farmers is used to produce ice cream,
contributing significantly to the economic well-
being of the nation's dairy industry."

—*www.idfa.org/key-issues/nutrition-health/
national-ice-cream-month*

I drove straight from Pippa's house to Omar's, hoping to find Marissa. Sure enough, through the screen door I could see her in the kitchen, sitting cross-legged on the floor in front of an open cabinet.

"Hey, Marissa," I called through the screen. "It's me again."

"Come on in, Kate," she called back. "It's not locked."

I let myself in.

"It's been so darned hot the last few days that I've been leaving the doors open," she explained, glancing up from her task: pulling out dinner plates and wrapping them in newspaper.

Grimacing, she added, "This kitchen is the worst. You'd think that in a fancy house like this, the air-conditioning would manage to cool off all the rooms."

Instead of wearing her maid's uniform, today Marissa was dressed in jeans and a pale pink tank top. Not only was this the first time I'd seen her wearing regular clothes; it was also the first time I'd seen her without her hair up. Her shiny dark locks hung halfway down her back, the long strands in front sweeping over her face in a way that highlighted how pretty she was. That was something else I hadn't noticed before.

"It looks like you're busy," I observed. "I hope I'm not coming at a bad time."

"Not at all," she assured me. "I'm just getting a head start on packing up Omar's things, since sooner or later, they'll have to be moved." She let out a long, deep sigh as she surveyed the stack of plates in front of her. "Frankly, it's nice to have some company." Rolling her eyes, she commented, "Aside from Federico, of course. Mitchell, too."

Trying not to sound too interested, I asked, "Oh, really? They're both staying at the house?"

"Federico is still here," she replied. "Mitchell's been in and out, dealing with paperwork. But Federico has been going through Omar's personal things. His clothes, mostly. He's been deciding what to give to friends and what to donate to charity.

"It's good that he's getting that done, since it's a tough task," she continued. "But I'm sure he's keeping plenty for himself. He and Omar didn't come close to wearing the same size, but I'm sure Omar had plenty of neckties and cufflinks and who knows what else that Federico is helping himself to."

"What about Omar's more valuable things?" I asked. Gesturing vaguely in the direction of the sculpture garden, I added, "His art collection, for example?"

"I imagine that Omar made provisions for everything he owned in his will," Marissa said. "I guess the lawyers will sort all out those details."

"I suppose they'll figure out how to handle Omar's business, too," I mused.

"Oh, no," Marissa said. "Mitchell is doing all that. After all, he's been involved in all the details of Omar's various companies from the very start. I can't imagine a bunch of lawyers trying to figure out something so complicated without any background."

"I guess it's lucky that the two of them can help get things settled," I commented.

"I suppose so," Marissa said. "It's just annoying the way those two bicker all the time. Anyway, what brings you here?"

"Believe it or not, I realize I left behind a few other things," I told her, hoping my nose wasn't growing any longer. "I'm afraid the events of this past week have turned me into a complete scatterbrain."

"Be my guest," she said, making a sweeping motion toward the kitchen. "In fact, if there's anything here that you'd like, feel free to take it. I don't think Federico or Mitchell or anyone else is interested in Omar's pots and pans. I wouldn't be surprised if all this stuff ended up being donated to charity."

In order to continue my charade, making it look as if I'd actually had a legitimate reason for this visit, I riffled around inside a big cabinet until I found a large metal cookie tray. It was pretty banged-up, the kind of thing no one was likely to want. That kept me from feeling bad about turning this poor unsuspecting tray into a pawn in my little deception.

"Here it is!" I cried. "I wonder how this ended up in here?"

My Oscar-level performance was wasted on Marissa. She was barely watching me.

"How about some coffee?" she asked. "I'm ready for a break."

"Coffee sounds great," I said. Of course, all the coffee I'd just drunk at Pippa's house was sloshing around in my stomach like the water in a Los Angeles swimming pool during an earthquake. As for the caffeine . . .

"I don't suppose you have any decaf," I said.

"I do," Marissa said.

She stood up and began bustling around the huge kitchen like the lady of the house, measuring out coffee and pulling cups off the shelf. She stepped into the pantry, coming out a few seconds later with a box in her hand and a triumphant expression on her face.

"We're in luck," she said. "I found a long-forgotten box of biscotti hidden away in back."

A few minutes later, the two of us were sitting opposite each other at the rustic wooden table.

"So how long have you worked for Omar?" I asked conversationally.

"Almost three years," she replied, mixing two large spoonfuls of sugar into her coffee. "Before that, I worked for a cleaning service." Wrinkling her nose, she added, "That was pretty awful. The idea of working for only one person on a regular basis sounded much better."

I nodded, meanwhile dipping what looked like a chocolate almond biscotti into my coffee. As I bit into it, I discovered that I was right. I also realized that I'd just come up with an idea for a brand-new flavor: coffee ice cream with pieces of biscotti in it. I could call it Coffee Break in Milano.

Then I remembered that Federico had said he was from Milano. And decided that instead I'd call it Coffee Break in Rome.

"Did you just work for Omar here in the Hudson Valley, or did you also work at his apartment in the city?" I asked. Maybe I should throw some extra almonds into my new Coffee Break ice cream, I thought.

"I work—*worked*—at both places," she said. She helped herself to a vanilla biscotti, dipping it into her coffee before stuffing half into her mouth. "Hey, these are really good!"

Which made me wonder if I should develop several different flavors that used biscotti. Sometimes I was overwhelmed by all the possibilities for fun ice cream flavors. So many add-ins, so little time . . .

I reminded myself that I needed to stop obsessing about ice cream and instead take maximum advantage of the golden opportunity that had fallen into my lap. After all, Marissa had spent three years getting a firsthand look at Omar De-Vane's life. And she was someone who a lot of people undoubtedly considered invisible, meaning they were likely to show their true selves in front of her without even thinking about it.

"Working for someone like Omar sounds so glamorous," I commented. "You must have seen him interact with all kinds of famous people. And probably some who aren't so famous but are really powerful . . ."

"To tell you the truth, a lot of those people are actually pretty disappointing once you spend some time with them," Marissa said. "Some of them are amazingly rude, and some are egomaniacs. Some are just plain dumb."

"What about Omar?" I asked. "The one time I met him, he seemed really nice. Was he?"

"He was a prince," she said without a moment's hesitation. "He was amazingly talented, a true genius. The fashion empire he built is proof of that. But despite his success, he never became one of those people who are full of themselves. He was kind, generous, thoughtful . . ." Marissa's voice had grown hoarse. "I always figured it was because he came from such humble roots."

"Humble roots?" I repeated, surprised. "But the biography I found online makes it sound like he was born with a silver spoon in his mouth. I read that he grew up in New York City, where his father was a successful businessman and his mother was a high-society type, and that he went to the best schools before studying fashion in Paris and Milan. . . ."

Marissa smirked. "You can thank his PR firm for spreading that pack of lies."

I had to admit that I knew exactly what she was talking about. When I'd worked in public relations, more than once I'd been assigned the task of reinventing some celebrity's past.

"Mitchell, who was in charge of things like that, decided that a glamorous upbringing would make a much better story than the truth," Marissa said. "Starting with his name. Omar's real name was Elmer. Elmer Szabo—that's spelled S-Z-A-B-O. It's Hungarian.

"Omar's parents were immigrants," Marissa continued. "They had a second son, too. I never met him, but Omar used to talk about his brother all the time. His name was Arthur." Laughing, she added, "As far as I know, he still has his original name."

"I guess Omar figured 'Omar DeVane' would look better on the label of an expensive designer creation than 'Elmer Szabo,'" I said.

"Exactly," Marissa agreed. "And he really did grow up in New York City. That part, at least, was true. But he came from the Bronx. Not exactly Park Avenue or the Upper East Side. When he was a teenager, he got an after-school job working for a tailor to help his family make ends meet. That's where he learned everything he knew about fashion—by altering men's polyester suits and hemming cheap cocktail dresses."

I had to admit that while the real story behind Omar DeVane may not have been as romantic as the one he preferred to tell, I felt he deserved a lot of credit for pulling himself up from his humble beginnings. Yet I could see that he might feel the rich and famous folk he wanted to design for might not be as appreciative of his roots as I was.

"Mitchell was his best friend back in those days, which is

why Omar trusted him to manage his business," Marissa went on. "He had the same modest upbringing. But he's never pretended otherwise. With Mitchell, what you see is pretty much what you get."

"Interesting," I commented thoughtfully. "Two men who truly lived out the American dream. Of course, Gretchen did, too, and she's not even American."

"True," Marissa agreed. "And like Mitchell, she played a key role in Omar's career." She shook her head sadly. "Too bad Gretchen and Omar had a falling out, and that Omar passed away before they had a chance to resolve their differences."

My heart immediately began beating faster. "What happened?" I asked.

Marissa shrugged. "Apparently there was a clause in Gretchen's agreement with ODV, saying she couldn't launch her own line of clothing as long as she was under contract with Omar's company."

"I knew she was interested in fashion design," I replied, "but I hadn't heard anything about being restricted by a legal agreement." The wheels in my head were turning. So everything wasn't peaches and cream between Omar and Gretchen, I thought. At least not lately.

Needless to say, that immediately got me thinking about Peaches and Cream ice cream, and how it would be so much tastier with just a hint of almond flavoring . . .

"And now Gretchen's starting to get a little older," Marissa said. "Not that she's old by the real world's standards, of course, but when you're a model it's a whole different thing. And she's been thinking about creating her own label. Because of her contract, she couldn't. At least, not without getting sued."

"Omar wouldn't release her from that contract?" I asked. "Even though he was such a generous person?"

"It was Mitchell who wouldn't allow it," Marissa said.

"How do you know?"

"Because I heard Mitchell and Gretchen arguing about it."

"When?"

Marissa thought for a few seconds. "It must have been last week, since at the time we were all up to our ears in preparations for Omar's party."

I was about to write off that bit of information as irrelevant, given the fact that it was Omar who had been murdered, not Mitchell. But then Marissa said, "Of course, now that Omar has passed away, she's no longer bound by that contract."

My ears pricked up. If there was ever a motive to kill someone, that was it.

"How do you know *that*?" I asked.

"The same conversation," Marissa replied. With an odd smile, she added, "Maybe walls don't have ears, but the hired help sure does."

And there's clearly a lot going on in this house that's worth listening to, I thought.

"And Federico?" I asked. "What's his story?" I could see that Marissa was in a mood to gossip, and since I was in a mood to listen to gossip, we were well-matched.

Marissa laughed.

"Federico the Great?" she said, smirking. "I think you mean Fred Miller."

"I'm talking about Federico," I explained patiently. "Omar's personal assistant . . ."

"Right. Fred Miller." That same cold smile reappeared. "It sounds as if good old Fred has you totally convinced that he's exactly who he's pretending to be. Now that's what I call a first-class phony. He dyes his hair, he wears tinted contact lenses, his forehead is so smooth that he's obviously had Botox treatments . . ."

"What about his accent?"

"You meana thees accent?" she said, doing a perfect imitation of Federico. She let out a loud guffaw that was so raw that the sound made me jump. "That's totally made up. Can you think of a place anywhere in the world where people really speak English with an accent like that?"

I guessed that Milan, Italy, wasn't the correct answer.

"His accent is as fake as everything else about his supposed life story," Marissa went on, her voice dripping with disdain. "The real story is that Omar met him at a bar in Brooklyn. Once Fred realized the identity of the older man who was trying to pick him up, he latched onto him like a starving leech."

"Still," I said thoughtfully, "you've got to admit that Federico—Fred—does have a sense of style."

"Ninety-nine percent of which he picked up from hanging around Omar and the other fashionistas in his entourage," Marissa said. "Let's just say he's good at copying. But when it comes to having an original idea, I don't think Fred Miller ever had one in his life. That is, aside from deciding to leave his postage-stamp-sized hometown in Indiana and moving to the big city to try to make a name for himself."

So absolutely everything about Federico was a lie. He'd certainly fooled me.

I was trying to digest this fact when another thought struck me: If Fred Miller was so good at lying about his name, his background, and even his accent, what else was he good at lying about?

By that point, our coffee cups were empty, and the plate of biscotti contained nothing but crumbs and the inspiration for some fabulous new ice cream flavors.

Still, I'd gotten even more than I'd hoped for.

What I was learning was that when it came to the world of fashion, nothing was the way it appeared. And binder clips and double-sided tape were only the beginning.

* * *

Just as I'd hoped, Arthur Szabo turned out to be an uncommon enough name that tracking down Omar's brother was as easy as pie.

Even easier than pie, actually, thanks to Google. No rolling out of a pastry crust was required. All I had to do was type the words "Arthur Szabo New York City Bronx" into the Google search page on my phone.

I found his address and phone number easily. I jotted down both, but it was the first bit of information I was more interested in.

A phone call wouldn't do. Instead, I wanted to meet the man in person.

Next stop, the Bronx.

Chapter 13

Dairy Queen's "phenomenal story began with the
10-cent sale of a then unnamed product on
August 4, 1938, in Kankakee, Illinois. A father
and son partnership in Green River, Illinois, had
been experimenting with a soft frozen dairy
product for some time. They contacted Sherb
Noble, a good friend and customer, who agreed to
run the 'all you can eat' trial sale at his walk-in ice
cream store. Within two hours, he dished out
more than 1,600 servings of the new dessert."

—*https://www.dairyqueen.com/us-en/Company/
About-Us/?localechange=1&*

Getting to Arthur Szabo's home turned out to be even easier than I'd expected. After an hour on the train and a
short subway ride, I found myself standing in front of the address I'd found online for Omar's brother.

Yet I was certain there must have been a mix-up.

"This has got to be wrong," I muttered as I stood in front
of the building. "There's no way Omar DeVane's brother
lives here."

But both the name of the street and the peeling numbers
over the front door matched the address I'd scrawled on a
scrap of paper. And Marissa had claimed that Omar's beginnings had been humble.

This place, however, went far beyond humble.

The five-story brick building looked like something out of *West Side Story*. The resemblance to the sets of one of my favorite movies ever was made even stronger by the zigzag of fire escapes along one side.

Still, as I studied the building more carefully, I saw that while it was a long way from Greenaway, it wasn't exactly awful, either. True, it looked as if it had been around for a long time, with little sign of renovation or even regular maintenance. But aside from being a tad shabby, its worst fault was being nondescript.

I stepped up to the front door and studied the intercom. Next to each button was a name. Some were handwritten and some were typed. A couple of them were barely legible beneath the yellowing tape that protected them from the elements.

Sure enough, there was the name Szabo. Apartment 4B.

So I'd found an Arthur Szabo. I had yet to see if it was the *right* Arthur Szabo.

I pressed the button, holding my breath and hoping this wouldn't turn out to be a fool's errand. Or something worse: something I'd regret having gotten myself into.

"Who's there?" a male voice came through the intercom a few seconds later. It was barely audible through all the static.

"Um, I'm a friend of Omar's," I began, yelling back at the device. "My name is—"

But he had already buzzed me in.

The entry hall was completely without charm. The walls were painted a dingy shade of yellow and were clouded with so many scuff marks I found myself wishing I'd brought along a bottle of Windex and a roll of paper towels. I had the same reaction to the cracked black-and-white tile floor, which was caked with what was probably decades' worth of grime.

I trudged up three flights of stairs, instinctively holding my breath amidst the tsunami of smells. Cooking smells, mostly. Some were fresh, but some were old, as if they'd been lingering in the air the whole time that the grime in the foyer had been accumulating. But I also picked up on the distinct odor of oldness. To me, it seemed to come from a lack of fresh air, if it's possible for the lack of something to have a smell.

I was pretty much out of breath by the time I reached the fourth floor and spotted 4B on a metal door that was painted dark green. I paused, waiting for my pulse rate to get back to normal. But before that happened, the door opened.

Peering out at me was a man about Omar's age. I knew immediately that I had the right guy. While he didn't exactly look like Omar, he had the same stocky build, the same round head, and the same basic facial structure.

But that was where the resemblance ended. When it came to his demeanor, he and his dapper brother were a million miles apart. Arthur Szabo was wearing a faded Grateful Dead T-shirt with a pair of baggy black sweats. The front of his pants was sprinkled with orange dust that had probably come from nacho-flavored tortilla chips. Possibly Cheetos.

I was about to concoct a recipe for nacho-cheese-flavored ice cream—perhaps with real bits of tortilla chip mixed in—when he spoke.

"Can I help you?" he asked, his tone both cautious and friendly.

"I hope so," I replied. "My name is Kate McKay. I live in the Hudson Valley, not far from where your brother has—had—a weekend house."

"Ah," he said with a nod. "So you're a friend of Elmer's. Or Omar, as you probably know him." He opened the door wider. "Please come in."

I half-expected to be astonished by the interior of Omar DeVane's brother's apartment. I thought it might be sleek and modern, like Pippa Somers's place. Or possibly tasteful English Cottage, with flowered chintz fabrics and lots of charming touches like masses of ruffled throw pillows or a tea cup collection displayed in a glass cabinet.

Instead, I felt as if I'd stepped into a time warp. Suddenly, I was back in the 1970s.

Immediately to my left was the kitchen, where the glory days of the avocado refrigerator and the harvest-gold dishwasher were preserved with all the accuracy of a well-curated museum. The furniture that was crowded into the tiny living room just beyond the front door consisted of a well-worn La-Z-Boy chair and a sagging couch upholstered in brown chenille. A clear-glass coffee table with a silver metal frame sat on top of an orange shag rug. The lamps were so ornate they bordered on gaudy. As for the personal touches, those were more along the lines of a collection of Star Wars action figures crammed onto the shelves of a faux-wood wall unit than Staffordshire cups and saucers.

This was not a home that had moved into the twenty-first century with the rest of us. In fact, I would have been astonished to learn that it had Wi-Fi. Or even cable TV.

Arthur appeared to be amused. "I can tell from the look on your face that this isn't what you expected," he said.

I was about to protest, then realized there was no point. Even if he hadn't noticed me lurking outside, hesitant to ring the bell, he had undoubtedly faced the surprise of others who learned he was the famous designer's brother.

"No," I replied. "I guess it's not."

"I like it this way," he said with a shrug. "I grew up here. It's my childhood home, the place where my parents lived their entire adult lives. And since it's so comfortable—so familiar—I never saw any reason to change anything."

Glancing warily toward the kitchen, he commented, "Although I don't know how much longer that dishwasher is going to last. Every time I run it, a mysterious brown liquid oozes out of the bottom."

I laughed. While I hadn't known what to expect, I hadn't anticipated that Omar DeVane's brother would be so likable. Or so down-to-earth.

"My whole history is here," Arthur continued. "While other people notice the cracks in the ceramic tile in the entry-way, I see the floor that Elmer and I used to look at while we sat on the bottom step, putting on our roller skates. The plastic cover on this La-Z-Boy chair is split, but that's not what I see. Instead, I see my father, stretched out on it with a big glass of iced tea, telling funny stories about what happened at work that day.

"And that gash in the wall? That's from Elmer and me horsing around. Our mother was always screaming at us about not throwing a ball in the house, but of course we didn't listen. And that hole was from the time Elmer dove over the couch to catch a baseball and smashed my parents' framed wedding photo clear into the sheetrock.

"Besides, I love this neighborhood," he added. "Sure, it's changed a lot over the years. But the changes were gradual enough that I've gotten used to them. The old couple that used to run the dry-cleaning shop around the corner may have sold it quite a while ago, but the new owners have been here so long by now that they're as much a part of the neighborhood as the old owners were."

"Personally, I'm a big believer in sticking with whatever is comfortable," I told him. Glancing down at the black sleeveless shirt and khaki pants I was wearing, I added, "You can see that by the way I dress."

"I'm with you on that," Arthur said with a chuckle. And then he grew serious. "Elmer loved this place, too. More than that big flashy apartment on Park Avenue, the one with the huge windows and the six bedrooms and the doorman.

Whenever he came here, he'd plop down in this chair and say, 'Arthur, there's no place in the world that feels as good as it feels here.'"

His eyes had filled with tears. I impulsively reached over and gave his arm a squeeze. "I'm so sorry for your loss," I said. "I know what it feels like to lose someone you love. Both my parents died when I was still a child."

Arthur nodded. "That's probably even worse."

"I don't know how anyone can compare one person's grief with another," I said. "Sadness is sadness. Pain is pain. Who's to say how much it hurts? Besides, what's the point?"

"True," he said. "But I'm being a terrible host. Can I get you something? Coffee or tea?" With a self-deprecating laugh, he added, "Believe me, my coffee maker works a lot better than my dishwasher. It's a French press. State of the art."

I laughed. "Actually, that would be great." I hadn't intended to stay very long. But Arthur was turning out to be such a congenial host that I already felt as if the two of us were old friends.

Besides, I got the feeling he welcomed the company.

"Come into the kitchen so we can talk while I make the coffee," he said, even though the rooms in his apartment were small enough and close together enough that we could probably have conversed easily no matter where we stood.

"My parents moved here in 1968," Arthur said chattily as he bustled around the kitchen, filling a dented copper kettle with water and setting it on the electric stove. "This apartment has two bedrooms. Elmer and I shared a room our whole lives. He's two years older than I am, and I couldn't wait for him to move out so I could have our tiny bedroom to myself. But once he left, I missed him terribly."

"It sounds as if you two were best pals," I said. I'd just sat down at the rectangular kitchen table, blue Formica with squiggles all over it.

"We were extremely close," he said. "From the time we were little, we used to lie in bed at night, chattering away into the wee hours. We used to talk a lot about what we wanted our lives to be like when we grew up. Elmer always wanted a grand, glorious life. He used to dream about riding around in limousines and having famous friends.

"As for me," Arthur added, "I never wanted any of those things. I knew I was destined for something much simpler." Glancing around, he said, "Which, as you can see, is what I got. I never married. I used to keep dogs, two at a time so they'd have each other for company. But it hurt so much when they got old and passed away that I decided I couldn't keep putting myself through that."

As he poured hot water into the French press, he said, "In high school, Elmer was always the popular one. The guy with the big ideas. Like for one of the school dances, he came up with the theme 'Night in the Black Forest.' He created a fairy-tale extravaganza. The gym was decorated like the woods in a storybook, with gingerbread houses and a castle and even a pond for the Ugly Duckling display. Strings of tiny white lights were hanging everywhere, glittering like stars. The musicians dressed up like elves, and some of the kids came in costume . . . The whole thing was pure magic.

"But everything Elmer touched was special," Arthur went on, sitting down opposite me. "He was so focused. He'd decide he wanted to do something, and he'd just go ahead and do it. That's harder for most people to pull off than you might think."

I knew exactly what he was talking about. Everyone has dreams. But how many people actually make them come true?

"Speaking of Elmer's childhood," I said, trying to sound casual, "I understand your brother and Mitchell Shriver were quite close while they were growing up."

"Mitch? Sure," Arthur replied. "He was practically part of

our family. The two of them were inseparable. Mitch came over pretty much every day after school. Weekends, too. Most nights, my mother would automatically set a place for him at the table without even asking if he planned to stay for dinner."

"So he was almost like a third brother in the family," I observed.

"Yes and no," Arthur said. He thought for a few seconds. "It's funny, but I remember that even as a kid, I always got a sense that there was some competitiveness on Mitch's part. Elmer was definitely smarter than Mitch, always coming up with the big ideas. He was more popular, too. Mitch was more of a follower, if you know what I mean.

"He seemed happy enough to come along for the ride, but I couldn't help wondering how he really felt about always being the sidekick," he continued. "He always backed Elmer up, but he never got any of the glory. Like when Elmer came up with the fairy-tale theme for the school dance, Mitch was the one who stayed up half the night stringing those little lights all over the gym. But of course Elmer got all the credit."

I wondered if that feeling of always being in Elmer's shadow had followed Mitchell into adulthood.

"Still, they were always together," Arthur said. He paused to pour us each a cup of coffee, then brought a carton of milk and a ceramic sugar bowl over to the table. "A lot of people hate their high school years," he went on as he sat down opposite me. "Me included. But I think the fact that Elmer and Mitch had each other made it one of the happiest times of their lives."

"And it seems as if they remained fast friends into adulthood," I commented, wanting to push him a bit further.

"Mitch was with Elmer throughout his whole career," Arthur said. "He and I lost touch, though. I haven't spoken

to him in years." Shaking his head sadly, he added, "But I'm
sure he's as crushed by this as I am. It's almost like he lost his
brother, too."

"There are so many people who are devastated by his loss,"
I observed. "Not only those who knew him personally, but also
the ones who knew him as a designer. In fact, I imagine you've
been inundated with calls from people who want to interview
you about your brother. Magazines and newspapers and television stations . . ."

"On the contrary," he said. "Hardly anyone has bothered
to track me down." Gesturing toward his surroundings with
both hands, he said, "You can see that I was not part of the
same world as my brother."

With that, he rose, opened a cabinet, and pulled out a
package of Archway oatmeal cookies.

"These are my favorite," he said, almost as if he'd read my
mind. "I've loved them ever since I was a kid."

I smiled. "And Elmer's favorite was hot fudge sundaes."

A look of surprise crossed his face. "Yes!" he cried. "I'd
forgotten all about that!"

Arthur's eyes clouded over. "It's not that surprising that
I've forgotten little details like that, given how things between Elmer and me changed over time," he said. "If there's
one thing you learn in life, it's that nothing lasts forever. As
adults, Omar and I spent less and less time together. He was
always flying off to Paris or Milan or some exotic island for
a fashion show or an opening or a photo shoot. He was so
darned busy.

"We'd get together maybe four or five times a year," he
continued. "He'd come over for the big holidays, and we'd
have a quiet dinner. Just the two of us. He always came over
on my birthday. His, too, whenever he could manage it. But
on his birthday, it was much more likely that a bunch of his
jet-set friends would throw him a big to-do at some fancy

restaurant in Manhattan. Elmer always invited me, but I rarely went. As I said, I've never felt as if I fit into that world."

Shaking his head sadly, Arthur said, "Over the years, I had no choice but to get used to being without him. And then, of course, in an instant everything suddenly sped up. When I got the terrible news last spring, without any warning, I had to start getting used to the idea of being without him forever."

"Terrible news?" I repeated, frowning. "I'm afraid I don't know what you mean."

Arthur looked taken aback by my response. "You didn't know? I suppose I shouldn't be surprised. It wasn't exactly public knowledge. I guess I simply assumed that you and Elmer were pretty close since you bothered to come all the way to the Bronx to find me."

I could hear my heart pounding as I asked, "Didn't know what?"

Arthur swallowed, shifting his gaze down to the floor. "He was sick."

The air in the room suddenly felt strangely thick. Or maybe it was just that I was having difficulty catching my breath.

"Sick?" I asked. "How sick?"

Arthur cast me a wary glance. "Sick as in dying. Elmer only had a few months left to live. At least, that's what his doctors were predicting."

It took me a few seconds to fully comprehend what Arthur had just told me.

Omar DeVane had had a fatal disease.

This put a new spin on everything. The fact that someone had murdered a man who was going to pass away within a few months made the whole episode even more of a shock.

"How much of a secret was his illness?" I asked, my head still spinning. "Who knew about it?"

"Quite a few people," Arthur replied, "at least in his inner circle. Elmer cared about the fashion empire he'd built very, very much, and he wanted to make sure it would continue after he was gone. So most of the people who were close to him knew how sick he was. He was working with all of them, deciding how his estate would be divided up, who would take on which set of responsibilities after he was no longer around to run things, and other important details."

I struggled to digest this bolt from out of the blue. This new bit of information had cast new light on absolutely everything. If Omar had told everyone in his entourage that he had only months to live, that meant just about everyone on my list of suspects had no reason to kill him. Federico, Pippa Somers, Gretchen Gruen, Mitchell Shriver . . .

Each and every one of the people I'd considered suspects, in fact.

I was going to have to do some serious rethinking.

It wasn't until I was standing by the front door, about to leave, that I remembered one more thing I'd wanted to mention.

"By the way," I said, "Pippa Somers, the editor of *Flair*, is holding a memorial service for your brother this weekend. I don't know if she remembered to invite you, but I thought you might like to come. I'm sure you'd be more than welcome."

Arthur shook his head. "Thanks, but I'll pass. I meant what I said about not fitting into his world."

"I understand completely."

Instinctively I leaned over and hugged him.

As we separated, I noticed that his eyes had filled with tears.

"I'm glad so many people cared about my brother," he said in a choked voice. "But none of them loved him the way I did."

*   *   *

As I made my way home, I was reeling from what I'd just learned from Arthur.

That same thought kept playing in my head: If Omar De-Vane had had a fatal disease and only a short time left to live, why would anyone in his inner circle have wanted to kill him?

Did that mean his murderer was someone other than the four people I'd been considering the main suspects? Here I'd thought I was getting close to figuring all this out, and instead it was turning out to be very likely that was I merely trekking further and further in the wrong direction.

I was exhausted by the time I got back to Wolfert's Roost.

When I drove back from the train station and 59 Sugar Maple Way came into view, I felt like throwing my arms around the entire house. Arthur had been right about the importance of home. I was struck by the fact that, just like him, I was living in the place I had always thought of as my real home.

And my certainty that I'd made the right decision was reinforced as I walked inside and found Grams sitting at the dining room table, sipping a cup of tea.

I noticed that she was wearing a nice outfit once again: a lavender tunic top with a string of bright purple beads and button earrings to match. Yet I immediately picked up a negative vibe. Something was off.

"How was the senior center today?" I asked cautiously, joining her at the table.

"Fine," she said. She let out a deep sigh, then added, "I suppose."

Just as before, I was surprised by her ambivalence. "What did you do there?" I asked.

"Quite a bit, actually" she replied. "A nutritionist came in and gave us all tips for healthier eating. And then there was a Scrabble tournament. There were eight different games going on at the same time."

"That sounds like fun," I commented. "And the lecture must have been informative."

"Yes, it was definitely worthwhile," Grams agreed. But she still looked deflated. "It's just that . . . I wish we could do *more.*"

"What do you mean?" I asked.

She frowned. "Here's this group of smart, interesting people with plenty of time on their hands," she said. "And we're simply wiling away the hours, playing Scrabble and learning about new ways to use spinach. I wish we could find a more productive way to put all our energy and our knowledge and our life experience to good use."

She let out another sigh, this one even deeper than the first. "I mean, it's wonderful that we're all getting together and making new friends and learning things. But I'm frustrated that we don't have any real *purpose.*"

I had to admit that she had a point.

"What do you have in mind?" I asked.

"I'm not sure, exactly," she replied thoughtfully.

I reached over and gave her hand a squeeze. "If anyone can come up with a good idea, it's you," I told her. And I meant it.

Before long, I was back to obsessing about Omar DeVane.

But rather than thinking about the fact that he had apparently had a fatal illness, what I was fixated on was what his brother had told me about his childhood friend and current business manager.

According to Arthur, even when Omar and Mitchell were kids, Mitchell had felt competitive toward his more accomplished pal. And Arthur's use of that word—*competitive*—continued to gnaw at me.

I wanted to talk to Mitchell Shriver again.

Fortunately, the man had given me an excuse to do exactly that.

Chapter 14

In the late 1970s, New Jersey ice cream shop
owner Richard LaMotta created the Chipwich.
The treat consisted of four ounces of ice cream
sandwiched between two chocolate chip cookies
and studded with chocolate chips. Vendors with
carts, most of them students, sold them on the
streets of New York City for a dollar each.

—*https://en.wikipedia.org/wiki/Chipwich*

On Saturday morning, as soon as I went through the
usual routine of opening Lickety Splits for what was
bound to be another quiet day and leaving Emma in charge,
I headed back to Greenaway.

This time, it was because I wanted to talk to Mitchell.
What had impressed me most about my conversation with
Arthur was the realization that Omar's business manager
probably knew Omar better than anyone else in the world.
Perhaps even better than his own brother, given the way that
Omar and Arthur had grown apart over the years.

If anyone had insights into what was going on in the man's
life that may have motivated someone to kill him, it was
Mitchell.

I was also curious about those file folders he always
seemed to have with him. He acted almost possessive of

them. Or maybe he was merely an efficient business manager, someone who was constantly worrying about numbers.

I certainly wanted to find out.

The back door at Greenaway was open, just like last time. But through the screen I could see Marissa in the kitchen, surveying stacks of dishes that were lined up on one of the counters. It seemed to me that she was trying to decide what to do with them. Not wanting to barge in on her, I knocked.

"Hey, Kate!" she called to me. "Come in. It's nice to see you again."

I smiled at her warmly as I went inside. "Nice to see you, too. But I've come to see Mitchell. Is he here?"

"Everyone is here," Marissa replied with an exasperated sigh. "Pippa is upstairs, sorting through some of Omar's things. Sheets and towels, souvenirs he picked up on his travels around the world, that sort of stuff. It's actually very helpful, since no one else has the heart to do it. Gretchen is here, too. She decided it's not worth going back to the city since she'd have to come up again tomorrow for the memorial service at Pippa's. The last time I saw her, she was tweaking her eyebrows or filing her nails or doing some other self-improvement task. Federico is holed up in his room, packing his own things."

"And Mitchell?" I asked.

"He's in his office." Marissa gestured toward the room with the desk near the kitchen.

His office? I thought. And here I'd assumed it was Omar's office.

My knock on the closed door was greeted with a gruff, "Who is it?"

I opened it and stuck my head in. "Mr. Shriver? I'm Kate McKay, the caterer who—"

"I know who you are." He stuck the papers he'd been studying into a manila folder, closed it, and placed it on a stack of others. "Is there something I can help you with?"

"As a matter of fact, there is," I replied. "I can see you're busy, but if you have a few minutes . . ."

"Have a seat," he said, motioning toward one of the two chairs opposite his desk. Protectively he ran his hand over the top of the manila folder he'd just put down. I wondered if he was making sure I couldn't see whatever it was that he'd been studying so intently.

I hadn't been inside this room before, only in the hallway. But I wasn't surprised to find that the décor fit in perfectly with everything else in Omar's mansion. The grandness of this room made it look as if it had been created by someone who designed sets for movies.

Lining two of the walls were floor-to-ceiling bookcases that appeared to have been made from some exotic wood. An ornate, dark red Oriental carpet covered the floor, and two padded leather chairs sat side by side facing a fireplace. A particularly dignified touch was the bust of a man I was pretty sure was Plato. A large window composed of a grid of small panes of glass overlooked the sculpture garden—a window that would have been very much at home in an English manor house.

The big wooden desk Mitchell was sitting at was undoubtedly an antique, perhaps something Teddy Roosevelt had donated to Goodwill while he was redoing his office.

He looked at me expectantly.

"I've, uh, been thinking about what you said the other day," I began, trying to keep my voice steady so he wouldn't pick up on how nervous I was. "About the possibility of moving into the world of franchising."

"Ah," he said. He leaned back in his chair and crossed his legs. "Smart lady."

"Not that I'm ready to actually *do* anything," I added hastily. "Right now, I'm still getting Lickety Splits off the ground. The idea of bringing it to the next level seems—well, kind of ambitious. But I keep thinking about what you said, and I figured I owed it myself to at least find out how something like that would work."

"It's always wise to stay informed, especially where possible business opportunities are concerned," Mitchell said. He narrowed his eyes and leaned forward, as if he was about to say something really important.

"Franchising," he said, pronouncing the word with reverence, "is the ladder to success." Shaking his finger at me, he added, "And the beauty of it all is that that ladder can have as many rungs on it as you want it to have."

He sat back in his chair and fixed his gaze on me. "First of all, we'd have to come up with a unique idea. Something that makes your shop—what's it called again?"

"Lickety Splits."

"Cute name," he said, nodding. "But we'd need to find a way to make your ice cream shop different from anything else out there. At least, in the public's eye."

We, he'd said. Not *me.* I wondered when we'd gone from the one to the other.

"Then, of course," he went on, "we'd need investors . . ."

Mitchell launched into a long, boring monologue about financing and legal constraints and various states having different laws. I couldn't have understood half of what he was saying even if I'd forced myself to listen. Earning-claim statements, monitoring systems, working capital requirements, accrual-based accounting . . . I felt as if I was auditing an upper-level course at the Harvard Business School. I did learn that there are franchise registration states, franchise filing states, and non-registration states. What the difference was, however, I couldn't have said if my ice cream freezer's life depended on it.

"And of course I'd be happy to take you through this process," he finally said, a sign that the lecture was about to end. "You'd be wise to take advantage of the experience and connections that someone like me has, not to mention my financial savvy—"

His cell phone rang just then. He glanced at it, then said, "I'm sorry, but I have to take this."

I waved my hand in the air, sign language for "Do what you have to do."

But I couldn't have been happier that he considered his call private enough that he went out into the hallway. The diminishing volume of his voice told me he was walking farther and farther away.

This was exactly what I'd hoped for. Without wasting another second, I pounced.

I grabbed the stack of manila folders on his desk. I assumed it was the same one I'd noticed him carrying around ever since Omar's death. Eagerly I opened the first folder and scanned the top page. It looked like some sort of financial record: a list of expenditures, with names of what appeared to be suppliers on one side and a column of corresponding dollar amounts on the other. If there was anything meaningful here, it was lost on me.

The rest of the pages looked like more of the same. So I opened the next folder in the stack.

This folder contained contracts. They appeared to be agreements between ODV and various manufacturers.

It all looked very important. Yet I wasn't seeing anything that was the least bit helpful.

Frustrated, I opened the next folder. And immediately zeroed in on the title of the thick stapled document inside it: "The Last Will and Testament of Omar DeVane."

Now *that* was something interesting.

But as soon as I started to read, I heard Mitchell again.

"Look, just get back to me as soon as you can," he was saying, sounding exasperated. His increasingly loud voice told me he was heading back to his office.

I shut the folder quickly and put the entire stack back on his desk.

"Now, where were we?" he asked, sitting back down.

"You were telling me why you'd be a good person to team up with," I said.

And I leaned forward to show that I couldn't wait to hear more.

Even though Marissa had said she had a full house today—with not only Mitchell there, but also Federico, Pippa, and Gretchen—no one appeared to be around when I left Mitchell's office.

It struck me as the perfect time to do some snooping.

I wandered through the countless rooms on the first floor, not exactly creeping around but taking care to make as little noise as possible. I'd been inside most of them already. But I spotted a small room off the living room that I hadn't noticed before. It contained hardly anything besides a small couch, a couple of tables, and a TV.

There wasn't much of interest in what looked like a television room that belonged to someone who didn't actually watch much TV. But I instantly zeroed in on the one thing in that room that was interesting.

A door. Posted on it was a handwritten sign that stopped me in my tracks.

"ENTER ONLY WITH OMAR'S PERMISSION!"

If that wasn't an invitation to snoop, I didn't know what was.

I glanced behind me, just to make sure I was still alone. Then I reached for the doorknob tentatively, expecting to find that the door was locked.

Instead, the knob turned in my hand.

My heart was pounding, even though I told myself that I would probably find nothing more interesting than, say, a closet filled with fabric.

Instead, when I flung the door open, the only thing I saw was completely darkness.

I blinked hard, trying to get my eyes to adjust faster. As I did, I thought I heard footsteps directly behind me.

Instinctively, I started to turn around. But before I had a chance, I felt someone give me a hard shove from behind.

The next thing I knew, I was tumbling down a set of stairs.

I let out the long, low cry of an animal as I bounced down one step after another, a guttural moan that was the result of surprise, pain, and fear. But even that didn't block out the sound of someone slamming the door shut and locking it.

Chapter 15

"David Evans Strickler, a 23-year-old apprentice
pharmacist at Tassel Pharmacy, located at 805
Ligonier Street in Latrobe, Pennsylvania, who
enjoyed inventing sundaes at the store's soda
fountain, invented the banana-based triple ice
cream sundae in 1904. The sundae originally cost
10 cents, twice the price of other sundaes."

—*https://en.wikipedia.org/wiki/Banana_split*

"Ow-w-w-w!" I groaned as I lay at the bottom of the
staircase like a heap of laundry.

I reached over to rub my sore hip, the part of my body that
had borne the bulk of my weight as I'd slid down the entire
flight of stairs. Thirteen of them. I'd counted as I'd hit the
edge of each and every one.

Yet while I expected that a huge black-and-blue mark was
in my future, my hip didn't appear to be broken. Neither did
anything else. In fact, as I dragged myself up, I realized that,
miraculously, no other body parts hurt at all.

Slowly my eyes adjusted to the dim light. I began to make
out some of my surroundings.

And immediately let out a terrified gasp.

Looming in front of me were several people. I could see
their silhouettes just a few feet away.

And then, for the second time in the past two minutes, I felt someone push against me.

This time, the blow came from the side. And there was surprisingly little force behind it.

Still, I instinctively pushed back. As I did, I felt something cool slink down my calf, then curl around my ankle.

"Ugh!" I cried, instinctively swatting at it.

And then, nothing happened. The slithering animal didn't attack me, the person who had assaulted me didn't move.

Fighting off my growing feeling of panic, I glanced down and focused on a solid white torso, lying right in front of me.

And realized it was a mannequin.

I jerked my head up, studying the row of scary individuals standing in front of me. They, too, were mannequins.

As for the slithering being that was now resting on my foot, it was a length of shimmery silk fabric.

A feeling of tremendous relief washed over me. I finally understood where I'd landed—literally.

I was in Omar's design studio.

Relieved, I ran my hand along the wall near the bottom of the staircase. When I found the light switch, I found myself in a spacious workroom that was painted a stark shade of white. The bright overhead lighting practically made the walls shimmer.

But this was clearly the room that served as the designer's studio while he was at Greenaway. What a thrill it was to be in the very place where Omar DeVane created the clothes and other items that people all over the world clamored to wear!

I had to remind myself that I was only here because someone had pushed me down the stairs.

And that same someone had locked me in.

Which meant one of three things.

The first was that that someone was trying to get me out of the way for a while, most likely to give him or her time to do something to cover his or her tracks. The second was that

that someone was trying to scare me, since that person had figured out that I was trying to identify Omar's killer.

The third possibility was the most chilling. And that was that whoever had pushed me down the stairs had been trying to kill me.

The good news for me was that I hadn't been killed. Or even hurt, aside from my hip, which was no doubt developing that giant black-and-blue mark at that very moment.

The bad news for whoever had done this was that this little maneuver had done nothing to diminish my resolve.

That person had also forgotten that most of us carry a cell phone at all times. So getting out of here wasn't going to be that difficult. Still, now that I was here, I couldn't resist taking advantage of the situation. This was my big chance to get a peek at the inner workings of a world-famous fashion designer's empire. And despite the circumstances that had gotten me here, I couldn't help feeling a flutter of excitement.

I glanced around eagerly, anxious to take it all in. In the center of the large room sat two large tables. Each one was at least the size of a Ping-Pong table.

One of the tables was printed with a grid. That, I figured, was for cutting fabric. The fact that a few bolts of fabric were lying on it haphazardly, along with a device that looked like pizza wheel but which I'd learned from Grams was called a rotary cutter, told me I'd gotten that right.

The other table was covered with sketches. Hand-drawn on big pieces of paper were what appeared to be evening gowns. Some were black-and-white renderings—charcoal, perhaps—while some were more finished-looking. A few were even colored in with watercolor or something smeary like chalk or pastels.

Nearby, bolts of fabric jutted out of barrels. They reminded me of oversized bouquets of colorful flowers. Several sewing machines were pushed up against one wall. But the other three walls were lined with floor-to-ceiling shelving. On two of them were clear plastic bins filled with scissors and other gadgets related to sewing. There were also piles of spools of thread in every color imaginable. I saw more fabric as well, some of it rolled up, some of it neatly folded.

The third set of shelves contained more personal items. Books, for one thing, rows and rows of them. When I studied them more closely, I saw that they were all about fashion. Histories of fashion, picture books featuring the works of various designers, serious-looking tomes on technique, biographies of Coco Chanel and Yves St. Laurent, giant coffee-table books on hats and corsets and sleeves. Yes, an entire book on sleeves.

A few personal mementos were displayed on the shelves, as well. Ceramic vases that were clearly handcrafted, a glass elephant, a fabric doll with straw hair and an evil-looking expression that looked as if it had been made in some exotic, faraway land.

But what interested me most were the photographs.

Most of the photos were big, probably eight-by-ten, and polished enough that they had most likely been taken by professional photographers. One was a picture of a younger version of Omar, posing with a very youthful Gretchen Gruen. Another photo was of Omar and Pippa Somers. Once again, both of them were considerably younger. They appeared to be posing at a fashion show since there was a runway behind them. It could have been Omar's first big show. Or at least an important one.

One of the smaller photos, stashed on a lower shelf, was faded, making it look as if it had been taken a while ago. I couldn't be certain from where I stood, but I was pretty sure it was a snapshot of Omar, back when he was still Elmer, standing with his arm around Arthur. The two brothers had probably been teenagers when it was taken, judging from the jeans and T-shirts they were both wearing. Their shaggy hair, too. One thing I could see, even from far away, was that both were wearing huge grins.

I noticed another older snapshot, also faded. This one was of a young Omar posing with Mitchell. They were both holding up a check. I assumed it was the first big payment Omar had ever received, back when he was just starting out as a designer. Again, big grins lit up both men's faces.

In one corner of the huge space, I spotted a folding room divider. It was covered in elaborate pale green brocade that to my untrained eye looked like silk.

Peering behind it, I found a desk covered with papers and other clutter. Off to the side was a table with a laptop, a printer that was also a copier and fax machine, and a shredder.

Apparently Omar had had a home office here at Greenaway, just like Mitchell.

I wasted no time in going through the things Omar had kept here. I touched as few of them as possible, and I made a point of putting everything back in exactly the same spot. I also used a tissue I found in my pocket to pick things up so I wouldn't leave any fingerprints.

First I poked around the pile on top of his desk. In addition to more sketches and a few handwritten notes, I found pages torn from fashion spreads in fashion magazines, most of them seemingly featuring the work of other designers.

Continuing to exercise the same caution, I opened one of the desk drawers. It contained a neatly arranged collection of the usual mundane office supplies, like a stapler, a box of paper clips, and a package of colored pencils.

The drawer below it, however, contained files.

I could feel the adrenaline rushing through my veins.

I crouched down and read the neatly typed labels on the tabs. Bloomingdale's, Nordstrom, Neiman-Marcus . . .

More business files.

None of them struck me as worth examining. Or, to be more accurate, I didn't know enough about Omar's business and how it might be related to his murder for them to interest me.

Then I noticed the file at the very back.

Rather than having a typed label like all the others, this one had a single word written in pencil.

"Will."

Eagerly I grabbed it, forgetting all about the possibility of leaving fingerprints. My heart was pounding as I opened it.

It was Omar's will, all right. And it looked like an official document, complete with stamps and seals and signatures.

I skimmed the list of his holdings, all the property that constituted his estate. His New York City residence, which was a townhouse in the East Sixties. Greenaway, of course. An island retreat in the Caribbean. His company's headquarters in New York, a multistory office building on Madison Avenue with a ground-floor boutique. Other office buildings all over the world, too, as well as apartments in London, Paris, and Milan.

That was just the real estate. Then there were bank accounts and investments, all kinds of business-related assets ranging from factory equipment to stashes of fabric . . . the list went on for two single-spaced pages.

The wealth the man had accumulated was truly mind-boggling. Still, I was much more interested in the way his estate was to be distributed.

Fortunately, it was all laid out clearly. Omar had left half of his estate to his brother. He had left a generous amount to Marissa and some of his other longtime employees. The rest was to be divided among Gretchen, Pippa, Federico, and Mitchell.

Aside from being blown away by the magnitude of Omar's wealth, nothing else here surprised me.

In fact, I was about to close the folder and put it back where I'd found it when one last thing caught my eye. Stuck in back was a single piece of lined loose-leaf paper, the kind with holes punched along the sides. On it was a single paragraph, handwritten in a script that looked similar to the one used to write all the other notes I'd spotted on Omar's desk.

"I, Omar DeVane, revoke all previously executed wills and codicils . . . ," it began.

I checked to see if he'd written a date.

Sure enough: there it was, right on top. August 1. Just a few days earlier. And just a few days before he had been killed.

My mouth was dry as I started reading again.

"I leave my entire estate, including all my business and personal holdings, to the Omar DeVane Foundation . . ."

I gasped. I knew exactly what I had just found. In my trembling hands I was holding a new version of a will that Omar had been working on at the time he was murdered, one designed to replace his earlier will. And instead of dividing his fortune among the people around him, once death was imminent he had decided to leave everything to charity by way of his foundation.

I suddenly understood why a dying man had been murdered. Omar had been killed in order to prevent him from changing his will.

My head was spinning. It looked as if I had been correct in my belief that his murderer had been one of the people closest to him.

And that person's motive had been greed.

I hurried over to the copier, switched it on, and made a copy of Omar's handwritten revision to his will. I checked the copy to make sure that everything had been printed clearly—especially the date. Then I tucked the original back into the folder and put it back in the drawer.

The person who had pushed me down the stairs and locked me in had undoubtedly been trying to scare me away from the investigation of Omar DeVane's murder. Instead, that individual had done me a huge favor by bringing me one giant step closer to discovering his or her identity.

"I'm surprised you got into Omar's studio, since this part of the house is always kept locked," Marissa said as she unlocked the door and freed me from my glamorous basement prison.

"That's funny," I replied. "The door was unlocked."

"But what surprises me even more is the fact that you got locked in once you were down there," she added.

Another shrug. "I guess the door locked automatically when I closed it," I said. Ignoring the puzzled look on her face, I casually asked, "Do you know who has a copy of the key besides you, Marissa?"

Marissa frowned. "Federico, certainly. Mitchell, too. But aside from those two, I have no idea who else Omar gave the keys to."

The image of Gretchen draped across the couch a few days earlier, holding a long silver nail file, popped into my head. I'd seen enough spy movies to know that when it came to picking locks, nail files were the number-one tool of choice.

It occurred to me that there was someone else who had the keys, too. And that was Marissa.

She *was* the housekeeper, after all.

The idea that she might actually belong on my list of suspects was one I'd never taken seriously. But just as I'd seen plenty of spy movies, I'd also read tons of murder mysteries. And in the classic tales, it was always the butler who did it.

Once I was home, I realized I should tell someone about what had happened that afternoon. After all, the fact that someone might have been trying to kill me, or at least inflict serious bodily harm, was worth mentioning.

But I didn't think that someone should be Emma. The last thing I wanted was for my teenaged niece to start worrying about her wayward aunt. As for Grams, she was even lower on the list of people I wanted losing sleep over my sleuthing-related activities.

That left Jake.

Right after dinner, just as I was getting ready to call him, I heard a footstep on the creaky front porch. It was heavy enough to sound definitively male. It seemed the man had saved me the trouble of phoning him.

I figured that Digger must recognize his smell by now, since the scruffy little ball of fire was standing with his nose pressed against the door, wagging his tail wildly.

Which is why I was shocked when I threw open the door and found Brody standing in front of me.

"Brody!" I cried. "What a surprise!"

"A good surprise, I hope," he said, grinning. He thrust out a stack of shiny bags printed with pictures of mountains and pine trees. "I brought us some snacks."

I had gotten over my surprise enough to hope that he'd brought something sweet and tasty, snacks that would go well with ice cream. That, of course, was always my first priority when it came to anything edible.

Brody crouched down to give Digger a good head-scratching as I looked through the packages.

"Oh, yum!" I said, swallowing hard. "Peanut-and-Dried-Cranberry Quinoa Fuel Bars!"

"There are protein balls there, too," he pointed out enthusiastically. "And fruit leather. No sugar added, of course. And there's salmon jerky!"

Could I ever be serious about a man whose idea of a snack is a protein ball? I wondered.

But then Brody abandoned Digger, coming over to plant a kiss on my cheek. At the same time, he gave my shoulder a little squeeze.

"It's so nice to see you again, Kate," he said softly, practically whispering in my ear.

Okay, so maybe snacks weren't the most important thing in a relationship.

"I should put these into bowls," I said, even though I wasn't quite sure if foodstuffs like these belonged in a bowl. Surely the people who liked this kind of thing didn't eat out of serving dishes. They were more likely to cram this so-called snack into their mouths straight from the bag as they fought the white waters of the Colorado River or kicked snow off their boots at the top of Mount Everest.

And I certainly had no idea about the proper way to serve salmon jerky. Perhaps on a silver tray lined with paper doilies?

But before I had a chance to consult Martha Stewart's web site on that issue, there was another knock at the door.

No, I thought, my heart sinking. It couldn't be happening. Not again.

Sure enough, when I opened the front door as tentatively as if Freddy Krueger was my next-door neighbor, there was Jake. He, too, was bearing gifts.

"I brought you some fancy hot fudge I found in a gourmet market!" he greeted me, proudly holding up a glass jar. "It's guaranteed not to be as good as yours, but I thought you might be interested in keeping an eye on what the competition is up to."

Jake definitely won that one.

But as soon as he stepped inside and saw that Brody had already marked this territory, the air became so charged with electricity that I was surprised my hair didn't stand up.

And I'm not talking about good electricity, the kind that

makes toasters—and ice cream makers—run. I'm talking about the kind that means that trouble is a-brewin'.

Every muscle in Brody's body seemed to grow tense as he glanced up at the man he clearly thought of as an interloper.

"You again," Jake said under his breath.

"Funny, I was about to say the same thing," Brody shot back.

Digger was the only one who was pleased about what was happening here. Ecstatic, in fact, leaping around gleefully and barking and generally acting as if two six-foot strips of rawhide had just entered the room.

It was definitely time to call for backup.

"Emma!" I yelled, my voice edged with hysteria. "Could you please come down here?"

A second later, I heard her bedroom door open. My niece came trotting down the stairs with a sketch pad under her arm, her halo of curly black-and-blue hair pulled back into a haphazard ponytail. She froze when she saw that, once again, we had a bit of a situation on our hands.

"My goodness!" she cried with forced cheerfulness. "Jake! Brody! How nice to see you both again!"

"I'm going to get some bowls," I said, dashing toward the kitchen.

But of course I couldn't stay in there forever. Not without some excellent excuse that, at the moment, I was much too flustered to think up.

So I had no choice but to go into the living room with my mouth-watering offerings: dried fish, dried apricots, and cold quinoa with protein powder. Digger was underfoot the whole time, sniffing the air hungrily and poking his nose around the coffee table. He was obviously a much bigger fan of dehydrated food products than I was.

"We'll have ice cream later," I reassured everyone as I set the bowls down.

"I imagine that Brody can't stay very long," Jake commented. "Someone in the adventure industry probably has to get up really early. I imagine that sunrise hikes are a big part of that business."

"They are," Brody replied, grabbing a handful of that peanut-and-quinoa thing and gulping it down. "But aren't cows famous for needing to be milked super early in the morning?"

"I don't actually milk the cows myself," Jake retorted. "I have people to do that."

"Ah," Brody said. "And here I thought milkmaid was no longer a viable career path."

Emma and I exchanged nervous glances. Even Chloe, curled up on the window seat, seemed to be wearing a tense expression. This was going to be a long night.

Unless one of us did something. Fast.

"Let's play Trivial Pursuit again!" I said. "That was so much fun."

Jake glanced at me warily. "I really don't think—"

"That's a great idea," Emma agreed. Her eyes were shining in a way I wasn't sure I liked as she added, "Only this time, let's do things a little differently. Let's play the girls against the boys."

Alarms went off my head as loudly as if I'd just burned a pan of chocolate brownies and the smoke alarm went berserk.

"Emma," I said, "I don't know if that's such a great idea."

"Sure it is!" she insisted. She'd already pulled the game off the shelf. Before I could suggest that she and I talk in the other room, she was setting it up, this time on the dining room table.

"Jake, Brody, come on over and take a seat," she insisted in an impressively no-nonsense voice. "The boys' team can even go first."

Reluctantly, the two men pulled themselves out of their seats and shuffled over to the next room. I had no choice but to do the same, bringing along a couple of bowls of snacks.

"Brody, why don't you go first, since you're the new guy in town," Emma said as soon as we'd all sat down at the table.

"Sure." He picked up the dice, threw them, and moved his team's marker to a pink square.

"Pink!" Emma cried. "That's the Entertainment category. I'll read out the questions, Kate, if you don't mind."

"Be my guest," I replied. Frankly, I was happy to have as little to do with this misadventure as possible.

"I never know the answers to the Entertainment questions," Jake mumbled, looking sullen.

"Me, either," Brody added, his level of enthusiasm just as low.

"Okay," she said, peering at the card. "Here's the question: Who played the lead role in the 1986 movie *Aliens*?"

"I didn't see that movie," Brody said.

"Me, either," Jake said.

"Come on, guys," Emma prompted. "You have to give me an answer."

"Hey, I think it was that dark-haired actress," Jake said.

"Which one?" Brody demanded. "There's only like a hundred of those."

"She has a funny name," Jake said.

"Great," Brody muttered. "That's really helpful."

"I think she was in *Ghostbusters*," Jake said. "But, darn, I still can't remember her name."

"Give up?" I asked, feeling I needed to contribute something.

Jake leaned back in his chair and did a man-spread thing, suddenly taking up more than his share of room at the table. "Yeah, we give up."

"I didn't give up yet," Brody said sharply.

"I thought you said you didn't know," Jake challenged.

"I don't, but that doesn't mean I'm willing to give up already," Brody said. "We should at least guess."

"Okay, guess."

"Uh, Jodie Foster?"

Jake glared at him. "She doesn't have dark hair."

"Nobody said the star of *Aliens* had dark hair."

"I distinctly remember that she had dark hair," Jake insisted. "I can picture the movie posters."

"Fine," Brody shot back. "Then, I don't know, Debra Winger."

"No way was it Debra Winger!"

"Maybe we should have a time limit," I suggested. Either that or start passing around antacids.

"Let's just say Debra Winger so we can move on," Brody said.

"Fine," Jake grumbled. "Whatever."

"So your answer is Debra Winger?" Emma said.

"Yeah," the two men mumbled.

"The answer is Sigourney Weaver," she told them.

"There's the funny name," Brody grumbled.

"I told you I never get these," Jake said.

"Yeah, me either," Brody added.

"Our turn!" I said brightly.

The girls' team also landed on pink. But Emma and I both knew immediately that the planet Superman came from was Krypton.

"That's an easy one," Jake complained.

"I thought yours was pretty easy, too," I told him, letting my irritation show.

"Everybody knows Superman is from Krypton," Brody declared.

I cast a look at Emma that said, "Tell me again why we're doing this . . . ?"

She and I got the next question wrong. Our green Science and Nature question was, How many of the planets in our solar systems have moons? Neither of us knew the right answer. For future reference, the answer is six.

It was the boys' team's turn again. This time, they ended up on an Arts and Literature square.

"I never get these either," Jake said.

"This is an easy one," Emma insisted as she glanced at the card. "What was British novelist C. S. Lewis's full name?"

"Never heard of him," Brody said with a sigh.

"I have," Jake said. "He wrote those Narnia books."

"Oh, yeah?" Brody said. "I liked those. When I was a kid, I mean."

"Me, too," Jake agreed. "But I have no idea was his name was."

"We should guess."

"I know: his full name was Debra Winger Lewis."

Even though the two men had barely made eye contact up to this point, Brody looked over at Jake long enough to glare at him.

"Your answer?" Emma prompted.

"Charles Steven Lewis," Jake guessed.

"That's not what I was going to say," Brody insisted.

"Oh, yeah? So what's your answer?"

"He was English, so how about Cecil Something?"

"Cecil 'Something'?" Jake repeated scornfully. "You think that's better than Charles Steven?"

"Not 'Something,'" Brody shot back. "I'm just saying if he was British, maybe his name was Cecil. I have no idea what his middle name was."

"I'm thinking we need to have a time limit," I suggested once again.

"I'm starting to agree," Emma said. "So what's your answer?"

"Cecil Steven," Brody said at the same time Jake said, "Charles Steven."

"I'm afraid both answers are incorrect," Emma said. "C. S. Lewis's full name was Clive Staples Lewis."

Our turn again. We got Literature, and I knew that the musical instrument Sherlock Holmes played was the violin. Then we got Science again and struck out on what atmospheric layer lies between the troposphere and the mesosphere. (Answer: stratosphere. We should have been able to guess that one.)

"Your turn again," Emma said, handing over the dice.

Jake scooped them up and rolled them half-heartedly.

"Orange!" Emma announced. "That's Sports and Leisure." She picked up a card. "This is a tough one, but let's give it a try. Ready? How many Super Bowls have the Denver Broncos won?"

"I sure am glad we didn't get that one," I commented.

But no one seemed to be listening to me.

"They won in 2016, that's for sure," Jake said.

"Defeated the Carolina Panthers 24 to 10," Brody added.

"Really?" I said. "Guys remember this stuff?"

"That was some game," Brody said. "Peyton Manning at his best."

"He was a quarterback, right?" Emma asked, blinking her eyes innocently.

Jake snorted. "Only one of the best ever."

"His stats at Super Bowl 26 were almost identical to John Elway's first Super Bowl win," Brody noted.

"And of course the Broncos won two consecutive Super Bowls in 1998 and 1999," Jake said.

"Right," Brody agreed. "In 1998 they won against the Green Bay Packers, and in 1999 they defeated the Atlanta Falcons."

"Go, Broncos!" Emma exclaimed. "So . . . what's your final answer?"

The two men looked at each other. "Three," they said simultaneously.

"So your answer is three?" Emma said. "Jake? Brody? You both agree on that?"

"Yup, three," Brody said.

"Yeah, three," Jake seconded.

"That's right!" Emma announced, slapping the card down on the table.

"Hey, we finally got one!" Brody cried. "Good job!"

"You, too!" Jake returned.

When the two of them high-fived each other, I nearly fell off my chair. I glanced over at Emma and saw the triumphant look in her eyes. It had turned out that my clever niece had known exactly what she was doing.

"So we get to go again," Brody said, rubbing his hands together.

Jake rolled the dice and moved their marker. "Geography!" he cried. "We got this."

"We've *totally* got this," Brody agreed.

When the boys' team won, whooping and hollering and slapping each other on the back, I was thrilled. Emma and I simply smiled at each other as we watched the two members of the boys' team carrying on as if they'd just won the Super Bowl themselves instead of a mere game of Trivial Pursuit.

"And now," I announced, standing up, "I'd say it's time for some ice cream."

As I lay in bed that night, I couldn't help smiling. It wasn't as if Jake and Brody were about to become best buds. But it was interesting the way in which two men who'd started out as enemies had managed to work together once the stakes were high enough.

Suddenly, I stopped smiling. In fact, I sat bolt upright in bed.
Oh my, I thought, my head spinning and my heart pounding. Oh my, oh my, oh my.

A very bright light bulb had just flashed on in my head.
What I'd witnessed tonight, I realized, could be applied to
much more than a board game.

Chapter 16

The popular Ben and Jerry's flavor, Cherry Garcia, was proposed by a fan in Maine who sent a postcard to the company's headquarters in Burlington, Vermont. Created as a tribute to Jerry Garcia, the leader of the rock group the Grateful Dead, it is made with cherry-flavored ice cream, rather than the traditional vanilla that's usually used in Cherry Vanilla ice cream.

—http://www.benjerry.com/whats-new/2015/cherry-garcia-story

Another sleepless night.

I couldn't shake off the gnawing feeling that I'd stumbled upon the answer to the question that had been dogging me for the past week.

Jake and Brody. Federico and Mitchell.

Two men who had acted as if they'd hated each other . . . or perhaps really *had* hated each other . . .

Yet when there was reason to work together, they were able to put aside their differences in order to get the job at hand done.

Was it possible that Federico and Mitchell had done exactly what Jake and Brody had done? Had two rivals acted together to do away with Omar before he had a chance to cut them both out of the will?

All the information I'd gathered over the past few days

was so jumbled in my head that I had to struggle to focus on the few pieces that suddenly seemed the most important.

One of the most crucial bits had come from Omar's brother. I remembered what Arthur had said about Mitchell when he'd talked about the three of them growing up together.

"Even as a kid," Arthur had told me, "I always got a sense that there was some competitiveness on Mitch's part."

He had gone on to say that his brother was smarter and more popular than his best friend. That young Omar had invariably gotten all the credit even though his sidekick Mitchell had often done most of the scut work. That Mitchell was always backing up his best friend but that he never got the glory.

Then there was Federico. Everything about the man was a lie. He wasn't from Italy; he was from Indiana. His hair was dyed. He wore tinted contact lenses—and eyeliner.

His name wasn't even Federico. It was plain old Fred.

But he hadn't been content to be plain old Fred. He'd wanted more, much more. And based on what Marissa had told me, it sounded as if he had played Omar from the very start.

As far as Federico was concerned, Omar was his ticket to greatness.

But perhaps it wasn't coming fast enough—or to a large enough degree. And to lose out on being one of the primary heirs to a fortune the size of Omar's must have been devastating for him.

Then there was the fact that at times I'd observed that there was something almost theatrical about the constant bickering that went on between Federico and Mitchell. At the time, I'd written it off as Federico's flair for the dramatic combined with Mitchell's in-your-face New York style.

But now I wondered if what had really been going on was that they routinely made a point of acting like enemies whenever anyone was within earshot.

Even me, a mere ice cream caterer.

And then another thought popped into my head. I suddenly remembered what Federico had said to me the first time we spoke on the phone.

"Is this party going to be some sort of celebration?" I'd asked him when he'd told me about the event he was planning.

After thinking for a few seconds, Federico had replied, "I suppose we're celebrating Omar's life."

I now wondered if he'd already known that the night of the party would turn out to be the *end* of Omar's life, which would have given him all the more reason to celebrate it.

I tried to keep my mind from racing at a hundred miles per hour. I was desperate to find Omar's killer, which I knew could cause a person to distort facts and remember things incorrectly. I had to remember that it was possible I was simply reading more into what I'd seen and heard than there really was.

I wasn't doing a very good job of keeping my racing thoughts in check.

And my desperation was worsened by the realization that once Pippa had held the memorial service, the members of Omar's entourage would scatter. Marissa would find a new job, Federico and Mitchell and Pippa would head back to New York, Gretchen would run off to Paris or Milan to continue her modeling career or even launch her own line of fashions . . .

And Wolfert's Roost would be left with its horrible status as the Home of Omar DeVane's Unsolved Murder.

Sunday afternoon's memorial service, I knew, would be the last time that all the people who knew Omar would gather together—including whoever had killed him.

Which meant the amount of time I had to solve this mystery was growing shorter than a 1960s miniskirt.

The next step was to test my theory that Mitchell and Federico had worked together to murder Omar. Fortunately, I already had an idea.

Not surprisingly, it involved ice cream.

There's something about eating ice cream that makes people let down their guard.

Maybe it's because the experience is always so pleasurable. The melt-in-your-mouth creaminess, the perfect amount of sweetness, the infusion of some delightful flavor like rich chocolate or soothing vanilla or tangy berries . . . It's no wonder the stuff has such a magical effect. It's as if whoever is eating it becomes so consumed by the simple, joyous act that they go back to being their true selves.

Since my goal was to uncover the true nature of the relationship between Federico and Mitchell, ice cream was the most obvious weapon.

My plan wasn't exactly foolproof. Then again, ice cream had never let me down before.

Thanks to the fact that I'd already been to Greenaway several times, I was pretty familiar with the way things worked there. So I parked my truck on the driveway, far away enough from the house that no one inside was likely to spot it. Then I hurried across the expansive front lawn, darting among the trees in the hopes that they would shield me from view.

Under one arm I carried a tub of Chocolate Almond Fudge ice cream wrapped in a towel to protect my skin from freezer burns. The thick terry cloth also kept it from banging against the tender black-and-blue mark on my hip, which was the size of an ice cream scoop.

Chocolate Almond Fudge was a flavor that few people could resist.

When I got close to the house, I began tiptoeing around the edge, peering through the windows. I felt like a cat burglar in a Looney Tunes cartoon.

Except that instead of stealing something *out* of the house, my intention was to put something *into* it.

The kitchen appeared to be empty. And just as I'd expected, the back door was open.

My heart was pounding as if I were committing a crime. I reminded myself that sneaking ice cream into someone's residence wasn't exactly cause for an arrest.

Then again, trespassing was.

I tried to put aside the legal debate and instead concentrate on doing what I'd come here to do. I placed the tub of ice cream on the counter closest to the door that opened onto the hallway that ran past Mitchell's office.

That was the easy part. The hard part—the really scary part—came next.

And that was hiding in the pantry.

I had an excuse ready in case anyone found me. A weak excuse, granted, but I didn't expect that there would be much cooking going on at Greenaway today. Not with Pippa's memorial service only a few hours away.

And if anyone did happen to open the pantry door and find me crammed inside, it was most likely that someone would be Marissa.

I didn't think she'd call the cops on me. Not if I explained that I'd come back to retrieve one more forgotten item, found that the back door was open, and taken it upon myself to come into the house to get it without bothering anybody. As for the hiding-in-the-pantry part, I figured I'd just say I heard someone coming and was afraid I'd get in trouble.

By that point, I hoped to be halfway out the door.

It was stuffy in the pantry. Boring, too. Fortunately, there was enough light creeping in from under the door that I could at least read the labels on the foods that were lined up neatly on the shelves.

Extra-virgin olive oil from Italy, raspberry-flavored bal-

samic vinegar, fancy Greek olives, eggplant caponata from
Sicily . . .

Some of the bottles and jars, I noticed, were actually dusty.
I figured they were items that had looked enticing in the
store, but once they were brought home no one ever found a
use for them.

The labels on gourmet food items didn't exactly make for
the most scintillating reading. Fortunately, less than ten minutes had passed before I heard footsteps, followed immediately by a booming voice.

"Hey, check this out," I heard Mitchell say. "Some idiot
left a whole tub of ice cream out."

"It's just sitting there, melting," Federico said disdainfully.
I noticed that his Italian accent had been replaced by one that
was more Indianapolis than Milan.

"We should put it in the freezer," Mitchell said.

"I have a better idea," Federico said. "Let's eat it."

"Why not?" Mitchell said.

"Here's a spoon," Federico said. "Dig in!"

Fireworks were going off in my head. I'd been right! The
two of them were secretly friends. Or at least two people
who got along just fine when they thought no one else was
within earshot.

I still didn't know for sure if they were the killers, however.

There was silence for a few seconds. Then Federico cried,
"Wow, this is incredible! That ice cream lady may be too
nosy for her own good, but she sure knows ice cream."

"Yeah, this is good stuff," Mitchell agreed.

Lowering his voice, Federico said, "You don't think she's
going to—you know—make any trouble for us, do you?"

"Hah!" Mitchell replied. "She's nobody, Freddie. Believe
me, we have nothing to worry about. Especially now."

I wished I'd thought to bring along a voice recorder. Or

that I'd at least set up my phone to record what they were saying. Then again, I hadn't expected my ice cream trap to do
much more than give me some insight into whether Mitchell
and Federico really were the archenemies they pretended to be.

Yet I was now more convinced than ever that they had
worked together to kill Omar.

There was more silence as they both continued to pig out
on ice cream. Even though I couldn't see them, I could tell
that was what they were doing by the slurps and sighs of
pleasure I heard through the closed door.

And then Mitchell said, "You know, Freddie, it's too bad
that you and I didn't figure this out years ago."

"Figure what out?" Federico asked.

"That you and I would have been better off working *with*
each other instead of *against* each other," Mitchell replied.

By this point my heart was pounding so loudly that I was
sure the sound must be resonating through the entire house. I
hoped I wasn't about to blow my cover.

But then something even worse happened.

I felt a sneeze coming on.

The dust on the shelves that surrounded me was clearly
having an effect. I inhaled sharply and held my breath. But
the tickle in my nose wouldn't go away.

And then: *Ah-chooo!*

It was one of the softest sneezes ever made by a human
being. But it was apparently loud enough that Mitchell and
Federico heard it.

"Hey, what was that?" I heard Federico say.

"It sounded like it came from inside the pantry," Mitchell
said.

I knew I had to act. If they opened the door and found
me, I'd be cornered. And there were two of them and only
one of me . . .

So I flung open the door and burst out of the pantry, making a beeline for the back door.

"Hey, it's her!" Federico cried.

"Grab her!" Mitchell yelled. "You! Kate! What do you think you're doing?"

But I was out of the house by then. I sprinted toward my truck, my breaths coming out as gasps as I ran as fast as I possibly could.

As soon as I climbed behind the wheel, I locked the doors, turned the ignition, and drove off lickety split.

As I careened around a curve in the road, I spotted Mitchell and Federico in the rearview mirror. They were both standing outside the back door, waving their arms and yelling. I could still see them as I grabbed my cell phone to call the police.

Detective Stoltz was unavailable, I was informed by whoever answered the phone at the precinct.

So I left him a long, detailed voice-mail message. I tried not to sound too crazed as I laid out my theory. I even quoted the words I'd overheard Federico and Mitchell say. Fortunately, Detective Stoltz knew that I'd been helpful in solving a murder once before. I hoped that would give me enough credibility that he'd take me seriously and call me right back.

But for now, as bizarre as it seemed, I had an event to cater.

I'd barely had a chance to catch my breath before I sailed into Lickety Splits. I found Emma and Willow already dressed in their cheerful bubble-gum-pink Lickety Splits polo shirts and spanking-clean white pants. They were busily packing up tubs of ice cream, silver serving trays, and a big supply of Sterno to keep the chocolate fudge sauce hot.

I could have used Ethan's help, too, but he had claimed he wasn't available. Perhaps he was busy brushing up on European languages. But what was much more likely was that he and Emma still weren't on speaking terms.

I dashed into the back of the shop and changed into my Lickety Splits shirt and white slacks. As I did, I kept my phone in full view, glancing at it every five seconds as if I could will Detective Stoltz to call me back.

I also rifled through the drawer underneath the counter, pulling out a pair of poultry shears I kept on hand and sticking it into my back pocket. They weren't the sharpest, just scissors I kept around for cutting into boxes or snipping herbs into tiny pieces. But they would have to do. Besides, if I was going to start carrying a concealed weapon, it had to be one that wouldn't tear through my clothes.

And as my 'Cream Team and I loaded up the truck, I also kept my phone in my pocket. I wanted to make sure I felt it vibrate if Detective Stoltz called.

Nothing.

I had no choice but to carry on, acting as if everything was fine as I drove to Pippa's house. Emma, who sat beside me, could barely keep still.

"I know this is a really sad occasion, but even so, I'm excited about being at such a big event," she chirped. "And I can't wait to see Pippa Somers's weekend house! Were you kidding when you said that practically everything in it is white?"

"That's pretty much the case," I replied, veering around a sharp curve. I was silent for a few seconds. "By the way," I went on, trying to sound casual, "I'm going to let you and Willow do the serving today. I think I'll stay behind the scenes."

I didn't tell her that it was because I was avoiding two of the event's guests.

"Okay," Emma agreed. "But you'll miss out on seeing all the celebrities!"

"That's okay," I assured her. "My main concern is making sure that everything runs smoothly. I think the best way I can do that is by holing up in the setup room, doing all the backup work."

"You're the boss," Emma said with a little shrug. I got the

feeling that her eyes were so filled with stars in anticipation
of the afternoon ahead that that arrangement suited her just
fine.

It turned out that "behind the scenes" was exactly where
Pippa wanted us to base our operations. As soon as we arrived at her snow-white mansion, her housekeeper, Katarina,
led Emma, Willow, and me to a small room off the kitchen.
She referred to it as a butler's pantry.

Why a butler needed his own pantry was beyond me. But I
instantly knew that I wanted a butler's pantry even more
than I wanted a butler. Especially at Lickety Splits.

Everything in the small room was white, just like the rest
of the house. White walls, white counters, white cabinets
with glass-paneled doors that reached all the way up to the
ceiling. Inside them I could see rows of neatly stacked white
plates, white mugs, and white mixing bowls. The backsplash
was composed of white subway tiles.

While the compact, windowless room was stark, to me it
was the ideal workspace. It felt so clean and simple and efficient that I couldn't wait to get busy.

"Okay, let's get this party started!" I told Emma and Willow.

Almost immediately I became so absorbed in doing that—
literally—that I lost all sense of time. I stood at the counter,
rolling Classic Tahitian Vanilla and Meyer Lemon ice cream
balls in coconut and placing dollops of cinnamon ice cream
on oven-warmed donuts. Perhaps most important, I heated
pots of hot fudge on the stove, then placed serving bowls
filled with the stuff over the cans of Sterno I'd brought to
keep them warm.

Even though I was tucked away in the butler's pantry, I
could hear the crowd in the living room growing larger and
larger. Getting louder and louder, too.

Emma kept sticking her head in, not only to replenish her
supply of ice cream goodies but also to report on the celebri-

ties she'd spotted. It seemed that those stars in her eyes paled beside the actual stars who were standing around in Pippa Somers's living room, eating my ice cream.

"Kate, you wouldn't believe who I just saw out there!" she cried as she dashed in to refill an empty tray. She named a hunky movie star who had been the model for Omar De-Vane's line of men's sunglasses. She gleefully added that the actor's date was just as famous, a young actress whose legs were as long as the list of movies she'd made.

"How about Omar's business manager, Mitchell Shriver?" I asked casually, pretending to be absorbed in getting exactly the right amount of coconut to stick to the vanilla ice cream ball in front of me. "Is he out there?"

"Yup," Emma replied. "He was talking to that super-model who used to do ads for Calvin Klein. He was bragging to her about a trip he's about to take. Apparently he's planning to dash off to a really exotic place."

That certainly got my attention. "A trip?" I repeated.

"He said he's leaving tonight, right after the memorial service," Emma reported breathlessly. "Isn't that glamorous?"

"Very," I said, doing my best to sound only minimally interested. "Did he happen to mention where he's going?"

Emma shook her head. "He kept acting flirtatious with the model, refusing to say where he was going no matter how much she teased him about how secretive he was being."

Alarms were going off in my head. So Mitchell was about to leave the country—for a location he wasn't willing to reveal. And I had a feeling that the reason he'd decided to disappear so suddenly had nothing to do with a fashion show.

"And Federico?" I asked as calmly as I could. "Did he come, too?"

"Oh, yes," she said. "You should see him! He looks like he's here for a fashion shoot instead of a memorial service. He's wearing a suit that's the same color as that vanilla ice cream. And his necktie is turquoise silk, and there's a matching handkerchief sticking out of his pocket . . ."

I'd have bet a month's rent for Lickety Splits that there was a plane ticket in his pocket, too.

As soon as Emma left with her refilled tray in hand, I tried calling Detective Stoltz again.

"It's Kate McKay," I began my voice-mail message, trying to keep my frustration out of my voice. "Detective Stoltz, the two people who I'm nearly certain murdered Omar DeVane, Federico and Mitchell Shriver, are at Pippa Somers's house right now. She's holding a memorial service for Omar. But Mitchell is planning to leave the country tonight. I suspect that Federico is, too. They have to be stopped! I have a piece of evidence that I'm dying to show you, one that supports my theory . . ."

My head was spinning as I tried to come up with a way to keep Federico and Mitchell from leaving Pippa's house—especially since I had a feeling they planned to drive straight to the airport to escape to a safe haven far, far away. And as long as they weren't convicted of murder, they would still be in line to inherit a huge piece of Omar DeVane's estate and live happily ever after . . .

I was wracking my brain, trying to think up a way to keep them here until Detective Stoltz showed up, when I heard footsteps behind me.

"Back already?" I asked, assuming it was Emma. "Those people certainly eat a lot of ice cream."

When I didn't get a response, I turned.

But it wasn't Emma who was standing in the doorway. It was Mitchell and Federico.

And in Mitchell's hands was Federico's turquoise necktie.

Chapter 17

"Grocery stores didn't start selling ice cream until
the 1930's, and by WWII, ice cream had become
so popular that it turned into somewhat of an
American symbol (Mussolini banned it in Italy for
that same reason). Ice cream was great for troop
morale, and in 1943, the U.S. Armed Forces were
the world's largest ice cream manufacturers!"

—*http://www.almanac.com/content/*
history-ice-cream

My heart pounded with sickening force, and I could feel
the adrenaline coursing through my veins.

Meanwhile, my mind was racing so fast that I bordered on
panicking.

Stay calm, I told myself. Act as if everything is normal—at
least until you can figure out what to do.

I thought of yelling, but by this point the amount of noise
generated by the crowd outside was on par with a Led Zeppelin
concert.

Instead, I moved on to Plan B. Casually I reached across
the counter and adjusted the flame on the three Sterno cans
that were keeping the bowls of hot fudge warm. While the
flame was currently at a moderate setting, I turned them up
to the highest possible level. I also stuck a ladle into one of
them, pretending I needed to give it a stir.

"Hey there, you two," I said with forced gaiety. "This is turning out to be a big ice cream eating crowd. I just hope I brought enough!

"I'm so glad my ice cream is such a bit hit," I went on. "Not only the hot fudge sundaes, either, which of course were Omar's favorite food. But the guests really seem to like the Coconut Balls. The Donut Sundaes, too. Of course, it's hard to resist anything that's smothered in hot fudge . . ."

As I babbled on, I noticed that Mitchell didn't appear to be listening. He seemed much more focused on stroking the necktie he was holding in his hands. Yet his piercing eyes were fixed on me.

As for Federico, I watched in horror as he reached back and closed the door.

My attempts at warding off panic were starting to fail. But I did my best to act as if nothing was wrong as I said, "If either of you would like to help yourselves to a few of these Coconut Balls I just made, feel free to—"

"You couldn't leave it alone, could you?" Federico hissed. I noticed that once again, there wasn't even a trace of an exotic European accent.

Not that it mattered anymore. At the moment, the man's country of origin was the least of my concerns.

"When you pushed her down those stairs," Mitchell growled, "you should have pushed a little harder. I knew I should have done it myself."

"Who knew that a lady who sells ice cream for a living would turn out to be such a snoop?" Federico shot back.

"Hey, I do a lot more than sell ice cream!" I exclaimed indignantly. "I create unique flavors, I cater events like this one . . . then there's my new Lickety Light line!"

I had to remind myself that this was hardly the time to get defensive. At least not about something like my career.

Not that Mitchell or Federico were even listening.

"Federico and I had such a good thing going," Mitchell said, spitting out his words. "At least until *you* came along."

"We were just trying to keep from getting cheated out of something we deserved," Federico added. "If only Omar had left everything the way it was—"

"But you both loved Omar!" I cried. "What about all those lovely things you said about him, Federico? You said that he was such a warm person, that he was a genius, that you'd always miss him . . ."

"I *will* always miss him," Federico replied coldly. "And he was special in many ways. But that doesn't mean he wasn't foolish when it came to his money. Imagine, giving his entire fortune away to a bunch of do-gooders.

"What about us?" he went on, his voice becoming angrier. "What about people like Mitchell and me who really deserved his money? The people who stood by him, who helped make him who he was . . . who enabled him to make all that money in the first place!"

"He's right," Mitchell said, his tone tinged with the same bitterness. "I spent my entire life helping Omar make money. We sat next to each other in practically every class since the third grade, for heaven's sake. Even back in those days, I was always lending him lunch money or helping him get an after-school job.

"And ever since he started his own business, I was the one who advised him," he went on. "I bargained with suppliers to get him better deals. I found investors when he needed to expand, talking complete strangers into backing a young designer that no one had ever heard of. The day he opened his boutique on Madison Avenue, who do you think was there at six a.m., washing the windows and polishing the doorknob?"

"I worked at least as hard as you did," Federico piped up. "Do you think I *liked* kissing up to editors and buyers and all those other people whose support Omar needed? If I had a nickel for every endless phone conversation I endured, feeding the ego of some—some *fabric* salesman or some idiot who wrote for an insignificant web site or even some obnoxious socialite who was making ridiculous demands on Omar but who we had to keep on our good side because she was a regular customer . . ."

"But he paid both of you, didn't he?" I couldn't resist pointing out.

"He paid me well enough," Federico replied haughtily. "But it was nothing compared to what *he* had. I mean, just look at Greenaway. It's like Versailles. Have you seen my studio apartment in the West Village? It's the same size as Omar's bathroom. His *guest* bathroom!"

"Same here," Mitchell grumbled. "Although my house in Scarsdale isn't too shabby. Still, it's not like I was able to come even close to living the way Omar lived."

"And finally, it was our turn to get *our* share!" Federico cried. "Once he died, we were each going to inherit enough to live like kings for the rest of our lives." Scowling, he added, "Until he came up with that ridiculous idea of changing his will and leaving all his money to charity instead!"

"What a waste," Mitchell commented with a sneer. "Giving it all away to strangers!"

"He *owed* us!" Federico shrieked.

"Leaving his fortune to his foundation instead of to us—" Mitchell began.

"It was preposterous!" Federico cried. "The man had to be stopped!"

I stared longingly at the locked door, wishing I could will myself onto the other side of it. But I knew I couldn't make that happen. I considered screaming, but the level of noise out there, combined with the fact that the kitchen separated me from the rest of the gathering, made me afraid that all that would accomplish would be making the two men in front of me even angrier.

I moved my right hand to my waist, then eased it around behind me to the back pocket of my white pants. When Mitchell suddenly came rushing toward me, his face red with fury, I pulled out the scissors I'd hidden away in my back pocket.

"Don't come any closer!" I cried, holding the scissors out in front of me so they were pointed right at his chest.

Mitchell stopped in his tracks.

But only a second or two passed before I felt the scissors being yanked out of my hand.

Federico had come up next to us, catching me completely off guard, and snatched them away before I realized what was happening. For someone who was so spindly, he was surprisingly strong.

I stood facing my attackers, aware that I probably had only seconds to come up with a way to defend myself against two men, both of whom were determined to get rid of me.

Fortunately, I'd had the presence of mind to think a few steps ahead.

So instead of panicking, I reached across to the counter and grabbed the ladle that was sitting in the bowl of fudge sauce. As I expected, the handle had gotten really hot.

No wonder, since I'd turned up the Sterno so high. In fact, the fudge sauce had started to boil.

Death by chocolate, I thought.

With that, I quickly dunked down the ladle as deep as it would go, filling it with steaming fudge sauce. Then I flung it at Mitchell, splattering his entire face with boiling hot liquid.

"Arghhhh!" he cried, dropping the necktie as his hands flew to his eyes. "That burns! Ow-w-w-w-w!"

"What do you think you're—" Federico was already reaching down to pick up the fallen necktie.

But I was ready for him. I dipped the ladle again, then

threw a big glob of hot molten fudge right at him, once again aiming for the face.

"Ah-oo-oo-oo!" he moaned, swiping at his eyes.

By that point, both men were yelling, their voices much louder than I knew mine would ever be. A few seconds later, the door of the butler's pantry flew open.

Pippa Somers stood in the doorway, her eyebrows knit with concern. Peering behind her, I saw that a few other people were coming toward the butler's pantry, curious about what was going on.

Pippa froze. "What on earth is going on in here?" she cried. "Kate? Mitchell? Federico? What's happening?"

I looked over at Mitchell and Federico, both dressed in their fine clothes but with globs of hot fudge sauce all over their faces and hands. The molten chocolate had also dripped down to their collars, the fronts of their shirts, and, I was pleased to see, Mitchell's necktie. As for Federico's tie, it still lay on the floor, splashed with big brown stains.

Pippa frowned. "Honestly, do you really think this is the best time for a food fight?"

"This isn't a food fight," I replied calmly. "This is the conclusion of a murder investigation. Call the police, Pippa. Omar DeVane's murderers have finally been identified. These two men just tried to kill me, too. They came in here to strangle me with a necktie, the same way they murdered Omar."

Mitchell and Federico glanced at each other, their expressions horrified. I could practically hear the gears inside their heads turning. And then, moving at the same time like two dancers doing a carefully choreographed step, they both turned and headed for the door.

But Marissa was blocking it.

So was the man who I assumed was her escort, given the fact that one arm was draped protectively around her shoulders.

I'd never been so happy to see Pete Bonano in my life.

Especially since he was wearing his police uniform and everything that went with it. Including a gun. And handcuffs.

He wasted no time in cuffing the two killers together.

"You are both under the arrest for the murder of Omar DeVane," Officer Bonano announced seriously. "You have the right to remain silent. Anything you say can and will be used against you in a court of law—"

"It was all his idea!" Federico cried, glowering at Mitchell. "He's the one who found out that Omar planned to change his will! He's the one who masterminded the whole thing and even came up with the idea of leaving the country . . . Anyone who knows me knows I'm not *smart* enough to plan something like this!"

"Be quiet, you idiot!" Mitchell shot back. "Did you hear what he said? They can use anything you say against you!"

"But you planned the whole thing!" Federico whimpered. "I'm the one who kept telling you we'd never be able to pull it off, remember?"

He was still whining as Pete Bonano led them away, meanwhile calling for backup. Mitchell kept trying to shut him up, scolding him like a child.

They were back to bickering. But this time, it was for real.

It took only a few minutes for a police van to arrive and take away the two suspects. Detective Stoltz showed up, too, his face expressionless and his posture rigid. His four-star-general-style demeanor gave absolutely no indication that something momentous had just happened.

After the van left, he paused at the edge of the living room, surveying the stunned crowd of guests, who were standing around awkwardly. I assumed he was looking for Pippa, the homeowner. Instead, he walked straight over to me.

"I got your messages, Ms. McKay," he said seriously. "A little too late, it seems."

I was trying to decide whether to respond politely with "No problem!" or more honestly with "Y'think?"

But before I had a chance to say either, he said, "You've done a good job here." He hesitated for a moment, then added, "A really good job."

I didn't know the man well enough to be able to read him, but I was pretty sure I saw admiration in his eyes.

It vanished as quickly as it had come.

"But next time, if there ever is a next time," he went on in a stern voice, "I'd appreciate it if you'd leave the investigating to the pros."

He didn't wait for my answer. Instead, he turned around and left.

I blinked a few times, trying to process what had just happened. I *thought* I'd been paid a compliment. Then again, I wasn't completely sure.

Once the excitement was over, the guests went back to standing around in cocktail-party-style groups. But the entire atmosphere had changed. A feeling of heaviness hung over Pippa's house.

"Perhaps we should all just go home," she suggested, not speaking to anyone in particular.

"No, we should stay," Gretchen insisted. "We came here to honor Omar and his memory, and that's exactly what we should do."

"All right," Pippa agreed with a little shrug. "As long as Kate is willing to keep going, we should all carry on."

"I'm up for it," I assured her. And I was, aside from the fact that I felt so weak that I needed a hit of ice cream. *Fast.*

In about ten seconds flat, I gobbled down three Coconut Balls and two Donut Sundaes. Pants came in all kinds of sizes, I reminded myself. Meanwhile, the rest of the guests were chatting away loudly about the drama that had just unfolded in front of them.

Willow came over to me, her face distraught. Emma was right behind her, her expression almost identical.

"Are you sure you're all right?" Willow asked anxiously.

"Those two creeps tried to kill you!" Emma exclaimed.

"I'm fine," I told them both. "Really."

Emma threw her arms around me and gave me a big hug.

"Okay, 'Cream Team," I told them. "We've still got a job to do. Let's keep that ice cream coming."

I was about to do exactly that when I felt someone touch my shoulder lightly. I turned and found myself face to face with Marissa.

"Are you okay, Kate?" she asked breathlessly.

"I am now," I replied. "Thanks to Pete. Speaking of Pete, how long have you two been an item?"

Marissa's cheeks immediately turned pink. "We met the night Omar was killed. I know it sounds crazy, given everything that was going on, but somehow we liked each other from the first moment. But it wasn't until a few days later that Pete called me. He asked me to go see a Spanish movie at the Rhinebeck Cinema."

Grinning, she added, "We never got there. We were so busy talking and laughing and just getting to know each other that we decided to skip the movie and go out for coffee instead. The next night, we went out for dinner. And the day after that—"

"I certainly owe both of you," I told her sincerely. "The next time you two are out on the town, please stop by and I'll force-feed you so much free ice cream you won't be able to move."

She laughed. "It's a deal."

As soon as I went back into the butler's pantry to pick up where I'd left off, my heart sank. It looked as if there'd been a chocolate explosion in there. The entire room was covered with splatters of dark brown sauce. The floor, the walls, the counters, the cabinets . . .

But I was even more dismayed by the sight of a huge batch of hot fudge sauce that by now was so badly burned it was hardly recognizable.

Fortunately, I'd brought along a lot more.

Chapter 18

Chocolate syrup is the most popular ice cream
topping in the world.

—*www.icecream.com/icecreaminfo*

Goodness, it felt good to be home.
As soon as I got inside, I threw myself on the couch,
facedown. I was suddenly exhausted and shaken and exhilarated and overwhelmed—and totally confused by all those
emotions that had finally decided to set themselves free.

Gram and Emma both gave me plenty of space. So much
space, in fact, that when there was a knock at the door, no
one but me was around to answer it.

Standing on the threshold was Jake, his face tense with
concern.

"Jake!" I cried. Sure, I was surprised to see him. But I was
even more surprised by how happy I was that he was here.
"You're not going to believe what happened—"

"I know all about what happened," he interrupted. "Word
travels fast in this town. Especially when one of your oldest
friends is Pete Bonano. Are you okay?"

"I'm fine," I replied, even though I wasn't sure that was
true.

As he came inside, he held out a jar.

"I brought you this," he said. "More hot fudge sauce, but

one made by a different company this time. I figured you might as well learn everything you can about the competition."

"I'm always looking for a chance to eat ice cream," I told him. "And you've just given me one."

"I'm up for ice cream, too," he said. I wasn't sure if he was kidding or not as he added, completely deadpan, "Especially if there are hot fudge sundaes on the menu."

Ten minutes later, Jake and I were sitting at the kitchen table. It turned out he'd been serious, and in front of us sat two of the most beautiful hot fudge sundaes I had ever created. Mine consisted of a huge scoop of Classic Tahitian Vanilla and a scoop of Dark Chocolate Hazelnut topped with a generous slathering of gooey hot fudge sauce. Maybe the sauce he'd brought wasn't as good as the one I made, but it was certainly in the Exceptional category. Then came the requisite mountain of whipped cream, an avalanche of chopped pecans, cashews, and almonds, and of course a cherry, so shiny you could practically taste its sweetness just by looking at it.

Jake's hot fudge sundae was identical, aside from the ice cream flavors. He'd opted for strawberry and Chocolate Marshmallow, two choices that showed excellent taste on his part. It was a good thing I kept a nice big selection of flavors at home for emergencies like this one.

"Quite a day, huh?" he said once he'd tasted his sundae and agreed that life didn't get any better than this.

"That's what we call an understatement," I agreed. "I'm so glad that Omar DeVane's murderers have been caught and Wolfert's Roost can go back to being its normal self."

He looked at me earnestly. "And I'm glad you came through this without getting hurt."

Once again, I had to agree.

"I admire your spirit, Kate," he continued, "and I know you felt that you had to do everything you could to find out who killed Omar DeVane. But now that it's over, is there any chance I can get you to promise that you'll stop doing dangerous things like investigating murders?"

I gave him a funny half-smile. "Honestly, Jake, what are the chances that there'll be another murder around here anytime soon?"

"Good point," he said. "Even so, I worry about you."

I immediately felt my blood pressure rise. "I don't need you or anybody else to worry about me, Jake!"

"I can't help it," he replied with a little shrug. "That's what happens when you care about someone."

This time, I was at a loss for words.

He, too, suddenly seemed tongue-tied. He put down his spoon, folded his arms, and leaned forward.

"I get the feeling you're not sure you're interested in seeing anybody right now," he said, looking at me so intensely that it was difficult not to squirm.

"I never said that," I insisted. At the same time, I was wondering how he'd managed to read my mind.

"Maybe not in so many words," he said. "But I know you, Kate. Even after all these years, I can still read you pretty well."

I just stared at the cherry perched on top of my sundae.

"Then there's that guy," he said, practically spitting out the words. "Brody or whatever his name is."

"He's very nice," I said, unable to resist the impulse to make Jake even more jealous than he already seemed to be.

"The guy is obviously into you," Jake said. "But there's something I want you to think about."

I glanced up, blinking. "What's that?"

With his blue eyes fixed on me in that same intense way, he said, "The fact that I'm the one who's here.

"You had a horrible thing happen today, Katy," he continued. "Two men—two *murderers*—tried to make you their next victim. And it's me, not that Brody character, who came to your house to be with you."

In a soft voice, I said, "I noticed."

Jake's voice was thick with emotion as he said, "The way I feel about you has never changed."

"Jake, I—"

"Kate, let me say this before I chicken out." He paused to take a breath. "I just want you to know that whenever you decide you're ready—*if* you decide you're ready—I'll be here. I'm not going anywhere. I made that mistake once, and I'm not about to mess up like that again."

That, I decided, was information that was worth filing away.

Even though I slept surprisingly well that night, the next morning I decided not to rush into Lickety Splits.

Not today. I needed time to decompress.

Besides, while I was looking forward to business finally picking up for the rest of the summer, chances were that it would take a day or two for the news about Omar DeVane's murder having been solved to spread.

So I slept wonderfully late. Then I lingered over my breakfast coffee, luxuriating in the simple act of just doing nothing. My relaxed mood was improved even further by the fact that Chloe was curled up in my lap, purring happily. And Digger was at my feet, mainly hoping for random table scraps to fall but also offering companionship and an impressive amount of cuteness.

I was also enjoying the quiet of the house, not to mention the rarity of having it to myself. I'd only slept until ten, yet both of my human roommates had apparently rushed out before then. What they were up to, I couldn't imagine.

The stillness was beginning to wear thin when I heard footsteps on the front porch. Digger dashed over to the door to greet Emma, who came bounding into the dining room seconds later, sketch pad in hand.

"You're here!" she cried when she spotted me lounging at the table. "I figured you'd be at the shop by now."

"I'm taking the morning off," I said. "And gearing up for what I hope is going to turn out to be a crazy-busy week."

"You definitely earned the chance to play hooky," Emma said.

"And what have you been up to?" I asked, noticing that there was a streak of charcoal on her cheek. "You have that intense Frieda Kahlo look, as if the creative wheels are turning in your head."

"I've been working on a drawing I want to give Ethan," she replied. "I was just down by the river, making some sketches."

Ah, Ethan.

"So I take it things between you two have been smoothed over?" I asked cautiously.

Emma was grinning as she plopped down in the chair next to mine. "Things couldn't be better, Kate. Last night, after we got home, Ethan called to tell me that he's decided to postpone his trip to Europe until I'm free to come with him."

Her big brown eyes were bright as she added, "He said it just wouldn't be any fun without me. He even recited this quotation: 'In life, it's not where you go, it's who you travel with.'"

"Seneca again?" I asked.

She shook her head. "Charles Schulz."

I could picture Snoopy saying those exact words to Woodstock.

"That's great, Em!" I told her. "I'm so glad the two of you found a way to resolve this."

"That's not the only thing I wanted to tell you about," Emma went on, suddenly sounding a bit nervous. "This might not be the best time to bring this up, but if it's okay with you, I thought I might sign up for a couple of courses in the fall. I'll check with Mom and Dad, too, of course. But after I talked to Ethan last night, I couldn't sleep, so I started looking at the community college's web site. They have some cool studio art classes starting in September. Sketching, oil painting, watercolor . . . Some great computer classes, too. I could even sign up for evening classes so they don't interfere with me working at Lickety Splits during the afternoon—"

"Emma, I'm sure I can work around your schedule," I assured her. "I'm absolutely thrilled that you want to take some classes. I know your parents will be happy about it, too."

My niece was still beaming as Grams came through the front door. When she strolled into the dining room with Digger prancing around at her feet, I immediately did a double take.

"Wow!" I cried. "You look like . . . like a model on the cover of *Flair* or *Elle* . . . or even *Vogue*!"

She laughed. "Or at least the cover of the AARP magazine."

Grams positively exuded elegance in the pink linen suit she was wearing. The jacket was short and boxy, with slight padding in the shoulders that gave it a crisp, tailored look. The skirt was A-line, falling mid-knee. Maybe it hadn't actually been designed by Chanel, but it had certainly been designed by someone who was a fan.

She also wore beige pumps with a little heel, along with a tasteful string of pearls and matching pearl studs. Her gray pageboy had been carefully styled, making me wonder if there was a can of hairspray lurking in her bathroom cabinet somewhere. While she often wore a touch of blush, pink lipstick, and a bit of eye makeup, today she was wearing much more of all three than usual.

With a sly smile, Emma said, "I bet the way you're dressed

has something to do with a gentleman friend. Perhaps someone you met at the senior center?"

"Not at all," Grams replied, looking indignant.

I folded my arms across my chest. "Okay, so spill it. There's obviously something going on. I want to hear all about what the special occasion is."

"It's not a special occasion at all," Grams insisted. "It's more like a special mission."

"Now you've really got my curiosity up," I told her.

"I still think there's a guy behind this," Emma quipped. "Some white-haired hottie, probably with a fancy sports car . . ."

"You couldn't be further from the truth," Grams said. "My special mission had nothing to do with anything remotely connected to my social life. Or any aspect of my own life at all."

Emma and I exchanged an exasperated look.

"Okay, Grams, enough with the woman of mystery act," Emma said. "Tell us where you went today."

"I paid a visit to a friend of Kate's," she said, pulling out a chair and joining us at the table. "Pippa Somers."

"Pippa Somers!" Emma and I repeated in unison.

She and I exchanged another look—but this one was of complete astonishment.

"I dropped in at her weekend house," Grams went on. "And as soon as I explained to her housekeeper that I was the grandmother of Kate McKay, the famous ice cream entrepreneur and amateur sleuth who had just solved the mystery of Omar DeVane's death—and risked her *own* life in the process, I might add, despite her grandmother's disapproval—"

"Go on," Emma urged, waving her hand in the air impatiently. "Did Pippa actually let you in?"

"Of course she did!" Grams replied. "And she couldn't

have been nicer. She said I reminded her of an aunt of hers, a woman who lives in Cornwall and is an expert rose gardener and has had a huge crush on George Harrison throughout her entire life. Pippa even invited me to come visit her at *Flair*'s headquarters the next time I'm in New York.

"And she insisted on serving me tea," she continued. "My goodness, it was like something out of the Victorian era. Her housekeeper, Katarina, brought us a tray with a silver tea set and tiny sandwiches and the most delicious scones . . ."

"I'm so pleased that you have a new friend," I commented dryly. "But surely there's a reason why you decided to drop in on one of the most famous, influential women in the world."

"Of course there's a reason," Grams replied. "Money. I went to Pippa Somers's house to ask for money."

It took a few seconds for her response to register. Once it did, I was horrified.

But before I had a chance to say a word, Grams calmly said, "Oh, not for me, of course. For the senior center."

I was still confused.

"You know that I've been complaining about how wasteful I find it that all those lovely, experienced people who have so much to offer are wiling away their days playing bingo and gossiping over coffee," she said. "One of the men who's a regular there used to be a professional basketball player. And one of the women I've gotten to know ran an entire hospital. Our group consists of artists and psychologists and businesspeople and people who have decades of experience in just about every field you can imagine."

With a shrug, she added, "And it occurred to me that there had to be a better way for them to spend their time. At least some of it, when they're not relaxing and flirting and trying to beat each other at bridge."

"You've got a point," I said. I was finally beginning to see where Grams was going with this. And I definitely wanted to hear more.

"So I came up with the idea of forming an organization," she explained. "Some sort of outfit that enables retired people to work with local youth. There are so many different things we could do! Go into high schools and tutor. Supplement instruction in elementary school classrooms by working with the children one-on-one, reading to them or having them read to us for practice. Use our connections in the community to arrange internships at local businesses, or even part-time jobs . . ."

I had a sneaking suspicion that Grams would be setting me up with Emma's replacement sometime soon.

"I don't think we'd need a lot of money to make all this work," Grams went on. "But we'd need *some*. I figured we'd certainly have to hire someone to run the organization. That person would have to coordinate with local schools and libraries and community organizations like the Girl Scouts and Boy Scouts . . . community centers all over the Hudson Valley, too, since many of them offer programs for children and teenagers that we could help out with. And down the road, people who go to other senior centers might also want to get involved. We'd also have to offer some kind of instruction to all the volunteers, I imagine. Possibly transportation in some cases, as well."

By that point her eyes were bright and her cheeks were flushed. I couldn't remember the last time I'd seen Grams so excited.

"There are so many details to work out!" she exclaimed. "I've been lying in bed awake for the last few nights, playing with all kinds of ideas. And when I read about Omar DeVane's foundation in the paper this morning and discovered that he had been trying to find ways to use his money to help people who were less fortunate than he was, all the pieces started coming together. The article also mentioned that Pippa Somers was handling his estate. So I figured I had nothing to lose by talking to her. I wanted to see if she might consider funneling some of the funds into the region he loved enough to make it his second home. And to make a long story short, she said she would definitely make it a top priority!"

I felt like giving her a hug. So I stood up and did exactly that.

"Grams, you are absolutely amazing," I told her.

Then it occurred to me that she wasn't the only woman in the room who deserved to be told that. I leaned over and gave Emma a big hug, too. "You're amazing, too."

"What did I do?" she protested. But she was clearly pleased.

I realized that this was one of those rare moments in life when it feels as if everything in life is right and nothing is wrong.

Emma was going back to school in the fall, taking classes in the two different fields that interested her most. She had also faced her first real challenge in a relationship that was important to her and worked through it.

Grams, meanwhile, was about to start a new chapter of her life, getting involved with a community-outreach program that was going to pull together all kinds of people, from senior citizens to kindergarten students to local business owners to teenagers.

As for me, I was looking forward to going back to my daily routine at Lickety Splits, scooping out Cappuccino Crunch and Honey Lavender and concocting Bananafana Splits and Hudson's Hottest Hot Fudge Sundaes and just generally making the world a better, sweeter, creamier, tastier place. I'd created the ideal job for myself. Actually, one that was much more than a job. It was living out a dream.

The possibility of romance also hovered in the distance.

While I still wasn't sure how I felt about that, just thinking about either Jake or Brody made me smile.

As difficult as it was to imagine, it was one of those moments that didn't even require ice cream to be as close to perfect as it gets.

Heavenly Hot Fudge Sauce

The secret to this utterly divine topping is whipping it up in a blender. Not only does beating it improve the texture, adding air to food, anything from carbonated beverages to whipped cream, always makes it taste better.

This hot fudge sauce is fantastic not only on ice cream, but also on pound cake, strawberries, or bananas, for a chocolate fondue . . . in fact, there's probably not a single food that couldn't be improved by dipping it in hot fudge sauce!

Be sure to use a better-quality cocoa powder like Ghirardelli. It may cost a little more, but it's *so* worth it!

2 sticks of butter
⅓ to ½ cup cocoa powder
2½ cups sugar
1 can of evaporated milk (12 ounces)
1 teaspoon vanilla
A pinch of salt

In a saucepan over medium heat, stir together the butter, cocoa, sugar, and evaporated milk. Bring the mixture to a boil and let it boil for 6 to 8 minutes. Add the vanilla. Pour the mixture into a blender and blend it for about 3 minutes.

It is best served immediately, but after cooling it, it can be stored in the refrigerator and reheated right before using. (A jar of this yummy stuff makes a great gift, especially when it's tied with a cute ribbon.)

Peach Basil Bliss Sorbet

While the light, fresh flavor of peaches just screams summer, peach sorbet is a refreshing treat at any time of the year. The addition of basil gives its icy sweetness an extra punch.

Garnish each serving with a fresh basil leaf, sticking it out of the sorbet like a feather in a hat. The contrast of the basil's dark green color with the cool pastel shade of the sorbet is striking.

For an elegant feeling, scoop the sorbet into a wineglass. For a fun, homey feeling, serve it in a glass canning jar. And use small spoons, since this treat's delicate nature seems to lend itself to tiny mouthfuls!

1 cup of basil (loosely packed)
1 pound of peaches
¾ cup sugar
¾ cup sparkling white wine or sparkling white grape juice
2 cups water

Peel the peaches, take out the pits, and slice them. Put them in a medium saucepan with the other ingredients and heat to boiling. Reduce the heat and simmer for 10 to 15 minutes, stirring occasionally.

Let the mixture cool. Remove the basil leaves. Put the mixture into a blender and puree. Spread the mixture in a shallow baking dish and freeze for at least 4 hours.